"We can say good-night here, if you like."

"No, I'll take you all the way."

They ascended the winding driveway, the high white stone building looming in the moonlight like a castle.

Moving across the wide shadowed porch, Colby grasped her shoulders.

"So this is more than a simple drop-off?" she teased.

"Aren't you glad?" Crowding Tina against the door frame of the wide front door, he kissed her more wildly than he had at the park, with the heated pressure of his tongue. She could feel the solid wood against her back as he moved his hands underneath her jacket, then underneath her sweater.

Just then the door swung open, and there stood Marilyn. With a gasp, Tina fell limp.

"You want something, Marilyn?" Colby asked with as much dignity as he could muster.

"I want you to quit ringing the damn doorbell! It's a slow time for the hotel, but we do have some guests who might wonder if this is a loony bin."

Colby was properly chastened. "It won't happen again."

Sugartown

LEANDRA LOGAN

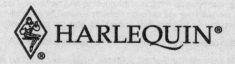

HARLEQUIN®

TORONTO • NEW YORK • LONDON
AMSTERDAM • PARIS • SYDNEY • HAMBURG
STOCKHOLM • ATHENS • TOKYO • MILAN • MADRID
PRAGUE • WARSAW • BUDAPEST • AUCKLAND

ISBN 0-373-75112-5

SUGARTOWN

Copyright © 2006 by Mary Schultz.

This edition published by arrangement with Harlequin Books S.A.

® and TM are trademarks of the publisher. Trademarks indicated with ® are registered in the United States Patent and Trademark Office, the Canadian Trade Marks Office and in other countries.

www.eHarlequin.com

Printed in U.S.A.

For Michele Hauf
A talented author and supportive friend

Books by Leandra Logan

HARLEQUIN AMERICAN ROMANCE

Chapter One

Tina Mills had forgotten about the miniature Royal Doulton tea set.

She set an Old Country Roses cup on a matching saucer and whimsically lifted it across the long table in salutation. "Your tea, Daddy, just the way you like it."

It was easy to envision jolly Bill Mildenderger seated opposite her, accepting his refreshment. As he had twenty-five years ago.

Hard to believe so much time had passed since her childhood parties here in the family dining room. Harder to believe she'd lost her dad completely in a pileup on the Long Island Expressway eight years ago. A pharmaceutical salesman, he'd been on the way home from one of his tristate trips that took in parts of New York, New Jersey and Connecticut. He'd had the same territory for decades, and judging by the Christmas gifts that had poured into their Brooklyn house every year, many customers found him as charming as Tina did.

Tina had been at Columbia University when it happened. Looking back, she remembered a strange feeling, midafternoon during a film editing class, around the time Bill's soul left his body at the crash site.

That was how close she'd felt to William E. Mildenderger.

Upon college graduation several months later, she'd left Brooklyn for Tribeca, finding a loft space to live in and starting up a small independent film company called Reality Flicks with her school pal Emmy Snow.

Tina had been surprised to discover that in his will her dad had left money to her separate from that which he'd left her mother, Angela. She hadn't thought about it much at the time and had just been grateful for the chance to make a financial contribution to Flicks along with her monied socialite pal.

Their venture had taken off eighteen months later when their documentary on battered women who were trapped in poverty won accolades at film festivals around the world. They'd been on a hot streak ever since, chasing one story after the next.

Tina had never stopped to look back until now, at age thirty, sitting in her old Brooklyn house on Hillerman Street. She set the tiny saucer down on the Irish lace tablecloth and studied the delicate red and gold floral cup in both hands. It was empty now. Back then it would have been filled with 7-Up or lemonade, anything that could be easily cleaned in case of spillage. Angela Winston Mildenderger had always hated mess, and would not have approved of the father-daughter tea parties with her china and on her lace, both handed down from the Winston side. Mother was all about taking sides. Building high walls around herself. She'd certainly keep an emotional distance from her only child.

Tina rose from her chair and moved back to the giant hutch standing open at the opposite end of the room. She'd been in the process of unloading it when she'd paused to sit for one last tea party. The back of the hutch was mirrored, and she couldn't escape her reflection as she resumed emptying the shelves of treasures. She'd always wondered why her mother had never warmed to her. Perhaps because she was so like her father, with his long, slender form, unruly black hair, high cheekbones and generous mouth. Tina had a strong Mildenderger personality, as well—boisterous, impulsive and direct. Not bad traits for a film producer, but a constant irritation to a repressed soul like Angela.

Mother liked rules. Structure. Self-control.

Still, it stood to reason that whatever she'd originally appreciated in Bill, she'd have found equally admirable in Tina. But even as a small child, Tina sensed that Angela merely tolerated her husband, and was frequently exasperated with him. It didn't stop Bill from making physical, spontaneous gestures toward his wife, a twirl around the kitchen, a surprise bunch of flowers, unexpected takeout Chinese. Sometimes in an unguarded moment with her sisters, Angela's face filled with humor and affection. But mostly her mother was a one-woman corporation.

Tears slid down Tina's cheeks as she thought of her mother's present state, robbed of coherency by a severe stroke, sentenced to a nursing home. Angela's life expectancy was only a matter of months. Incapable of communication, she wore a vacant stare, as if the vital part of her had already moved on to a better place.

Tina mourned what could have been between them. Intimacy. Joy. Chances lost forever. And because of all this Tina didn't want children of her own. She didn't feel she knew how to be a mother, after her own childhood experience.

The dining room was in the front of the house and because it was a warm September day, Tina had opened the windows for some fresh air. Hearing an engine in the driveway, she glanced out between the blinds and saw that she had company—her aunts Peggy and Jean. Tina watched Angela's younger sisters emerge from Jean's giant red van. The three Winston women were close in age and all were of similar make and model, with stout and plump bodies, pale-blond hair and dark-blue eyes. Peggy was the kindest of the trio. The pampered baby of the family, she at least had some humor and playfulness about her. Which was why Tina had chosen to contact her in particular, with a cordial message that she was going to be at the house, sifting through family things to hold an estate sale to help raise funds for Angela's care.

Car doors slammed. Hard.

They didn't ring the bell, and Tina didn't expect them to. The sisters were totally at home in one another's homes. Now they stood in the foyer like awkward children, staring into the dining room. Tina's heart squeezed in sympathy for them. They usually shouted, Knock-knock! to Angela and she would shout her location in the rambling two-story.

"Hello," Tina ventured softly.

They moved into the room, jaws slack, eyes riveted on the table stacked with china and glassware. Peggy was the first to recover.

"How are you faring, Tee?"

Tina smiled weakly. "It's been tough. Mom's always been so healthy. This is the last kind of trouble I expected."

With a passing glance to stony Jean, Peggy moved to hug Tina. "I know, Tee. Angela ate healthy and exercised. Sixty isn't all that old anymore by today's standards. Jeanie and me, we're only years behind her. It's all very scary."

Tina hoped to lose herself in her aunt's embrace, but it was too light and brief for any real comfort.

Arms folded across her chest, Jean stiffly moved to the open hutch. Her tone was as tight as her short, outdated perm. "Your message to Peg mentioned some kind of sale?"

"I hate to part with anything, of course. But Mom's hospital bills must be paid—"

"There is the health insurance!"

"Jean, her coverage is only eighty percent. Have you seen some of the itemized bills? Hundred-dollar pills? Ten-dollar bandages?"

Jean's haughty turn and lift of her double chin suggested she hadn't.

Tina traced a finger along the top of an ornate captain's chair at the head of the mahogany table, her voice even but firm. "We all know that Mom is never coming home. Seems best to use Mildenderger resources to make her final days as comfortable as possible."

"Bill sure owes her that much!" Jean stated.

Peggy gave her sister an elbow nudge. "You always did have a good head for things, Tee. While we understand and appreciate your intentions—"

"We want some say in what goes out of here!" Jean blurted.

Tina's voice held audible strain. "I called you here as a courtesy, because I'm sure certain items hold special value to you." *Because I thought you'd give me a boost in this latest crisis.* She wouldn't lower herself to reveal the weakness, the huge hole in her heart, drilled deeper and deeper with every passing year of their indifference.

"There are some things, Winston things, we will want, Tee," Peggy said, her voice tighter now.

"Winston things," Tina repeated warily.

"Things from our mother," she clarified.

"My grandma."

Jean inhaled sharply. Peggy shot her a warning look.

To Tina's own surprise, she was feeling more angry than sad. This was fortunate, as it kept the tears at bay. "What, exactly, is your problem?"

"Well…" Jean began, "we have reason to doubt your family loyalty. I mean, you changed your name and all."

"I shortened Mildenderger to Mills, yes," Tina said in surprise. "I did it because of my production company with Emmy. Instant name recognition is important. Dad would have understood, and it is his name at issue."

"Oh, sure, *he* would have gone for anything," Jean muttered.

Just as the Winston sisters went for nothing.

Tina briefly studied them, perplexed. "Are you mad that I didn't choose the name Winston?"

"No!" they chorused with a force that set her back on her heels.

Tina took a steadying breath. "I only wished to give you an opportunity to take a memento or two—" Her voice broke off as Jean feverishly grabbed a crystal butter dish.

"This belonged to *our* mother!" Jean plopped the dish on a free corner of the large lace-covered table.

"Fine. One butter dish for Jean."

"There is a whole set, the set must stay together." Jean edged between the open hutch doors and rooted through shelves. She triumphantly produced salt and pepper shakers, a creamer and a sugar bowl. Stacking it with the dish, she frowned. "The cover to the sugar is missing."

"Dad broke it years ago."

Jean nodded heartily. "He broke a lot of things."

"Jeanie," Peggy sniped.

Jean pointed jerkily at the loaded table. "You choose something, Peg. Hurry up! I already know what I want next."

Peggy took hold of one of Tina's coveted Doulton teacups.

"I want those, Peggy," Tina swiftly admitted. "Of everything here, they mean the most to me."

"But they are Winston pieces," Jean said primly.

Peggy held the china to her chest, uncertain what to do.

Tina was flabbergasted. "Technically, they all are my pieces."

The sisters looked as though they'd been slapped. And wanted to slap back. Pain and anger swelled through Tina, but she wouldn't let them see it. She'd never let them see it.

"I asked you over as a courtesy. Hoped at such a harsh time we could pull together."

"But the very idea of selling family treasures," Peggy said mournfully.

"Not all the treasures," Tina corrected. "Just things that no one really wants or needs. I don't like this, either, ladies. But it's my responsibility as heir and executor to see to Mom's best interests."

"As if Angela would want it this way!" Jean cried. "Bill set up the will. Angela didn't change it because she thought she had all kinds of time."

Tina gaped at her. "Are you telling me Mom wouldn't want me looking after her?"

"Jean is overreacting," Peggy said hastily.

Jean whirled on her sister in fury. "I am not! You know I'm not. We've been in complete agreement until the minute we walked into this house. Now you're getting all wimpy."

"Jean," Peggy cautioned. "Tina suffers, too."

Jean sniffed in dismissal.

"Never mind," Tina said. "Why change the habits of a lifetime? I was never good enough to play with your kids outside the holidays. Never said the right things or wore the right clothes or did any damn thing right!"

With a trace of shame, Peggy averted her gaze.

Jean pounded the table. "There are Winston things and there are Mildenderger things. We will want possession of all the Winston things! Period."

Tina gasped in outrage as Jean skirted the table and frantically began dividing pieces by origin. "How dare you?"

Jean's pudgy face flushed. "I am loading up my van. Just try and stop me."

"Slow down," Peggy ordered, wrapping plump arms around her sister.

"But she isn't entitled, Peg. She's not one of us."

"I'm not one of you?" Tina challenged in shock.

"Not a Winston at all!" Jean buried her face in Peggy's shoulder and began to sob. "Angela's already left us! It's all over. I miss her so much!"

"We shouldn't have come here. Let's go home." Peggy's voice was gentle but her intentions were forceful as she steered Jean toward the foyer.

Tina was in quick pursuit. "What is Jean talking about, Peggy?"

Peggy never stopped moving. "She is half out of her mind with grief. Pay no attention."

"How ridiculous. She basically said we're not related!"

"I spoke to Angela's doctor after I got your message," Peggy said breathlessly. "She's expected to last three months at the most. Surely there are enough savings to last that long."

"Maybe. Barely."

"Let's postpone all this for now—until the cash is needed."

Postponement. A typical, passive Winston reaction. Did any of them ever face an issue head-on? "Wait! Please, Peggy! I'm not who I think I am?"

Peggy yanked a despondent Jean down the stoop. "That's not for me to say."

"Oh, go on, give it a try."

Pausing on the walkway, Peggy wore a stony glare that would rival Angela at her worst. "Don't call me again, Tina. At least not right away."

Alone again, Tina moved through the house in a daze. Things were sad enough without this extra hit. A part of her wanted to run back to Tribeca, think no more about this until action was necessary. But how cowardly would that be, when she made a career out of probing other people's dilemmas through the unflinching eyes of the lens? She owed it to herself, to her beloved father, to sort out this mystery.

Collecting a bottle of whiskey from the kitchen cupboard along with a tall, cloudy glass nobody would ever fight for, she closed herself off in the den to sort through more Mildenderger family history.

Maybe she'd been made to feel an outsider for a simple reason that had never once occurred to her—because she was one. Was it possible her parents weren't her biological parents? It was true they both were around thirty when she was born, which might have been a little old at the time. Incapable of making a baby, had they adopted her?

She marched to the file cabinet holding the family's important documents. Grasping a file folder marked Certificates, Tina unearthed her parents' birth and baptismal certificates, as well as her own, everything in its proper place. Records of first confessions, first communions, all the milestones so crucial to Angela's sense of propriety. Again, in order.

She moved on to the photo albums, discovering something she'd never seen before—her parents' wedding album. Eagerly, she lifted the cover to unknown territory, Bill and Angela's relationship when it was brand-new. Bill wore a top hat and tails, Angela a traditional satin dress with a hundred tiny buttons down the back. She was still the same suppressed woman, posed rather stiffly beside giant footloose Bill. The smile was real, though, as was the excitement in her eyes. The pictures told her Bill had clowned around a lot on this important day. One photo revealed Bill's face covered in wedding cake. And he'd hoisted Angela over his head outside the church. She looked absolutely aghast, but actually was laughing!

Day turned to dusk as Tina flipped through album after album, reviewing the phases of her life. Like the paperwork, the photographs seemed in order, from the very start. There was even a shot outside Mercy Hospital, where she'd been born. Bill was holding her proudly.

Of course Tina was their child! It said so in black and white and faded Kodachrome. Her aunts were simply cold fish, who, if nothing else, *wished* she was never part of the family. So anxious to get their mother's stuff back, they'd have said anything. Right?

Tina spent a restless night at the old house on Hillerman Street. *She is not one of us* looped relentlessly through her brain. By morning she was ready to accept the unpleasant reality. Despite family records, something was wrong with her family story.

And she would waste no time cornering the man sure to have answers.

"LITTLE TINA MILDENDERGER, what a pleasure." Warren Ferguson, longtime attorney to Tina's parents, squeezed her hands. "It's been far too long, dear, considering we both live right here in Manhattan."

Tina was aware of his assessment of her chic navy dress and spiked heels, the black hair pulled away from her face with a simple gold clip. Her appearance was far from the soft, scruffy image she adopted to set her documentary subjects at ease. Even further from the innocent child Warren had once taken out for treats.

It was deliberate staging, as she had no wish to set him at ease.

"You still look the same, Warren."

The tall, distinguished man touched his thinning hair. "Kind of you to say. But I am sixty-three now. Moving much slower, and grateful to be retired."

Easing out of his clasp, Tina moved to gaze out his living room window, with its spectacular view of Central Park. "Thanks for seeing me so quickly."

"I would have preferred treating you to lunch at the Four Seasons, like your dad and I used to do. But I understand why you declined, probably wanting to discuss personal business, with your mother having so little time left."

"Privacy is a concern, Warren."

"I can assure you Mildenderger affairs, modest as they are, are in order. Come, sit at the table. Myrna made us coffee before she left. She was a little hurt that you wanted to see me alone."

"Warren, I don't think she would have been comfortable here today."

Was that a flash of panic in those normally steady pale-gray eyes? She congratulated herself for choosing the right source.

They adjourned to the grand kitchen, sat at the granite-topped table. Myrna had left them more than coffee. A huge platter of pastries and a bowl of cut fruit sat between two place settings. Dear Myrna, who'd tangled with four energized children, yet always welcomed Tina into their fold. Tina resisted the nudge of sentimentality. She had to stick to business.

Seated across from him, Tina accepted a steaming mug. "I called my aunts Peggy and Jean to the house yesterday because I was considering an estate sale to help pay for Mom's care."

His brows rose. "Is that necessary at this juncture?"

"Perhaps not, after all, as Mom may not last as long as they originally predicted. And I may have overreacted a little, faced with her steep bills."

"So tragic, as she no longer knows any of us. Myrna and I have visited several times."

"Yes. Thank you." She sipped from the mug. "Anyway, I ended up having a brutal run-in with the aunts. Things were said that made no sense to me."

His features hardened. "They aren't the nicest pair, are they?"

"No." She exhaled and spoke in a rush. "In a tussle for heirlooms, Jean actually stated that I am no relative of hers, no Winston."

"Oh, Tee, really!" Shaken, Warren struggled to recover. "Do you really care? Of all the Winstons, Jean is especially heartless. God rest your father, he always said so."

"I think maybe for the first time ever, Jean was telling me something significant. I'm determined to follow up on it. Through you."

He fumbled with a doughnut. "Nonsense, dear."

"Her inference was that I'm not Bill and Angela's biological child. As their lawyer and friend, you surely know the true facts."

"But you have a birth certificate."

"I do. But documents are easily forged."

"Not thirty years ago they weren't," he said heartily. "Why, I even recall a photo of Bill holding you in front of Mercy Hospital." His eyes wandered like a miscreant teenager's. "You happen to come across that?"

"If *you* recall it, Warren, odds are you took it."

He flushed profusely.

"You look absolutely tragic! C'mon, level with me."

He took a deep breath, then spoke with new determination. "Bill was my best friend since we were kids in Queens. Please, Tee, let it be. Whatever was done was out of love."

Tina turned her head one way, then the other. "Funny, I don't feel the love. All around me, Warren, no love."

"Only because Bill's been gone so long."

"I deserve to know why nobody else ever loved me the way he did."

"Myrna and I have always loved you."

"Quit dodging!"

He shook his head. "I promised Bill to never— Tee, I promised."

"There's no scandal in being adopted, then or now. But if Bill and Angela are not my true parents, my birth certificate was forged for some reason." She tapped her chin with a shaky finger. "So it has to be something of an illegal nature."

"The circumstances were rather irregular," he admitted reluctantly.

"Just tell me the truth," she coaxed. "I'm not here to condemn you or Dad."

"But you will judge us!"

"I am already judging you. My opinion of you is lowering with each passing minute."

His rueful expression suggested retrieving this information from him might be more difficult than she thought. "My reputation in legal circles is sterling. Though I can no longer be prosecuted for anything, I'd hate to lose that. Even my kids don't know."

"So I was stolen."

"Of course not. How unthinkable." He tried to pat her hand but she snatched it out of reach.

"I don't think I can go on *not* knowing, Warren."

"Very well, Tina. I only hope I'm doing the right thing."

Chapter Two

Tina couldn't breathe as she waited for Warren to unlock the secrets of her past. She hadn't been stolen. Had she been picked up on the roadside? Bought on the black market?

"As you've always believed," he said carefully, "you are indeed Bill's natural daughter."

"Excuse me?"

"Bill had had an affair on his sales route. The woman became pregnant. For reasons left unclear to me, she wanted to give you up. Being a natural-born salesman, Bill always saw opportunity in every event, good or bad. He and Angela both desperately wanted a baby and knew by then that Angela would never conceive. So he sneaked you into the house on Hillerman Street."

Tina sat back, stunned. Her dad, an adulterer? Incredible. Unbelievable. And disappointing. Mostly disappointing.

"How could Dad be so insensitive? The affair itself would have been bad enough, but to convince himself that Mom could ever accept me—his love child—is downright inexcusable!"

Warren smiled faintly. "He set out to trick her at first. Told her a baby was coming available on his route, that the pregnant girl was from a fine family who wanted a hush-hush adoption without red tape. Furthermore, he suggested the best way, the only way, to secure the baby without hassle from the authorities was to pretend Angela herself had conceived. Desperate for a baby, Angela played right along, announcing she was pregnant. Acted out the part to everyone but her sisters. It wasn't hard to pad her body for effect. Maternity clothes were looser back then. Women didn't display their condition as freely. In the final weeks of 'pregnancy,' Angela went on a business trip with Bill. The plan was to pick up the baby, claim that she'd given birth on the road.

"They went straight to a designated motel and waited for word that the baby had arrived. The call came, and a few days later a pickup was arranged at a roadside café. Unfortunately, things started to go wrong as soon as they met up with mother and child. Angela rightly sensed that Bill had an emotional connection to the mother.

"Back home, Angela eventually forced a confession out of Bill. Faced with the truth, Angela was outraged. Wanted to give the baby back! But she came to realize she couldn't do that without looking like an utter fool. And you know how Angela feels about propriety.

"I intended to have no part of the charade. But then Bill brought you over to my office. One look at you, honey, and I was in love, the way I'd been with my own babies. I'd have conquered a country for you that day. But all Bill wanted was a birth certificate, to make life smoother. So I produced one, pulling some strings at the county registrar's office. And we swung by the hospital to take that photo." He looked sheepish at this last admission.

"Dad had to know this wouldn't work." She paused, biting her lip. "He had to know I'd suffer in the long run."

"You give him too much credit. Bill was an operator

who routinely seized opportunities without proper thought to the consequences. When the fallout did occur, no one was more surprised than he. He felt remorse, tried to fix the damage with a charming maneuver. Sometimes he would succeed, sometimes not. I confronted him soon after the truth came out, concerned about your well-being. Your whole future was in the hands of a woman scorned. Bill was rather vague, a habit he had whenever things went sour. Insisted that he and Angela had come to some kind of terms."

"What kind?"

"I don't know. Obviously, it didn't work, considering she never did get over your origins."

They sat in silence. The clock chimed the hour, then the quarter hour. Warren refreshed their coffee.

Her beloved father was an adulterer. Tina looked back on the rocky results of her father's actions. All her childhood events that Angela had missed due to unavoidable circumstances. Her father's overcompensation in so many areas. All because his naiveté in thinking the three of them could ever be a healthy family. The sheer selfishness of it all scalded her.

To think now she'd continued to idolize him long after his death. Dad was her rock, her good example.

Suddenly her family wasn't even real. Bill, in particular, was nothing more than a charming stranger.

She finally spoke in a husky voice. "I can't help but wonder… Would I have been better off had Angela given me back?"

"Oh, Tee. That certainly would have disappointed us. And surely would have destroyed Bill."

"Probably wasn't even an option," she said bitterly. "My real mother never made contact in all the years. Plainly, she never wanted me either."

"I can only imagine how you must still yearn for motherly affection—"

She set tightened white fists on the table. "You're wrong! I reconciled those needs long ago."

His expression held doubt. "Please believe that Myrna and I have complete sympathy for you. Fact is, the three adults blessed by your birth totally let you down. Inexcusable."

Fresh questions overwhelmed Tina. If her parents' marriage was unhappy, why hadn't Bill started over with the other woman at the time of her pregnancy? If the woman cared for her baby at all, what would have compelled her to give it up and stay in the background?

"Exactly what do you know about my biological mother, Warren?"

"Nothing really. Bill was careful not to let much slip. Mentioned a town once, that's about all. Warren's mouth disappeared into a tight line, as if he hadn't meant to let that much slip. Tina let it go, for the time being.

"Wonder how she let this happen. If she has any regrets. If she's ever wondered about me…"

"Surely she must have! There could be any number of obstacles that kept her away that have nothing to do with you personally."

"Like what?"

He shrugged. "Maybe she anticipated a fresh start for the three of you and was furious to discover she'd been misled by Bill. Maybe she couldn't explain a new baby in the life she had and sacrificed you for that life. So much time has passed since the decisions were made," he said impatiently. "Could be the truth has died with the both of them."

Warren plainly liked the last idea best. But Tina wasn't buying it. The woman would be sixty at the very most. Might be even closer to fifty. Considering that women were now expected to live well into their eighties, her real mother might actively be enjoying middle age. Her gaze was steady. "Where, exactly, did this grand affair take place?"

He sighed in resignation. "Up in Connecticut. A place called Sugartown."

EMMY SNOW was on the telephone when Tina entered their trendy Tribeca headquarters later that afternoon. The spacious third-floor flat on Franklin was home to Reality Flicks Productions as well as home sweet home. Tina's relationship with Emmy was long-term comfortable, dating back to their sophomore year at Columbia when they'd roomed together in a dorm. Tina was already well-known on campus, making small films just for kicks. Emmy was a spoiled, aloof Palm Beach socialite who believed the world was after her money. Like her father, Tina felt it her mission to charm everyone, so she promptly made an ice-breaker video— *A Day in the Life of Emmy Snow, Socialite at Large,* which featured a hilarious voiceover. In gleeful retaliation, Emmy taped Tina yodeling in the shower and they entertained the masses in the dorm's common room with their "art." It was soon clear they shared similar dreams about filmmaking, and shared the opinion that true stories about real people were the best entertainment.

Tina's small blond friend paced near the window with the cordless phone, chewing out some incompetent soul. This was classic Emmy. Right down to the comfy mint-colored Betsey Johnson slip she often wore around home. If the person on the other end of the phone knew what she was wearing, it would certainly take the edge off her bite.

"You promised Monday delivery and guess what? It's

Monday!" Emmy's face softened when she spotted Tina. "This evening is fine. I'll be here."

The business area of the apartment was at the front, decorated in art deco style. The walls were painted in bold red, black and white, and the furniture was leather, glass and chrome.

Tina parked on a long black sofa, allowing her weary body to sink into the soft upholstery. "Was that call about the new lenses?"

"Yup." Emmy approached, setting a bottle of Diet Pepsi on the glass coffee table near Tina's briefcase. "You called hours ago to tell me about what you've discovered. Where have you been?"

"Back to Brooklyn again for a look at Dad's things. Hoping for a fresh perspective."

"Find anything?"

She gestured to the briefcase. "Hints of another large life in Sugartown, Connecticut. A side of him I knew nothing about, locked away in a trunk under the basement stairs."

"Everybody has secrets, Tina. Your dad was bound to have a few."

"But not from me! We were the best of pals. I had to pry the lock open with a screwdriver. I felt so awful doing it. He should've given me the key—the key to everything!"

Emmy's ivory features settled into a frown. "He didn't know he was going to die so suddenly. He probably would have given it all to you eventually."

"I doubt it. Warren politely suggested that Dad basically was a charming narcissist who put his own comfort first. Under the circumstances, I can't argue the point. Funny that Mom never told me, though, especially after Dad died. It would have been the ideal time to justify her distance, and to change the Mildenderger will to favor the Winston clan."

"It's hard to know why she spared you the ugly truth. But she was always careful to avoid emotional scenes. She had to realize any confessions about Bill or changes in her will would likely cause you a major meltdown that she couldn't escape."

"I think you're on the right track, Em. And appearances have always meant so much to her. By leaving well enough alone, nobody ever found out how she'd fallen for Bill's tricks, or how much she resented me and why. The sterling family image has remained intact." Tina pressed her achy temples. "If only I had found all of this out sooner."

"Then what, Tee? What could you possibly have done?"

"Oh, I don't know. Maybe tried to reach my mother from a fresh angle, woman to woman, mutual victims of Dad's lies."

"None of this is your fault. If anyone should have used that angle, it's Angela. She knew the facts all along. In any case, that option no longer exists for the two of you. Angela will never wake up again. It's up to you to put this crisis behind you."

"Warren said much the same thing. But I'm not sure I can go on without finding out about this woman, my biological mother." She shook her head, overwhelmed. "It's so hard to accept. I actually have another mother, out there someplace."

"I imagine Warren warned you that tracking her down could be risky business."

"Naturally, but he's always been conservative, cautious. You don't agree with him, do you?"

"Well…"

"Oh, c'mon," Tina complained. "We seek the truth for a living."

"But not from the inside out about ourselves! No, this

is something else entirely. A personal, potentially volatile situation. The woman you seek might cause you even more pain."

"So Warren pointed out. But how can I possibly go on examining the world when I have new questions in my own backyard?"

Emmy glanced at the soft-sided briefcase on the table. "What did you find back at the house?"

Tina leaned over and unzipped the case. "There were boxes of Dad's sales ledgers, listing clients and trans-actions. I discovered that by the time I was born, he had not a single client left in the Sugartown area. So his visits were off the official route and most likely strictly social." She sifted through papers. "There is a draft of a letter here to someone he called Honey Bee, obviously his lover, my biological mother. There are mushy sen-timents that are classic Bill. As well as a detailed account of Natalie's activities at age five. She's obvi-ously me. I remember riding without my training wheels that summer, just before kindergarten, and other small comments fit." She handed the letter to Emmy.

"So they called you Natalie." Emmy skimmed it with interest. "You would have thought you'd ridden that bike on water by this glowing report."

"Bill Mildenderger was a champion salesman, don't forget."

"So, Bio Mom—"

"Bio Mom, Em? That sounds so *Star Trek*."

"Do you want to call her Honey Bee? Bill's lover? Both sound so *As the World Turns*."

"Guess Bio Mom will do."

"This letter suggests she had at least some interest in you."

"I'd need to see proof of that in *her* writing. And there is none."

"I suppose Bill was already in too much hot water to keep anything from her. Except you."

Tina smiled thinly, and produced a photograph from the case. "I figure one of this trio may be my mother." She held up the faded four-by-six so they could study it together. Bill was clowning around with three attractive women, in front of an oversize stone mansion bearing the sign Hotel Beaumont.

Emmy shrugged. "Unfortunately, none of them openly resembles you. But the hotel is a solid lead, as I ran across it in some preliminary research on Sugartown."

Tina's face softened. "You already did some checking, Em?"

"Naturally. The town is located in Litchfield County, population three thousand. Their council seems set on keeping things simple, honoring history. This Hotel Beaumont," she said with a tap to the photo, "was mentioned as a cherished hundred-year-old landmark, a good representation of the stable, traditional town. A rather uneventful place. Though there was a little scandal about seven years back, when some con man pretended to be scouting locations there for an orange juice commercial. It made national headlines, I think, because the con crisscrossed the country doing the same schtick. Ironically, it was in Florida, genuine home to orange groves, that he ended up getting caught in his lies. Judging by the *Sugartown Gazette*, the locals weren't feeling too smart after treating him like a VIP for three weeks *and* giving him some very lovely parting gifts. But in their defense, these gullible citizens had plenty of company in several other states."

"Guess we all can be gullible, given the right pitch by a good salesman."

"Kids believe in their parents, Tee, with a built-in innocence."

"I've been too soft in my personal dealings, allowing all my relatives to push me around." Tina unscrewed her cola bottle and took a swig. "That's over. The gloves will soon be off with the aunts. And in the meantime I intend to approach Bio Mom aggressively, like a journalist."

"That could get tricky, if you have any respect for her privacy."

"I'm not going to trot through town with a burning torch, screaming for Bill Mildenderger's lover. I intend to give her a chance to explain, with no pressure. There could well be extraordinary circumstances for her giving me up. Though I can't think of anything that would justify her keeping her distance permanently."

"I can't either. But I'm prejudiced because I know you, can appreciate what she's missed. Who knows? Maybe in hindsight she's come to regret her decision."

"I won't allow myself that naive hope. My main goal is to find my way back to Dad. Put him in perspective. Allow myself—" she choked up "—allow myself to understand him, forgive him."

Emmy smiled gently. "With a little imagination we should be able to come up with a way to use the film company as a front, huh?"

"My thought exactly. I can be myself that way, as nobody is bound to connect Mills with Mildenderger."

"All we need is a subject for a Sugartown film."

"Too bad you didn't uncover any real sins there, Em."

"Damn. Where is sin when you need it?"

"How can I ever hope to profile boring?"

"Try thinking outside our usual box, Tee. Rise above hard issues."

Tina lifted herself off the sofa with a groan. "Guess I'll hop on the Internet and Google them myself."

THE NEXT THING TINA KNEW, Emmy was shaking her awake. She opened her eyes to discover she was on the living room sofa, where she'd crashed sometime during the night. Blinking in the morning sunlight, she slowly sat up. Before her on the coffee table sat a yellow legal pad full of notes. Emmy grabbed it as she sat down beside her.

"So you have an angle for the Sugartown story?"

"Maybe." Tina rubbed her eyes. "It's sort of a reality TV concept working off the quaintness of small-town life."

"Hmm… A contest program called My Town's Better Than Yours."

"The idea is to choose one town from each of the four corners of the country, Sugartown being the northeastern choice. I profile each one in a thirty-minute segment, give the nation a chance to vote for their favorite. A cable network will jump at it, like HGTV, History Channel, Lifetime."

"You don't sound very stoked about it."

"Oh, Emmy, the idea finally occurred to me about two this morning. I can't possibly get this thing off the ground."

"Why not?"

"There's Angela's care to consider. I'm constantly at the nursing facility. The staff reports to me. And there's the threat of her sisters invading the house in Brooklyn. I wouldn't be gone an hour and they'd be on the inside grabbing stuff. No, I simply can't get away."

"Look, these problems can be solved. First of all, Warren can easily take over as Angela's caregiver for the time being. As for the house on Hillerman, have security installed. If the Winstons choose to ignore the warning sign and enter, they can expect to belly-up to a squad car for an official police pat-down."

Tina chuckled. "You make it sound so simple."

"It can be. If you want results bad enough."

"So you've decided the search is a good thing."

"Sometime in the night, I put myself in your place and realized it's a necessary thing. The alternative is to settle for fifty percent of your attention for an indefinite period of time. And Reality Flicks deserves better. So go for it. Settle it. Come back at a hundred percent."

"So you like my contest scheme?"

"Sure. Just needs some tweaking. For instance, what does the winner get?"

Tina sat back on cushions, stupefied. "Get?"

"You need a prize for the contest, Tee."

"You are so material sometimes."

"Yeah. Just like the four corners of our country."

"Oh, we'll work out something." Tina stood and stretched, her confidence returning. "Can't mope here all day. I've got to talk to Warren about Angela. And find an alarm system with a hair trigger."

Chapter Three

The police chief of Sugartown hadn't been informed about the town council meeting on the third Friday night in September. Which is exactly why Chief Colby Evans decided to attend. It seemed unlikely that they were trying to do something in the town without his knowledge. The four men and three women who presently made up the council were a good mix in age, experience and temperament, respectful of his position and opinion.

Just the same, he'd endured the occasional flimflam since his sister Deidre's appointment to the council three months ago.

He and so-called Dizzy Deedee had always gotten in each other's hair. Dizzy was six years older than Colby and had long felt it her right to mother him and at times, smother him. Always in a way she sincerely believed to be helpful.

Women could be especially dangerous when trying to be helpful.

Despite the fact that Colby was thirty, Dizzy stubbornly treated him as years younger, as a hapless lad still in need of direction, much like her own teenage daughter or the kids under her tutelage over at the elementary school.

Admittedly, they had been doing more than their share of bickering lately over council issues—a curfew for students that she judged too early, a speed trap on a county road that she judged a waste of time. Sometimes he swung the council vote, sometimes she did. The worst part of the council meetings was that Dizzy really liked to hear herself talk. Town members sometimes slanted him pleading looks to just give in to her to stop the talking. And sometimes Colby did.

If there was a secret meeting going on, it likely pertained to Colby's biggest proposal yet, the use of municipal funds to install new playground equipment at the public park, rather than at the school where Dizzy was principal. A highly debatable issue, as the present school equipment was in better shape but used more often than the park's gear. Colby accused Dizzy of seeing only the school's needs in her line of vision. Dizzy tagged Colby's bid a trifle self-serving, as he was known to push lady friends on the park swings long after the children had gone to bed. With the board presently stymied for a ruling, it would be just like Dizzy to rally parents behind his back for one uninterrupted sales pitch.

Crossing Belmont Street in his uniform of pale-blue shirt and navy slacks, the representative of the law knew he shouldn't be jaywalking. But as it happened, there wasn't much traffic, apart from a cluster of young bicyclists and some teenagers bouncing a basketball. Strange, as a lovely autumn evening like this, with temperatures in the seventies, normally drew crowds. Especially to the park he was now passing, full of that old weather-beaten equipment.

Colby grinned at fleeting memories of those creaky old swings, feeling all the more determined to improve his future rides with that funding.

Council meetings were held in the basement of St. Bartholomew's Church on Belmont Street. As he walked along the side of the old building, he noted that the frosted basement windows were cranked open and a hum rose from the sills. Sounded like a full house.

Colby entered the rear door and went down the stone steps. If Dizzy had deliberately kept an entire meeting from him, it would be a new low. But it didn't escape him that if he had been blackballed, it was no less than a town conspiracy. For nobody had mentioned a word of it in his presence. And to add insult to injury, the station's only clerk, Grace Copeland, had made a mess of a file cabinet at the end of her shift around five. A deliberate ploy? Predictably, he'd insisted upon straightening it out himself. While she, rather unpredictably, had gone to the diner to fetch him a pot roast meal to eat at his desk.

Columbo would be curious. Sherlock would be furious. Colby was both.

Gently he creaked open the door at the back of the room. Mayor Husman was at the podium on the church's stage, overdressed as usual in a black suit with crisp white shirt and red tie, his blond hair parted neatly. Of all Sugartown's residents, Colby found Seth Husman a particularly big pain in the ass. Back in school Colby had been the cocky lower-middle-class jock and Seth the pompous rich boy, and they'd constantly dueled for the limelight.

They were still rivals at times. But these days, Colby was more amused by it than anything else. With age and experience came the knowledge that material wealth wasn't necessarily the key to happiness. As for Seth, he'd yet to pull a dollar bill far enough away from his face to see the bigger picture.

"In closing," Seth announced, "I'd just like to congratulate everyone for sprucing up their homes and storefronts. Now I'll hand it over to…ah…" Seth had just caught sight of Colby in the back and momentarily lost his stride. "…hand it over to our chamber of commerce president Jessie Miller, who made all this possible. With the invaluable help," he added with a smirk at Colby, "of our tireless council member Deidre Littman."

Dizzy Deedee *was* at work here. He knew it! But what was up?

Leaning a shoulder against a square plaster pillar, Colby tipped halfway out of sight. He still had a good view of Jessie taking the microphone, however. In her late twenties, the petite nurse was energetic, bubbly and eager to please. Colby and Seth had both dated her. Both had found her too bossy.

"Thanks, Mayor. Just a few final thoughts." Jessie crunched her nose and scanned her notes. "The park committee has some work to do on the gardens. They can go right now to catch the last light." She nodded approvingly as several males hustled out. "Now it's true that we believe only a location scout is coming tomorrow. But it isn't too early to go beyond sprucing our facade. We want to greet this person with courtesy, reflect a general impression of town tranquility. This means keeping noise levels down, abiding by traffic laws. It'll be good practice for when the mobile unit arrives, which includes a cameraman. And with release forms signed in advance, we'll have no editing power over what is released."

Colby expelled a long breath. What the hell had they gotten his orderly Sugartown into? Hadn't they learned last time how disappointing it could be when a project went sour?

Jessie's lips pursed. "My only real concern is the

trailer park at the edge of town. It houses some hooligans right now, those jailbirds on work release doing road repair. But," she added, "Chief Colby seems to have a pretty short leash on them, so I guess we can rely on him to restore order in a pinch."

Seth raised his voice loud enough to carry. "Speaking of the devil, Colby Evans will have to be told about this before daybreak, don't you think? Convince him in advance that the representative herself isn't a hooligan."

Colby wheeled round the pillar. "You've had your fun, Mayor." There was a tangible feeling of heightened anticipation, as there was whenever the rivals squared off.

"Somebody had better start talking straight," Colby boomed. "And I mean now."

Jessie cleared her throat. "Perhaps Deedee would like that honor."

His sister, seated in the front row, skipped up on stage. Still dressed in one of her school-principal suits, she looked, Colby thought, remarkably like their late mother. But he wouldn't allow the sentimental resemblance to distract him.

"Yeah, Dizzy, do tell." Hands on hips, Colby stalked down the center aisle, to stop just short of the platform. There was no mistaking the pair as relatives, with their thick brown hair and intense amber eyes.

Deedee grinned, taking the microphone. "I'd appreciate it if you'd take your hand off your holster, Cole."

"All in due time."

"Here's the thing," she said with a fluttering hand. "A production company called Reality Flicks is coming here to shoot a television program on small-town living."

Colby groaned and rubbed his face. "No, Dizzy, no."

"Part of a contest called My Town's Better Than Yours—"

"Nicknamed Four Corners Project by the crew," Jessie said importantly.

Deedee went on. "Four towns across the nation will compete for the title of best. It will air on cable television, and the viewing public will be allowed to vote for their favorite town. We—"

Colby had hopped up on stage and grabbed the mike from her in midsentence. "Do I have to remind all of you what happened the last time a stranger invaded Sugartown with an agenda?" Voices rose but so did his. "Don't you remember Vincent Plant, the orange juice king? Scouting commercial locations here, miles from any grove? I don't know what Chief Rodale was thinking when he embraced that creep, encouraged your open bribery to win the commercial shoot. He was no more a producer than he was a king. A con artist is what he was. Plain and simple."

The rumbles of protest that followed didn't surprise Colby. The general public thought Plant merely skipped out on his motel bill with a basket of Violet Avery's honey samples, a signet ring from the jeweler and some other minor bribes. But the real losses were far more costly. Plant had discreetly lured a few investors into a bogus scheme involving a hybrid orange crop that was supposed to contain antitoxins beneficial to cancer patients, then run off with the loot.

At the time, Rodale had kept details of the scam private to spare local investors any embarrassment. Colby only knew about it because his late wife, Diana, was among the victims. Young and eager to please, she'd plunked down their thousand-dollar savings to give them a surprise head start. He'd been angry at

Diana for about five minutes before putting the blame where it belonged, on the stranger who had invaded their town and the lawman who allowed the pillaging.

Upon his appointment to the chief position five years ago, Colby announced a no-tolerance policy toward solicitors like Plant—no doubt the reason he'd been completely shut out of this decision.

Deedee stood her ground next to him. "This is legit. I spoke with producer Tina Mills myself. Checked out Reality Flicks myself."

He glowered over her. "How did you check them out?"

"Through the Better Business Bureau." She nodded at the crowd. "Not a single complaint.

This wasn't enough to sell Colby, but he didn't have any ammunition of his own. Yet. "Even it is on the level, what do we stand to gain?"

"A hundred grand!"

Colby had to wait for a thunder of applause to die. "One in four odds aren't very good. We'll likely lose the contest and our privacy in one shot."

"Most of us don't mind that, Cole. We anticipate increased tourism."

"Why the hell would we want that?"

"People who come here will spend money. A welcome boost for business owners and our civic improvement fund."

"So it's all about money."

Deedee bit her lip, momentarily stumped. "Well, we'd be making new friends, too, I suppose."

His features sharpened. "I, for one, have all the friends I need. Good old trusted friends who have never struck me as this greedy."

"Oh, this is why nobody told you about this!" Deedee stomped her sensible pump, completely losing her composure. "Because you'd condemn the project without a fair hearing, spoil it for the rest of us. If you can't happily join us, we'd rather you just keep clear."

He rocked on his heels. "I see, unless a hooligan gets out of hand."

"Well, yes. It's your job to protect the town. The crew will be headquartered at the Hotel Beaumont," she said in a smaller voice. "And you could make a special effort to go by there each night. Just to make sure everything's buttoned up."

"But you want it done off the radar, to make it seem unnecessary."

Deedee pinched his cheek. "You've got it, exactly."

As SHE DIDN'T OWN A CAR, Tina had to give transport to her true hometown some hard consideration. Hire a car and driver? Though common in Manhattan, it seemed ostentatious for her destination. Take her mother's Lumina? Someone might trace the plates and discover it belonged to a Mildenderger and conceivably blow her cover. Though Bill's secret was kept in Brooklyn, there was no telling how many folks in Sugartown knew of Bill and of her existence. Bio Mom might have a whole town willing to protect her by trotting Tina in useless circles.

She'd settled for driving to Litchfield County in a rented sedan.

Impressions hit her as she wheeled through Sugartown's broad and tidy streets. Stately old homes with fresh paint. Neat lawns. Majestic old oaks and maples turning color. There seemed a tranquil energy and order to things. So unlike her usual choice of subject.

But surely she could get a story angle. It was a documentary producer's mission to peel away surface images like layers of onion for a candid look. Tina was adept at it. If only she could hang on to her trademark objectivity.

The town's municipal building was white brick,

situated on Main Street between the library and a small department store. It looked busy today, which was Saturday. She rolled into a narrow open slot in front of the store and popped out of the car, carefully smoothing her tight yellow dress and loose black hair.

No sooner had she taken the four stone steps of the municipal building's entrance than the double doors swung open.

"I am Mayor Husman. Greetings!"

Tina smirked at the tall blond man in a well-cut navy suit and polished shoes. Apparently being mayor meant a lot to him. She extended her hand. "Tina Mills."

He cradled her hand like a precious baby bird. "Glad to meet you, Tina. Come inside."

The building was a cool contrast to the hot autumn day. Husman led her along the wide corridor. Tina sensed he might have been lingering in the doorway waiting for her. If he was representative of the town's eagerness, her job would be a piece of cake!

"Please call me Seth. My office is up one flight. Biggest room in the building." He led the way upstairs, stopping at the first doorsill to allow her passage. "But I'm worth every square inch."

A woman of about twenty sat in the outer office and jumped at the sight of him. "Oh, Mayor, you're finally back. I—"

"Not now, Lindsay." Still making jolly sounds, Seth ushered Tina through the inner door. "Just make yourself comfortable." Seth stopped dead at the sight of the uniformed man seated in his big leather chair, low-cut boots propped on his ornate mahogany desk.

"I knew you'd want me to," the man said. "Make myself comfortable, I mean."

"Remove those feet!" Seth growled. "That piece is a prized antique."

"Or so the seller on eBay claimed." He tapped a neat pile of papers on the desk, swung his feet to the ground and came to greet them. "I'm not so easily convinced, Seth. By anyone's claims," he said pointedly to Tina. "I'm Colby Evans, Ms. Mills."

Colby did not cradle her hand as Seth Husman had. Rather, he clamped it. Tina admired his grip and the fact that he hadn't offered her his title. His authority was plain through his badge, his uniform, his hard, insightful eyes. Eyes that were, upon scrutiny, a unique shade of amber.

Her fighting instincts rose, but she quickly quelled them. It was reasonable that not all civil servants would tumble as easily as the mayor had. Too bad the groupie hadn't instead been Evans, though, as a cop in particular would routinely cruise the streets and be more likely to cross her path during filming. She especially approved of cop groupies with sexy strong dark features like his.

Preferring to flirt rather than fight, she flashed a winsome smile. "It does pay to be a little suspicious, at least of transactions on eBay."

Seth scrambled to wedge himself between them. "A local lady got many of us hooked on the auction site," he explained. "Marilyn Beaumont is her name. You'll meet her soon, as you're staying at Hotel Beaumont. It's a family-run place. I could take you over there right now if you like. Personally."

"Have a seat, Ms. Mills," Colby intervened.

She noted that he was holding the permits necessary for her production and promptly joined him in the guest chairs while Seth parked behind his antique throne. "Do call me Tina."

"Do call me Seth!"

"Settle down, Mayor," Colby said blandly, his eyes never leaving his prey. "Intriguing little contest you're running, Tina."

So it was. But, plainly, he didn't like it at all.

"There is so much junk on television now. We thought it might be fun to remind the jaded public that good, solid Americana is still alive and well."

Colby leaned forward, resting his elbows on his thighs. "A far cry from your regular beat on crime, corruption and misery."

She didn't particularly care for his stark description of her body of work. "It may be a little fluffier than our company usual—"

"My main concern here, Tina, is that you may put a negative slant on our town."

"But, Chief Evans," Seth said smugly, "last night you were worried about attracting tourists with a positive slant."

Colby shot the mayor a look. "I did my own research on Reality Flicks, and this new, bigger concern hit me." Back to Tina, he said, "It appears you routinely use exploitation to get a story."

Tina sat back, appalled. "We don't!"

"But your subjects often seem exploited."

"Not by us," she said angrily. "We work to uncover the misdeeds of others. Help fix the world's troubles by bringing them to light."

"Does this *show* have a sponsor yet?"

"The cable network LifeSource is behind us. They'll handle the contest details, provide the prize money."

"What other towns were chosen?"

"Towns in Washington, California and South Carolina."

"Is there any footage of them I can view?"

"Well, no. So happens I'm cutting my teeth on you."

"Are you?" He smiled, showing his teeth as if in challenge.

"Not you personally, Colby!" Seth reddened and

sputtered. "You aren't to be involved at all. *I* am to have the reins. Even Dizzy said so."

Colby stood abruptly and flapped the permits. "Let's talk outside."

"You certainly don't have to, Tina," Seth blustered. Snatching the permits, he presented them to her. "Tell him to get lost."

Tempting idea. Colby had way too much nerve. But she couldn't afford to make a powerful enemy in the first ten minutes. Tina stowed the valuable permits in her purse and stood with a tug to her short knit dress. "Okay, Marshall Dillon, let's take it to the street."

Outside, she leaned against her rented black sedan with arms folded. "So?"

In view of curious passersby, Colby lowered his voice. "I thought you'd be more comfortable settling things out here."

"Why?"

"Because, I *know.*"

Her heart wrenched. She stiffened against the car. "What do you know?"

"Your game." He took out a pad of paper and began to doodle on it. Saying nothing. Allowing her to stew.

The actual time didn't matter but she glanced at her watch anyway, just to appear hurried. "Care to make your point, Chief?"

"I read up on the Chicago thing."

She stared blankly. "The Chicago thing."

He rolled his eyes. "Don't play innocent. You went undercover at a sleazy club, consorted with gangsters and assorted creeps. Danced in a cage. In a peekaboo suit," he whispered urgently.

That was all he had? Who even said peekaboo anymore? She smiled sweetly and said with a purr, "They nicked me catwoman at the club, because of my fishnet body stocking. Find that bit of trivia in the report?"

"No. That bit of trivia was apparently not reported to the Better Business Bureau, either."

"Hardly their jurisdiction, is it? Look, I hate to see you rattled over some long-forgotten dance moves done in the line of duty."

"I am not rattled!"

"It by no means reflects my character or challenges my ability to do lighter fare. Would it help to know I made mental grocery lists during my act?" She gave him a sample shimmy. "Milk, bread, Gouda, raisins. That is, when I wasn't watching illegal activity at the bar. The reason I was there in the first place."

"You are reducing my concerns to a joke."

"I don't want to."

"But you are."

"I would like to see you lighten up," she admitted.

"That's your problem. I do think you were allowed in town on impulse. Wouldn't have expected it of Dizzy. Still, here we are."

"The mayor also mentioned this Dizzy person. What's up with her? She dangerous? The boss? Some kind of puritan?"

"She's all those things. As well as my sister."

Tina smirked. "So Dizzy wants me and you don't. A sibling battle over town policy."

"Imagine Bigfoot marching across a Monopoly board and you've got Dizzy Deedee's effect on Sugartown."

"Maybe you're more worried about trumping Deedee than you are about my little film."

"It's not clearly a sibling rivalry issue, like the swings, for instance."

"The swings?"

"I want new ones for the park. Oh, never mind. This

is about my job as chief, protecting the town. We've been embarrassed once before on a national level—"

"Ah, the orange-commercial scam."

"Right. I'm not about to let history repeat itself on my watch. Allow you to incite people, have them behaving crazy again for a chance to be on camera."

She leaned closer. "You overestimate my power. I'm not much of a threat without the fishnet number. Which I left at home."

"I suppose it's wrapped in tissue, until your own daughter grows old enough to wiggle in your footsteps."

"That would make for a lousy mother, wouldn't it?"

Her anger startled him. "Just trying to lighten up. Like you said."

Naturally he had no way of knowing he'd hit her central nerve. She drew a steadying breath. "Look, I only mean that if I had ambitions to be a mother—which I don't—I would try to be the best damn mother ever. Which I won't be."

He too was now a bit more unsettled. "Can you at least give me an idea of your general direction? Creatively speaking."

"I can't give it even if I want to. A documentary has no predetermined course. It shapes itself at random. Through people and place."

"I hate the word *random*. Means something can lead anywhere."

"Yes, that's the idea."

He shook his head. "What I wouldn't give for the right to yell *cut!* at you anytime I want."

True, the film project was a smokescreen, but she was still determined to pull it off by Flicks' high standards. Marshall Dillon be damned. "You sure won't be getting those rights, Chief. Your territory is restricted to enforcing the law."

"But I will be close by whenever possible." Colby peeled the top sheet off his pad and set it on the sedan's windshield under a wiper blade. "Any other time, you can reach me at that number." With a nod he stalked off.

Intrigued, Tina reached for the paper. It was a parking ticket for fifty bucks!

MAYOR SETH HUSMAN insisted on hopping into Tina's rental sedan to accompany her over to Hotel Beaumont. Tina found him a little overbearing, but all in all was pleased. The mayor had contritely taken back the parking ticket.

"Please don't let our chief's bullishness bother you."

No, she was more bothered by Colby Evans's disarming smile. Or was it his snoopy nature? His arrogance? His muscled chest? Those amber eyes? Hard to decide. The bullishness definitely was no problem. She matched him there.

"He had no right to challenge your purpose here," Seth asserted heartily.

"Probably doing his duty as he sees fit. Let's forget it."

"Not a chance. Just wait until the council sees that ticket he issued you."

"I was illegally parked."

"Only half the car was in the loading zone! And he only did it because he doesn't like your project."

"In any case, you ripped up the ticket."

"So I did." He pulled the shreds of paper from his jacket pocket. "Not too many pieces, though. I'll tape it back together." It occurred to Tina that the mayor was gleeful in his anger toward the chief, as if friction between them might be a jolly sport. The last thing she needed was another conflict on the side.

"I'd rather you let the whole matter go."

"We'll see. Take a left off Main Street here at the

light," he directed, with a wave that deliberately brushed her arm. "Roll up the hill past the gas station. It's just ahead. The property takes over the whole street corner."

Tina recognized the hotel from the one photograph she carried featuring her dad and those three mystery women. But it wasn't a full view and hardly did the large stone building justice. It had turrets and stained glass and a broad front porch with stone pillars.

Seth went on about landmark status, built over one hundred years ago, originally the estate of a newspaper publisher.

All she could picture was her father standing out in that front yard. Living secrets, days away from home. Shaping events that would lead to her creation. Tricking his restrained but surely faithful wife.

Oh, Dad... How could you?

She steered the sedan up the winding drive and eased into the lot on the north side of the building. Seth grabbed her large suitcase from the back seat and waited while she retrieved a smaller one. Together they rounded the house to the wide concrete staircase out front.

"They'll be expecting you by now," Seth said.

"You call ahead?"

"Didn't bother. There are no secrets in Sugartown."

Tina smiled faintly as he held open the beveled-glass door for her. *There* are *a few secrets around here. In the name of Mildenderger.*

The foyer had a regal Old-World air to it. The floor, expansive front desk and sweeping open staircase were done in polished walnut, the light fixtures in brass. There was a cheeriness about it just the same, with plenty of light from various windows and a three-tiered chrome shelf jammed with ivy, ferns and colorful azaleas. A woman stood at the shelf, carefully watering each pot.

"Good afternoon!" Mayor Husman called out.

The startled woman tipped her watering jug enough to splash her green pantsuit. "Oh, Seth." Recovering with a laugh, she set the down the jug and crossed the large accent rug between them. "You must be Tina Mills," she greeted with an outstretched hand. "Lizbeth Beaumont, manager and part owner of this place. I'm so pleased you chose the hotel as your headquarters."

"Pleased to meet you, Lizbeth." Tina felt a measure of awe as she took in the tall, elegant, middle-aged woman with reddish-gold hair. For, aside from a thickened waistline, some laugh lines and a shorter hairstyle, she might have stepped right out of the thirty-year photo! One of the mystery trio.

To think this could very well be her biological mother. Touching her, smiling at her.

Lizbeth looked concerned. "Are you all right, Tina? You look pale."

"Guess it's been a long trip for me," she said softly.

"We'll get you registered and to your room." Lizbeth briskly crossed the room and rounded the desk. "You'll find the place fairly peaceful. Autumn is a slow time for us."

Tina followed, sensing she still had the mayor in tow. "Thanks, Seth," she said brightly but firmly. "I'm sure you must have things to do."

He blinked and glanced at his watch. "Oh. I guess so. Meeting with the county commissioner. A plumbing problem on Main Street. Bye, ladies."

Tina turned to Lizbeth, who was impatiently tapping at a computer. "I hate these things. A friend—Seth's mother, Brooke, in fact—pushed me into updating our system. I've regretted it ever since. Give me back the old registration book anytime."

Tina perked up at the mention of the old system. Those books could give her the solid base she needed for placing her father in town, if she could locate his signature in them. "I suppose you've kept the old records," Tina remarked.

"Oh, sure. Figure it's part of the hotel's history. In the real old days, when I was a very young girl helping my grandpa around the place, people used to list their occupations along with home address. I guess license plate numbers eventually took over the occupation space. Too bad. I love to study people, discover what makes them tick. Part of the reason your film interests me so, I suppose. My natural curious streak."

Already something Tina had in common with Lizbeth.

The printer soon grinded to life and popped out a registration form. Lizbeth pushed it across the desk with a pen.

Tina began to fill it out. "Speaking of plate numbers, I'm afraid I don't know the one on my rental car."

"No problem. After all, we do know exactly where you're coming from, don't we?"

Tina averted her gaze and kept writing.

Lizbeth leaned against the counter rather dreamily. "We Beaumonts have always felt our hotel is sort of the heart of the town. Though some think it's St. Bartholomew's Church, while others believe it's the library. You'll get a good look at all of them during your stay, of course. But this place does film well. Was used in one of Humphrey Bogart's lesser-known gangster movies in the fifties. I was a toddler then. Mother and I got walkons. Marilyn, my mother, remembers more about it, if you're interested."

"I'd love to meet your mom. She help run this place?"

"Oh, no. She dabbled over the years to try and please her father, but never really got pleasure from it the way I do."

"Your Bogie story does sound fascinating," Tina said

with exaggerated interest. "Just the sort of human-interest stuff I need. Is your mother the type who enjoys telling anecdotes?"

"Hard to shut her up."

"I'd love to meet her. She around?"

"She lives with me in the family wing but isn't home today. She does on occasion stay over in Clarksville to visit friends and buy yarn at a discount mart for her knitting. I expect her back in the morning."

Tina tried to suppress her excitement. Marilyn was likely just the kind of witness she was looking for, a chatty old thing who'd been around in her father's day and who would know what had gone on here at the hotel.

The sooner Tina identified all potential Bio Moms, the quicker she could incorporate them into the Four Corners Project. Tina's sharp mind ticked off possible avenues to pursue and took a chance on her friendly innkeeper.

"I'm so happy you're pleased about the film, Lizbeth. I wonder, because it's the weekend and a slow time for you, if you'd consider inviting some of your female friends over for an informal get-together to start me off. Nothing grand, just coffee?"

Lizbeth was startled. "I know there was some discussion by the town council on how to best introduce you...."

"I advised Jessie Miller by phone to do nothing. I want to catch people being themselves, doing the usual. But it would be nice to get my bearings before I hit the street on Monday. Meet other successful business-woman like yourself."

Lizbeth looked a trifle harried. "I suppose something can be done on short notice." After a brief pause, she said, "It'll be my pleasure. Now, if there's nothing else, I'll get you settled in your room."

There were the reservation books, but she could wait. At least an hour.

Chapter Four

"You big dumb oaf!"

Colby barely gave his big sister a glance. "Hey, Dizzy."

"You gave our guest of honor a parking ticket in front of city hall!"

"Well…"

Fresh out of a Saturday faculty meeting, principal Deedee Littman wasn't dressed for the playground but sat on the swing beside his anyway, and produced the offending ticket, now a taped-up mess.

He inspected it. "There's an ordinance about tearing up tickets. Someplace on the books…"

"Seth is behind it all, of course, the ripping, the taping—"

"The tattling. It's high time he stop whining to you about me."

"He is what Mom used to call a pill, Cole. But that's not the issue. Did you have to insult this producer the minute she arrived?"

"The ticket probably was a mistake," he conceded with effort.

"No, duh. What on earth happened to set you off?"

"It wasn't all me!"

"So it was mostly her, I suppose?" Deedee's dark-brown hair swung at her chin. "I hear this kind of flimflam at recess every single day! It's strictly playground level."

He flashed her a wicked smile and reached over to give her swing a push. "Well, we are on a playground at the moment. So all's fair."

Feeling the old rivalry, they both began to pump their swings to gain height. Colby was in his element among the grand old trees, the basketball court, the fountain, the benches, the balding grass and the worn gym equipment that he was so intent on replacing with town funds.

"This shouldn't still be your favorite place," she complained in the face of his glee.

It went without saying that it always would be. The place he and big sister always came for a break during the years their frail mom couldn't tolerate noise in the house. The place he could let go, dream, relax. Even shout right out loud.

"But as this is still your favorite place," she went on, "the council wants you to have a new swing set, if we win the grand prize."

It seemed Dizzy was trying to bribe him instead of bully him on this one. "I have concerns about this documentary and made that clear to Tina."

Deedee almost smiled. "Oh, Cole. You have most of the women in town charmed to pieces. Why didn't you zap her with some of the usual?"

He slowed his swing back to a cradle motion along with hers. "Actually, I think she *was* rather charmed."

Deedee flapped the ticket in his face. "Excuse me?"

He tipped a flattened hand back and forth. "We had a sort of thing going on between us there for a while."

She almost smiled. "You truly live in a fantasy world, baby brother."

Not so. The world's harsh realities had him grounded, on and off duty. It was plain fact that he'd found Tina gorgeous, bold and expressive, a mystery like no local woman could ever be. And she *had* found him appealing. Of that he was sure.

So what had eventually spoiled the mood? His cop instincts overriding his hormones? This piece on quaint Americana just didn't fit the Reality Flicks pattern. He'd viewed some actual footage of films on their Web site and it was dynamite. She'd worn that fishnet suit at Club Bravado like a second skin, putting on some moves never taught at Arthur Murray. Sure, she'd helped bust the owner, notorious mobster Antony Flynn, freed his female employees from all sorts of nasty games. But every single story on the site fit a general pattern for gritty, provocative journalism. And she had no convincing reason for the abrupt change in direction.

Disrupted patterns troubled good cops like Colby. Add to that the fact that she'd been relieved at the mention of her club escapade, like she'd been worried he'd uncovered something else entirely. Mighty troublesome.

"Are you listening, Cole?" Deedee demanded.

He jerked back to the moment. "Not really."

"Lizbeth called to say that she's hosting a brunch reception for Tina Mills tomorrow at the hotel."

"Oh, yeah?"

"Down, boy. No men allowed. As she's never been one for kids or pets, there sure won't be any of those, either."

"Or hooligans from the trailer park," he chuckled.

She sighed. "You better get home before Dad begins to wonder. And let Tina alone from now on!"

Funny how Dizzy never gave up on issuing the orders. He had no intention of listening, of course. If Tina had something foxy hidden up those fishnets he was going to find out what.

"WEAR BLACK IF YOU'RE UNSURE," Emmy coaxed through Tina's cell phone the next morning. "People picture dedicated artists in black."

Tina was presently pacing around her cozy hotel room. While the pale-rose-colored walls, rosebud bedding on a comfy four-poster and framed artwork should have soothed her, there was no denting her sizzled nerves.

"There's already been some notice of my stint as catwoman, exotic dancer. So black might send the wrong message for this fluffier piece."

"Gee, guess that *is* right on our Web site. Setting the kick-ass tone."

"There wasn't much time to think of such details, but in any case, there would have been no transforming our image to fit this folksy gig."

"So who confronted you?"

"Colby Evans, chief of police. He is suspicious of cameras because of the orange-commercial con and troubled by our apparent shift in focus."

"Someone you can handle?"

"I don't know!"

"Ooooh, do I detect some sizzle?"

Tina leaned against the window frame overlooking the plush, sloping front yard. An older brown Chevy was roaring up the drive, veering off to the private detached garage. "He is a hottie."

"Better make sure he isn't your brother before you go too crazy."

She glanced over at her laptop, set on the small cherry desk. "Ha, ha. I already looked up his statistics. He was born three months before me, so his mother would have made national headlines if she'd given birth to both of us." Tina tensed as Emmy laughed. "What's so funny?"

"I'm just happy. That you had the desire to check. You can use a little romance in your life. Let go and fly."

"I'm not ready to trust *anyone* so soon after Dad's trick...."

"Just have some fun. Have a fling. Oh, and just a quick refresher on budding romance killers, Tee. Any mention of religion, politics or a dysfunctional mother makes men feel incapable of love."

"I already sort of mentioned to Colby that I don't intend to be a mother."

"Before he's even made a pass?"

"I know. It was dumb and made him squirm."

"But you think he likes you, right? He give you his number?"

"Sort of. On a parking ticket." Tina watched an older woman in faded jeans and a brightly colored poncho emerge from the private garage and follow the driveway back to the entrance. She was carrying an overnight bag and some shopping bags. Despite the energy in her step, the woman had a gray ponytail and looked well over seventy. Probably Lizbeth's mother, Marilyn, back from Clarksville.

"Try not to do any more damage until I get there," Emmy directed.

"You're joining the crew?"

"Definitely. Have a time frame in mind yet?"

"Let's plan for Thursday."

"No problem. Now be a good girl and think booty before duty." She punctuated her point with the dial tone.

Tina set a beige-and-green outfit on the bed, then wandered into the bathroom to find she had no bath towel. Realizing she was now limited for time, she slipped on her terry robe and opened her door to seek assistance. Two doors down, on her hands and knees in the hallway, was the aging hippie. Seeing she was in distress with gaping sacks, Tina advanced.

"Crap!" the woman squeaked. "You scared me!"

"Having problems?"

"Keep your voice down."

"Having problems?" Tina whispered, dropping to her knees.

"My sack handles broke. I need to get these things to my room before Beth sees."

Beth, presumably a nickname for Lizbeth. Tina couldn't suppress her grin. "You must be the mother."

"Marilyn Beaumont, mama to the tightest chick in town. Help me, will ya?"

Arms loaded, they stole off like a couple of thieves to the family wing of the hotel. There was a lock on Marilyn's door but it wasn't secured. Safely inside, Marilyn collapsed on the bed with her share of the stuff. "I really blew the budget this time—at least, that's what my girl would say if she saw all this."

Tina set Marilyn's other sacks on the bed as well. Skeins of yarns in various shades and textures rolled free, a kaleidoscope of color against the white bedspread.

"I do make good use of the yarn," Marilyn said, sitting up. "Beth just thinks I shouldn't buy so many kinds at a time. Must figure I'll drop dead before I have a chance to use them all." She slapped her long, skinny leg, thoroughly enjoying herself. "I always say she can return the unused skeins when I croak, if she can find my receipts." Pushing large owlish glasses up her nose, she peered hard at her guest. "By the way, just who the hell are you?"

"Oh!" Tina touched her heart. "Guess I didn't say. I'm Tina Mills."

"Oh, the movie gal." Marilyn inspected her with a nod. "Nice fishnets on the Web site."

Tina sighed. "You would be computer savvy. Seth mentioned your interest in eBay."

"My dear, I have my own Web site. I make these and sell them online." She peeled off her colorful poncho and handed it to Tina.

"Clever." Tina held it up over her robe in front of the dresser mirror. "Ponchos are hot right now."

Marilyn smiled to show some crooked teeth. "I could use the publicity, if you think I'm interesting enough for your documentary."

"I'll let you know."

The crinkles in her narrow face deepened. "Hmm, that old showbiz brush-off."

Tina laughed and draped the poncho on the back of a chair. "Hey, give me a chance. I haven't even had a shower yet. Which is why I was in the hall. I need a couple bath towels."

"C'mon, I'll show you a linen closet close to your room. Guests aren't supposed to use it, but I'm more than happy to do you a favor."

"I see. So I'll owe you."

Marilyn rubbed her palms together. "Well, as they say in the shower game, one hand washes another's backside."

"They say that, do they?" The wily old thing. If Lizbeth did prove to be her Bio Mom, Tina would have a granny in the bargain, too. "I do look forward to talking to you," she said as they exited the family wing. "Lizbeth is having a brunch for me in about thirty minutes—"

"I won't make that. Intend to take a little nap. When you get to my age, you have to sleep when you're tired. I don't get much rest during the night anymore."

Tina then noted that, despite her bravado, Marilyn did look weary. "I'll look you up later then, Marilyn?"

Marilyn set two folded white towels in her arms. "You know where I live, hon."

TINA ENTERED THE HOTEL'S main-level parlor and was touched to discover that Lizbeth had gone to some trouble on her behalf. Two uniformed waitresses were moving through a small group of women with a tray of appetizers and brimming stemware. She scanned the crowd, anxiously hoping that this ploy of hers had managed to reel in the other two Bio Mom candidates.

Lizbeth spotted her immediately and called for quiet. "Why don't we just go around the room and introduce ourselves to Tina." She deferred to the rather plain brunette in her midthirties on her right, dressed in a belted gray slacks and white blouse.

"I'm Deedee Littman, grammar school principal. My husband, John, is an electrician and I have two kids in junior high. Oh, and Chief Evans is my little brother," she added. "Who won't be bothering you again."

A redhead in her late twenties in a white uniform spoke next. "I'm Jessie Miller, the chamber of commerce president you spoke to by phone. I have to leave shortly for my nursing shift at County General Hospital, but you can call me anytime with concerns."

"I'm Brooke Husman," a chic middle-aged blonde in a pink Chanel suit announced. "My son, the mayor, told me how sweet you are. I am a reporter for the local paper and am at your service—as is Seth!"

"The name is Violet Avery," a tall, gaunt woman proclaimed, her age indeterminate due to a long, baggy blouse, heavy makeup and an unflattering shade of brown hair. "Happily single. Cat named Gus. Keep bees as a hobby. As head librarian, I can help you research any historical facts."

"Kaitlyn Schuler," a pregnant girl barely out of her teens piped up. "My mom was supposed to be here but she got caught up at the family flower shop, so sent me. If you need anything…" she said uncertainly.

"Lastly, I'm Ginny Royal," said a plump and jovial woman with black hair and flushed complexion. "My family has run Royal Diner on Main Street for over fifty years. Best food in town."

"Best short-order, Ginny. The hotel rules on sit-down elegance!" Lizbeth laughed, but Tina noted a serious determination in her words when she met Ginny's lofty gaze. Like herself, both women appeared to live for their jobs.

Tina mingled, taking a better look at faces. None of the women present resembled the ladies in Bill's old photo as clearly as Lizbeth had. She should have expected that was a lucky fluke.

The only one who bore her any resemblance at all was Ginny Royal, with her dark hair and direct personality. But the group in the photo looked extremely chummy. Could Lizbeth have ever been a close buddy to Ginny when their families had probably always been rivals of sorts?

Just as Lizbeth began moving them into the hallway toward the rear dining room, a young man who had been manning the front desk approached Lizbeth with a message. With a frown, she dashed with him to the foyer. All the women followed upon hearing Lizbeth's indignant cry. Tina moved to join her at one of the big bay windows overlooking the front lawn. There were at least twenty-five cars clogging the sweeping drive and over fifty people milling around! Some held signs. All about Tina.

Lizbeth opened the front door to rousing cheers. "You must disperse. Go home, please!"

Every woman stood as if frozen. It appeared no one intended to move. Tina felt awful. "Maybe if I spoke to them."

Lizbeth barred her way. "Don't!" she hissed. "They might trample my shrubs...and us to get inside." She closed the door again and locked it. "We better call the police."

COLBY TOOK UP his ringing cell phone, groaning at the sight of his sister's cell number. "Hey, Dizzy."

"Where are you?"

"Home." He stopped short of admitting he was ironing their dad's white uniform shirts. Ronny Evans worked part-time evenings as a security guard at an office complex that required a fresh, crisp uniform. Dizzy felt Dad should gab less and pitch in more around the place. But Colby couldn't bear to see him spend hours at the task with miserable results. If a little ironing allowed Dad a life outside their house, he'd gladly blow the steam to make it happen.

"About the reception, Cole—"

"Don't worry, I'm not about to crash your little tea party."

"Listen! Lizbeth already has her hands full with crashers. Yelling, sign-waving morons who want to charge the place to get to Tina."

"Just the kind of hassle I predicted. People go crazy over cameras."

"The cameras aren't even here yet."

"I know, sis."

"Cole, you gotta help."

Colby sighed. "Too bad I'm banned from Tina's air space."

"This is no time to be a nitwit."

"Gee, you add *please* to that and I'll skip right over."

"C'mon, Cole. They could tear up the lawn and worse."

"Of course I'll come. But you owe me for being so mean."

Her voice grew wary. "Your terms?"

"I want you to clean and press Dad's uniforms for two months. No, three."

"I knew you were still doing that for him!"

"Now you're going to do it. For a little while."

"How will he ever learn to take on more responsibility?"

"He's a fifty-nine-year-old windbag who struggles daily with sobriety. And makes my career possible. I figure he's got his hands full."

"Okay, okay. Just hurry."

Colby went for flashing lights and the siren as he zoomed up the hotel drive, intent on distracting the crowd. But he won nary a glance as his squad wormed through the narrow path left by clumsily parked cars. Stopping at the concrete bank of steps fronting the huge white stone building, he emerged from the driver's seat with bullhorn in hand. He knew he wasn't looking his authoritarian best in gray sweatshirt and jeans, but he did take the time to clip his badge to his belt.

Climbing half the steps, he turned back to the masses and spoke through the bullhorn. "What is wrong with you people! This is no way to greet a guest to our town." He was answered by a roar of discontent. "Not to mention that disturbing the peace and damaging property is against the law!"

He felt their semicircle closing in slowly but steadily. It deeply concerned him that there were so many vulnerable kids sprinkled in the path of a potential stampede. He thought frantically for some avenue of reason.

"May I remind you what happened when some of you got camera hungry for the orange-commercial huckster?"

"We want Tina! We want Tina!"

The chanting swiftly rose to a deafening level.

"I have half a mind to run you all in!" Just as he made the decision to call in all his officers and volunteers, he was startled by joyous shouts and applause.

No wonder. Tina was at his side, prying the bullhorn from him.

"Hey, everyone! I'm Tina Mills. Now, isn't it about time the chief let go of the orange-commercial-huckster disaster?"

The crowd roared her to silence. Colby couldn't help slipping an arm around her shoulders in order to push her behind him if necessary.

"But," she continued, "the chief is right to say this is no way to go about getting my attention. I can't see or hear any one of you properly. And this sure isn't anything I care to film. Mob scenes are already too common on the national news. My project is all about showcasing peaceful towns full of regular hardworking people. There's plenty of time for us to get acquainted."

Protests of "How" and "Where" cut her off.

Colby could feel Tina bracing her shoulders, but if people started running at her, she could get knocked over, hit her head and forget all about their little chemistry. And he'd hate to see that happen.

Pulling the bullhorn away from her face, she murmured in his ear. "Guess I haven't helped much. Maybe made things worse."

"Don't give up," he murmured back. "I think I may have the answer." Colby flipped open his cell phone and called Deedee. "Listen carefully. Have Lizbeth get hold of lots of those small tablets of paper she puts in the rooms—the ones with the hotel crest. And as many pencils as she can find. Bring them out here to me.

"I don't want to see anybody hurt!" Colby called out without amplification. "Think of your kids. I'm sure they're here because they're the cutest in town and oughta be in pictures." Cheers rose and Colby was relieved to hear a touch of humor now. "But they're small and deserve your protection from a stampede. Tina has wisely suggested that you jot down your names and phone numbers as well as any story or talent or achievement that might help Sugartown win the contest. That way she can look them over in quiet and make solid plans to contact you. We'd sure hate to see her dump us from the contest, wouldn't we?"

Lizbeth soon came scooting out with the supplies. Colby took half and instructed her to help him with distribution.

Tina set the bullhorn on a step. "Can't believe you just handed me the credit for such a good idea."

"They're in no mood to take direction from me."

"With your generous nature, you wouldn't last a week in showbiz."

"With your naiveté on crowd control, you may not last another five minutes in Sugartown. Go inside while I still have my finger in the dike."

Much to Colby's delight, Lizbeth invited him inside once the crowd dispersed. He accepted a bottle of the cold beer he was known to like and allowed Lizbeth to praise him in front of the grateful brunch guests. As he sauntered closer to join them, he was comforted by the aroma of his favorite Beaumont omelet with lots of onions and just a dash of cinnamon. During his child-hood, his parents used to bring him and Deedee here every Sunday for a buffet breakfast. Deedee had con-vinced him then that the building was a medieval castle. And he in turn had entered kindergarten thinking it was. How he was teased!

Even more tempting than food was the sight of Tina Mills sipping a mimosa. He'd been too wound up outside to appreciate the way she looked today, dressed in beige hip-hugger slacks and a jade cotton blouse that molded to her body. Her thick mane of black hair was captured by a barrette. He closed in.

Dizzy Deedee was saying something to Tina that had her tossing her head back in laughter. When the pair spotted him, Tina actually blushed, suggesting he'd been their subject.

"I was just telling Tina, Cole, about how as a rookie cop you were so determined to do a good job that you gave out enough tickets to paper the station!"

"Thank you, Dizzy." He gazed down on Tina to think how much good a proper night's sleep did her after her road trip. She looked far brighter with twinkling eyes and some sparkly gold jewelry. The diamond-encrusted initial *T* hanging on a chain around her neck was especially stunning. And way out of his budget. He wondered if a man had given it to her. Wondered what kind of men she generally went for. City slick and rich, most likely. He was all wrong for her, of course, and her probing would soon bear out the boring town routine that he loved. Still, his ego insisted there had been something between them.

"As you can imagine," Deedee forged on, "I was leading up to relaying your regrets for yesterday's ticket—"

"No need. I can do my own talking now that you've got me back on her security—"

"I what!"

"You were wise and mature to call me back in when you did." Stepping in front of his stunned sister, he took hold of Tina's arm. "This place has some wonderful patios on this level. Let's have a look at my favorite."

He escorted Tina out some French doors to the backyard.

"So you were called off my case and now you're back," Tina said.

"Yeah, that ticket I wrote you went places fast. It was ripped, it was taped, it was shaken in my face. More trouble than any ticket ever, except for maybe the time I cited feeble Mrs. Quale for jaywalking." He stopped.

"Look, here's the compromise offer, only half your car was illegally parked, making you half right. And I suppose you were also half right about my rivalry with Dizzy. She played a big role in your coming here—Nobody gave me any notice at all. I hate that!"

"So do those half rights get me out of paying a fine?"

"Yeah, this once."

"I want to thank you for rescuing me—and Lizbeth. But I hope you were teasing Deedee about watching me."

"Considering today's close call, I feel I have no choice but to watch out for you, after all."

"I've never needed security on the job before and surely won't start in a quaint town like this one."

"Funny how situations that look quaint on the surface can prove to be hazardous."

"Still, I doubt I'm in any real danger here in Sugartown. Or is this more about my posing a danger to the town?"

Battling both his suspicions and warming feelings for Tina, he regarded the danger ratio as a tricky calculation. "Without pinning blame, I'd rather not see any more skirmishes."

"But you do blame me."

"You are the biggest distraction to come through here in a long while, and it's already getting crazy. Maybe not as crazy as the Club Bravado stint—"

"You sure are stalled on Club Bravado."

"I've shifted into Park on Club Bravado and shut down the engine. That hard-edge stuff is you, Tina, not this Americana piece."

She watched him with a twinkle. "I think you want to like me, Colby."

He leaned against the waist-high railing enclosing the patio, smirking. "Oh, I do like you."

Finding his overconfidence aggravating, she turned to survey the expertly landscaped acreage, with bushes, small flowing fountains hosting birds, and stone paths cut in the emerald lawn to make it all easily accessible. "You're right. It is lovely out here."

"For many years this was *the* place families came for a fancy meal out. Followed by a walk back here."

"A fine place for a rousing joust, wouldn't you say?"

He groaned. "So Dizzy even told you about the medieval thing."

She smiled. "I was always pretending back then, too. You must have been a sweet little boy, Colby. Might have been fun to dream with you."

"Life would have been interesting if you'd lived here."

"Yes, a whole different life." With a soft smile she went inside.

Chapter Five

A glance at her travel clock told Tina it was near midnight. She had been encouraged to hear that Marilyn Beaumont was a night owl like herself. It could mean the chance for a private word while others slept. The older woman seemed the perfect objective source to tap into on the subject of her father's photo. Marilyn would know the identities of the two as-yet-unidentified women, and wouldn't be as jolted as her biological mother might be at the sight of her old lover. The task would be in introducing the photo into conversation. Slipping her robe over her nightie, she stole down to the family wing and Marilyn's unmarked bedroom door.

There was a light on under the door, but her soft taps brought no response. It was a nervy move, but she edged open the door for a look. Marilyn was nowhere in sight. Hopes still high, Tina decided to try the main level of the building.

She descended the staircase to the well-lit lobby area of the hotel. There was a plastic sign perched on the desk that gave Lizbeth's off-duty phone number in case of need, and explained that the front door was secured but could be opened with each room's key.

"Something I can get you, hon?" Marilyn's voice floated from the large, dimly lit doorway to the left.

Tina spotted her then, lying in the shadows of the room known as the parlor. "Just restless. Lizbeth mentioned they shot a Bogie film here. It must have been exciting to appear in it."

"I don't recall it very well," Marilyn said vaguely. "Had no lines." She beckoned then more cordially. "Join me for a bit and visit."

Marilyn was dressed in a bright-orange-and-gold caftan, seated in an upholstered rocker, knitting. Her normally tethered hair fell loose like liquid silver, and in place of her owlish glasses she wore some small reading specs.

A lamp on a small table holding scissors and a tape measure provided the only light. Marilyn gestured to a chair opposite. "Sit, enjoy this lovely room without all the blasted guests intruding on the space."

"A hotelier who doesn't like people, eh?" Tina teased.

"Hey, most probably don't. *Fawlty Towers* is based on a real hotel, you know. I, for one, don't apologize for my attitude. The whole generation in front of yours is a bunch of yuppie crybabies. Whining about their childhoods, spoiling their own kids into selfish rudeness." She smiled winsomely. "Want to film some of that attitude?"

"I think we'd need a whole one-woman show to do you justice."

Marilyn offered mild protest, but plainly she agreed. "I'm so grateful to Beth for learning the business when it was really my duty. If she hadn't begun to apprentice with my dad as a kid, we'd have been sunk when he died. But it's all turned out well in her capable hands." She sighed. "I'm the first to admit I've made mistakes in my life. Not that I'm a total slouch." She held up her knitting—a triangle of brown and white variegated yarn surely destined to be a poncho.

"I remember your business, Marilyn."

Satisfied, Marilyn studiously looped yarn over a needle. "Course my Beth isn't perfect, either. We coulda lost the place that one time when she went and got herself foolishly involved."

"Oh?"

"Happened decades ago." She crunched her wrinkled face smaller. "Beth married an older fella rather new to town named Arthur Porter. Turned out to be the sort of dandy who comes calling with flowers and candy and wants to know every single minute of your day. Then after the wedding everything is gone except their obsession with every single minute of your day. They call them stalkers now, but back then they called 'em fifty percent of the blasted male population! Anyway, he eventually got it into his head that she was having an affair with a long-term guest, and his dark side got even worse."

"Was she?"

"I sincerely hoped so. If only to give her a contrast in men. But to this day I'm still not sure what went on. In the end she was left to pursue her only true love, hotel management."

"What happened to Porter?"

"He was a barber by trade who ended up bombing on Main Street. He did all right at first, while he was still a charming bachelor winking at the ladies and handing out lollipops to the kids. But once rumors of his foul temper started, people worried for their very heads! Scissors are sharp, you know," she said impishly, clicking her small pair open and shut. "Scary in the wrong hands."

"I bet as her mother, you especially wanted to clip his ears back."

"Clip, scissors." She slapped knee. "Good one! What you're really asking is did I end up doing just that."

Tina grinned. "He does seem to be gone."

"Well, don't dig too deep in the back garden!" she cackled. "In all honesty, I only *wanted* to kill Arthur Porter. When you get to my age, you've felt that a few times in your life, I'm afraid. No, when I caught Beth with a nasty black eye and swollen lip, I went down to the basement for Dad's old shotgun only to use as leverage. I ended up having to blow a hole through the wall of an upstairs bedroom to get his undivided attention, but it got him packing." She held up the scissors again. "These were from his precious set, left behind in the commotion. I see them as a kind of trophy. Unfortunately, it wasn't all he left behind for me. He also left Beth in a miserable state. It's the only time in history I had to run the hotel myself for several months. Gratefully, nothing burned or exploded. Beth eventually recovered and once again became the sensible one."

Tina fought to maintain calm. Had Lizbeth been fooling around with Bill during her marriage? Had she become pregnant and gotten socked in the face for her deed? Then, left alone, had she given up the baby in order to keep running the hotel? It was all very possible indeed. But Tina wouldn't allow herself to jump to conclusions. There were the other two women in the photograph to track down. She glanced around to find full bookcases, some holding what looked like photo albums. Answers to a lot of things might be within easy reach. But how to handle it with subtlety? How could she continue to make Marilyn feel as if she was volunteering information?

"Lizbeth seems eager to showcase the hotel in my film," she ventured.

"Oh, it's true," Marilyn agreed with a clatter of needles.

"I wonder, are there any photographs that show the hotel through the years?"

Marilyn aimed a needle at a bookcase near the television. "Those burgundy books are your best bet for those." She watched Tina haul the four matching volumes back to her chair. "Feel free to take those back to your room, hon," she said on a yawn.

That wouldn't do, Tina thought in panic. She needed Marilyn's commentary. "Let's sit here awhile yet. This is so nice. Visiting."

In reply, Marilyn yawned again. So Tina began to flip through pages with some speed. She didn't find a single snapshot of Bill. But there were several featuring the three women at what looked like the same time period. It was while paging through that particular book a second time that Tina used a sleight of hand to take her photo from her robe pocket and drop it.

"Oops, this one must have been hidden behind another." She picked it up from the rug and handed it to Marilyn.

Marilyn wrinkled her nose and held it under the lamp for a good long study. "I can hardly believe it."

"What, Marilyn?"

She gazed up slowly at Tina. "That Beth looked so conservative even back then. Frumpy even."

"She doesn't!"

"I do think she still has that floral dress."

"She couldn't possibly."

"She still wears the same size and is frugal to a fault. I shall ask her."

Tina sought to redirect the old woman. "Do you remember when the picture was taken?"

"You mean, like, a day?"

"No, no, I mean a time in history."

"Guess it would seem like history to a kid like you." She held the photo a foot or so under her lenses. "Hmm, to think this gem was in that book all along."

"Must have been." Tina sought to control her impatience.

"Not many photos give such a good glimpse of the old maroon awnings we had on the windows. Gee, I liked those. But wouldn't you know the Royals copied us and put a couple on the front of the diner? We took ours down then."

"Who else is in this picture, Marilyn?"

"Well, the guy is Bill somebody. Real funny last name."

"He stay here?"

Marilyn pursed her lips. "Oh, yes. Lots of times. Salesmen flowed through here before motels littered the highway. We're still so much nicer here than any motel. Homey, with reasonable rates. Sometimes I think we should advertise more. But, hey, I'm mostly just the knitter."

"You liked Bill?"

"Oh, sure. He was real friendly as I recall. All three girls liked him, too."

Tina smiled bleakly. "Popular guy."

"Always clowning around, that whole bunch. The kind of friends Beth still needs to bring her out of herself."

"Who exactly are the other two ladies, Marilyn?"

"But you must already know. They had to be at the brunch."

"Then they must look different now."

"Go ahead, Tina," she said impulsively, drawing the photo back under the lamplight. "Guess who they are."

"Okay, I think one of them is Ginny Royal, from the diner."

This proved to be a hooting, knee-slapping mistake. "Ginny would be ornerier than a bull in a hornet's nest to hear you say so. She's nearly ten years younger than this bunch."

"She still could have been friends with Lizbeth," Tina said defensively.

"Nope," Marilyn said smugly. "You're just wrong. Capital *W* wrong."

Tina tapped her mouth. "Let me think."

"Weren't too many other choices."

"I have to place names with faces, don't I?"

"You're a journalist, for heaven's sake," Marilyn goaded gleefully.

Tina tapped the photo. "Violet Avery must be this one."

"Right you are."

"She'd be better off trying to match her true red hair than settling for auburn."

"Her current purple tinge is awful."

"She has lost some weight, though," Tina noted with respect. "Brings out her distinctive high cheekbones."

"Lost twenty-five pounds recently. She's in love, I think."

"Oh? With whom?"

"I have no idea."

"Marilyn, you do love games."

"I'm serious, hon. It's all hush-hush, with her lofty job at the public library and all the stuffed shirts who provide private endowments."

"I don't follow."

Marilyn rolled her eyes. "She's likely messing with one of the *home team*."

"You mean she's gay?"

"She thinks she is, I guess. At least on odd-numbered days. It's my understanding she's always been confused."

Tina chuckled. "Bisexuality isn't necessarily a confused state."

"You wouldn't catch me switch-hitting like that."

"I'm sure the males of Sugartown are grateful for your loyalty."

"Smarty."

"So was Violet 'confused' back when this photo was taken?"

"Probably. She'd date men for a spell, then withdraw." She grew thoughtful. "Might have been the liquor clouding her judgment at times, drawing her to the male species for experimentation. Then again, maybe she was simply in the mood for the mighty sword."

"Yeah, that mighty sword can be tempting. She ever marry?"

"No. But that's probably good, as she has little patience for children. They make noise in that library at their own peril."

Tina stared at the photo, choosing her words carefully. "She and this Bill would have made a cute couple."

"They flirted. All the girls did with the salesmen. I've long felt Violet liked them most of all because they always left as abruptly as they came, leaving her to her confusion."

Tina glanced at a grandfather clock as it struck 1:00 a.m. and moved on. "Brooke Husman must be the other girl in the picture."

"Yup."

"She was way too skinny then."

"Brooke was totally man crazy back then. Always on a grapefruit or fiber diet to keep trim, draw the looks. Despite the fact that she was already married to James. Settled down a little once Seth was born. At least she quit the man chasing. She still hung around here with Beth, though, still does, just like Violet."

"How old is Seth?"

"Twenty-nine. I know because it was all over his campaign posters last year that he was a boy wonder at twenty-eight."

"Younger than Colby Evans."

"By a year or so. Seth skipped first grade, which put him in Colby's second-grade class."

"Was the mayor that much sharper than the other kids?"

"Not at all. Education means so much to James that he shipped the kid to a special summer camp after kindergarten. Seth came back knowing too much for first grade so the principal caved and allowed him to jump a grade. Most folks heard about it in time, but back then it was hush-hush. Brooke happened to mention shortly afterward while a few of us were having drinks here at the hotel. Those Husmans have always cared too much about appearances for my taste."

Tina resisted a retort. Seth didn't seem that bad. And might well be her little half brother.

"I'm only telling you about Seth to stop you getting off on the wrong foot, thinking that he is near the delicious handful Colby Evans is."

No way could Tina ever have made that mistake!

Chapter Six

Tina kicked off Monday morning with breakfast down in the hotel dining room, a pleasant room with coral walls, scenic oil paintings and small, strategically hung chandeliers. Tina had taken over a spacious table near a large bay window overlooking the left side of the grounds. It was oversize for her, but she wanted to spread out the sheets of paper gathered at yesterday's mini-riot and didn't seem to be infringing on any of the guests dining around her.

She was enjoying coffee and a muffin while taking notes in a steno notebook when Colby, with a warm hello, slid into the chair beside her.

"Good morning," she murmured, finishing off a notation. She gripped her pen harder, feeling the pressure of the chief's incessant spying. His distrust of her could cause big trouble for her discreet search. In spite of the need for crowd control yesterday, she'd prefer to ditch...

She made the mistake of meeting his gaze, locking in on those strange amber-colored eyes, raven-wing brows and the smile with a wicked curl. A quirky combination that was too damn inviting for her own good. It was enough to handle this Bio Mom search without worrying about any chemistry with Colby. Right? But Emmy's encouragement to enjoy the mouthy footloose Colby for fun jabbed at her, too. Have fun with it. *Have fun with it.*

She knew she'd lingered on him too long when he patted his cheeks.

"I leave a trace of jelly or something?"

She fought a rising blush. "You eat a lot of jelly?"

"I like the grape stuff in the squeeze bottle. Aim it right and you don't even need to dirty a knife spreading it." He watched her with a maddening twinkle in his eye. "So do I pass inspection or not?"

Flashing a quick shy smile, she glanced back to her notes.

He eagerly made himself at home. Picking through the basket of pastries on the table, he set two doughnuts on his plate. Tipping his cup upright on its fancy saucer, he poured himself coffee from the thermal pitcher.

"This is nice, Tina, you know?"

"Having a second breakfast?"

He gestured to the open bay window. "Enjoying the beauty out there. I love the outdoors."

"Is this side of the building medieval, too, or another enchanted land?"

"I mean the warm fall breezes, the chirping robins, the cooing mourning doves. Harvey Beyer, our pharmacist, knows a lot about birds. Tracks all sorts of rare ones, I understand. Builds some clever houses to draw them in."

She eyed him wryly. "You actually helping me line up subjects now?"

"Let's just say I'm trying to make the best of our situation. I know there is no stopping this project, my next best move will be steering you to less embarrassing characters. Hey, neat little recorder," he said, reaching for the small rectangular gadget near her coffee cup. "Is it tapeless?"

She snatched it from him and stuffed it in her tote. "Yes, stores on a chip."

"Why so jumpy?"

"I use it for ideas on the run. Push the wrong button and you might erase something important."

"It's easy enough to operate, I'm sure. Given a fair chance, I could add ideas to yours. Our ideas could get all cozy on the tiny chip."

"Ideas like using Harvey Beyer."

Her frown startled him. "Got a problem with Harvey?"

"A pharmacist bird-watcher with carpentry talents is just the sort of visual story I'm looking for." Tina ruffled through the squares of hotel stationery in front of her. "Unfortunately, Harvey Beyer has another hobby in mind."

Colby was puzzled, until he read the slip handed him. "Why, that devil. As if a nude water aerobics demonstration followed by some special herbal wrap is bound to be a cure for anything. He's gotta be crazy."

"Crazy like a fox. There at the bottom he offers the wrap kit, including a video demo tape, for a hundred bucks."

"This is unthinkable without at least a Speedo," he muttered.

"He look good in a Speedo?"

"Not bad, probably. But you never mind," he said gruffly. "That's just the kind of goofy scheme that would embarrass us." He tossed the paper square back on the table and took up some others. "So, anybody a shoo-in yet?"

She tapped her pen on a notebook page of scribbling, reluctant to share. "Lizbeth and this place will be the film's centerpiece."

"That was a quick decision."

"The Beaumont is a landmark building with history, like the old Bogie shoot. And I like Marilyn's poncho business. Very inventive for a senior citizen."

"I doubt she'll care for that label. It suggests early-bird specials, blue hair and baking cookies."

"You're probably right."

"Anybody else?"

"Not really." Placing a strategic elbow over her notebook page to cover her doodling, she groped for a question. "You know anything about a group called the Think Tank? I heard mention of it at the brunch."

"Amateur poets who meet once a week. My dad belongs. I've gone to listen out of family loyalty."

"Your father's a bit of a poet, then?"

"He mostly likes the ladies in the group. At the price of composing a weekly limerick or gut-wrenching observation, he can flirt to his heart's content with no commitment and all the coffee and homemade treats he can handle."

"So your mother's out of the picture?"

"Died twenty years ago."

"Ill?"

"Always. Stricken with MS."

"I'm sorry."

He made a dismissive gesture. "Forget the Evans clan. We don't need the pressure of entertaining a nation." He busily began to shuffle through more papers. "I'll nail down a few sure things for you in no time."

She put a hand on his atop the papers. "Stop angling for control. And stop rushing me. For now I'm only dealing in possibilities. I'll be filming hours of footage. Allowing the documentary to take its own shape, remember?"

"But ultimately you'll edit the footage to your liking."

"Yes, Colby, I am responsible for the final cut. But it won't diminish the truth I find, only shorten it. In my experience, most everyone can use a little honest editing."

He exhaled. "A tough point to argue."

Lizbeth smoothly approached their table with an

apologetic smile for Tina. "Another contestant on the phone for you."

"Can't you field those calls for her, Beth?" Colby asked in surprised annoyance. "Take messages?"

The golden-haired proprietor somehow managed cool elegance even with an apron over her slacks and blouse. She eyed him as if he was a pesky fly. "Funny how suddenly you're interested in a project you tried so hard to nix."

"It was hardly a nix campaign. I only knew about it a day in advance!"

"Grumble, grumble, every time somebody causes a shakeup in your controlled jurisdiction."

He shook his head. "It's rough, Tina. Lose your mother early and gain a townful of spare mothers always itching to give you grief!"

"You've always been a smarty who needs attitude adjustment," she said with some affection. "Like now. Tina and I have a system here that suits us fine."

Very true. Though rather reserved in nature, Lizbeth seemed to instantly warm around her. Tina could only imagine sharing such a comfy cocoon with a devoted mother.

"But know I'm not a total fool, Cole," Lizbeth forged on defensively. "Only putting through select people, rewarding the ones who had the courtesy not to storm my hotel yesterday. It's Pastor Breck this time, Tina, from St. Bartholomew's."

Colby grinned as Tina closed the cover of her steno notebook and rose from her chair. "Tell her, Miss Not a Total Fool, about the pastor's talent."

Lizbeth cleared her throat. "He juggles."

"What does he juggle, Beth?" Colby pressed.

"I had to put him through, don't you see? Out of respect to the collar!" Lizbeth stomped off.

Tina put her hands on hips. "Okay, Colby. You're dying to tell me."

"He juggles water balloons. From the bell tower of the church. Singing 'Splish-Splash.' The lyrics mention 'takin' a bath.' Which is what you'll get if you get too close."

She rushed off to the lobby with his triumphant laughter curling deliciously up her spine.

Once Tina was out of sight, Colby couldn't resist picking up her steno notebook for a glimpse. Probably not ethical, but it was all for the greater good. He lifted the cover to find a single circle in the center of the page. Inside the circle written in bold black letters were three names. Lizbeth. Violet. Brooke. There were arrows jutting outward, which he suspected she'd been making while chatting to him, for the red ink matched the red pen on the table. Harvey. Marilyn. Ginny.

The red additions were small and scrawled, as if inconsequential to the bigger circle. Improvised misdirection meant to confuse the cop leaning across the table? He set the notebook back beside her tote, struggling to understand her creative process. He was in no way an artist. Even hard-pressed, he wouldn't be able to match his dad's cheesy, girl-chasing poetry.

Still, he couldn't get over the idea that those three boldly printed names in the circle were certainties in a plan that was supposed to hold only possibilities.

Lizbeth Beaumont, an angel who'd stepped up to bat when his mother died. A beautiful woman who didn't seem aware of her look, or at least never helped herself by sprucing up. Colby always felt she should get out and have more fun. Seemed a shame that she'd allowed the hotel to be her life.

Brooke Husman was pleasant enough. She'd made a name for herself reporting for the *Sugartown Gazette*.

Colby respected her and her bank president husband James for working hard. But their pretensions over class and possessions often tried his patience. Especially their pampering of their sheltered son, Seth.

Violet Avery was the single, orderly type who ran the library like a warden. Who preferred her honey-producing bees to people—especially to the children who invaded her library. Who insisted everyone under age forty address her formally.

What drew Tina's interest to them in particular? Did the secret of their charm lie in their relation to one another? Did they share something in common due to their lifelong friendship? Did she even know they were best friends?

Colby couldn't begin to figure this out. But he did know there was no separating this clique for any reason. They'd stood strong and loyal without fail.

When Tina returned to the dining room, Colby was standing by the window to distance himself from the site of his prying. She glanced at the position of her notebook before stowing it in her tote. To decide if he'd spied? He couldn't tell for sure.

"Where do you intend to begin your exploration?" he asked nonchalantly.

"Thought I'd hit Main Street today for leads."

"I better take you down in the squad car, send the message that a repeat of yesterday's mob won't be tolerated."

"People must have settled down by now."

"You're probably the biggest thing we've had here since Bogie himself."

"No way."

"Come along, and we'll see."

Colby felt some satisfaction over Tina's cry of dismay at the sight of Main Street, decked out like the

Fourth of July with ribbons on light posts and Welcome signs on doors. A banner reading Welcome Reality Flicks hung high over the width of the street near the town center where he'd nailed Tina with a ticket.

"I told Jessie Miller to keep life ordinary."

"To be fair, I think you'll run into this fever in every town you hit. We just happen to be your first." Colby eased into the grocer's parking lot on the corner of Fifth and Main.

Tina got out of the car with a door slam. Colby followed her to the sidewalk, where she looked up and down several times. "Well, I can't use any of this on film."

Suddenly Colby spotted Mayor Husman trotting down the government center steps, a rather prissy yellow tie flapping in his face. "Tina!"

"Good morning, Seth," she said curtly.

He came to a stop on the walk, speaking in breathless spurts. "Love the decorations? We worked half the night on them. All my idea."

"What were you thinking?" she demanded.

He was too busy running a comb through his pale, disheveled hair to catch her displeasure. "Ingenious, eh?"

The take-charge producer emerged in full force, to Colby's fascination and respect.

"I'm trying to capture normal life here in Sugartown and you're giving me a cartoon."

"Huh?"

"This is an exaggeration of your town, not the real deal."

Seth bristled as he caught Colby's smirk. "This is a contest, though. We need to stand out somehow. Red, white and blue represents the American way."

"The decorations will have to come down before my mobile unit gets here."

"Very well." He hung his head.

"If possible, I'd like you to speak to Jessie Miller right now. Get this straightened out quickly."

Seth accepted the dismissal, but not before leveling Colby with a deadly glare. As brief as Tina's visit was bound to be, Seth wanted to steal her away all for himself. Colby totally understood. Neither of them had had an interesting date in months. Tina was new, exotic, a fresh challenge between the dueling pair.

The Beyer Pharmacy was positioned near the beginning of their tour, and Colby was determined to steer clear of it altogether. But the decision was moot as Harvey Beyer himself popped into view on the sidewalk upon their approach. Colby would be the last to deny that the twenty-seven-year-old bodybuilder pharmacist with brown buzz cut might be able to pull off a healthy nude-swim/herbal-wrap video. But it just rang so carnival.

Colby literally barred Harvey's offer of a handshake to Tina. "You oughta be ashamed of yourself."

"Why?"

"That whole nude-swimming, herbal-wrap thing."

"Jeez, Cole, that was my uncle, Old Harve," Harvey whispered. "The idea that I'd—" He glanced at Tina with widened eyes. "I'm Little Harve. I build bird houses as my hobby. Nice ones. With my clothes on."

Tina mercifully shook his hand. "I made the identity mistake, didn't realize there were two Harveys."

"I never imagined Old Harve would even consider..." Colby said helplessly.

"Yeah," Little Harve murmured. "It is unimaginable."

Tina entered the drugstore, saving the awkward moment. "Chief Evans mentioned your houses. Have any on display in here?"

Little Harve led them down one of the narrow aisles of packed shelves and creaky flooring. Tina complimented him for not playing up to the camera on his turf.

Little Harve shrugged, as if such showboating had never occurred to him.

On the end of an aisle near the drug pickup window sat several wooden birdhouses of intriguing shape.

Tina took her time examining replicas of the local firehouse and city hall. "Do you copy lots of your public buildings?"

"Sure. Houses, too, if people commission them."

"You have a wonderful talent, Harvey."

The large, muscled man proved rather shy. "Filling prescriptions all day isn't very exciting. Carpentry and birding give me something to look forward to."

"I'd love to profile you," Tina enthused. "If you're interested."

"Well, sure. I guess."

Tina dug out her Polaroid and took some snaps. "We'll do some shooting of your daily work here, then visit your workshop for a look at your hobby. I'll be in touch later with the details."

As they headed for the door, a tall, spindly man with an egg-shaped head and receding hairline jumped into their path.

"Hey, Old Harve," Colby said laboriously.

He grabbed Tina's hand for a pump and squeeze. "I'm the Harvey you're looking for," he said on the quiet. "Sent you the note."

"The herbal-wrap man?"

"Whoa, missy! Keep your voice down."

"Why?" Colby demanded.

"Because I don't want anybody copying my idea before cameras roll," the old man snapped at the chief.

"No chance of that," Colby muttered.

Old Harve still held tight to Tina's hand. "The kid won't let me fill prescriptions anymore, so I need a new scheme. Marilyn's making a pile of dough selling her knitting on the Internet. Figure I can be a hit with my herbal wrap too, if you help me get the word out."

"Let go of her, Harve," Colby said firmly, moving Tina along.

"Marilyn said I can share her Web site if I can get some interest going."

"No, Harve!"

The couple rushed outside only to burst into laughter, though Colby was a trifle rueful. "I never meant to embarrass Little Harve like that."

"Interesting guy. Never met a shy bodybuilder before."

"He's very kind and terribly bright. Smart enough to overcome his nerd image by bulking up during college. Then he returned to help run the pharmacy, still kind and bright, plus more able to stand his ground."

Colby and Tina spent a good part of the day dipping into establishments, meeting and greeting owners and managers and customers, Tina scribbling details in her notebook. The jeweler could wiggle her ears. The barber could recite *Hamlet,* playing all the roles himself. The shoemaker did a stand-up comedy routine while he repaired leather goods.

By five o'clock that afternoon, Tina's ears were ringing, her feet were sore, she wanted nothing more than to head back to the hotel for some peace and a chance to review her notes. But Colby wouldn't hear of it. The Royal Diner had been closed this morning due to some electrical problem, and it was important Tina see it before setting up her filming schedule. He would treat her to dinner there, in fact. Tina admitted to being hungry. They'd only stopped for a quick sandwich at a sub shop for lunch.

Ginny was punching keys at the register when they entered, dressed in some kind of pink nylon uniform with a small plastic crown on her head, along with the rest of the female staff.

"What the hell…" Colby looked around. Pink and yellow lights were strung everywhere and blinking madly. Tables and booths held glittery centerpieces. He glanced to Tina, who was busy reading the menu, posted above the register.

"How much of this is ordinary?" she asked.

"I think the paper napkin holders have been spared."

Ginny rounded the counter with an air kiss for Tina that she called West Coast hospitality.

"Ginny, I'm not even from Hollywood. Reality Flicks is based in New York."

"No way!" She stomped a pink slipper.

"Ginny," Colby blustered, "we've been up and down the street and your getup is the most outrageous."

"Why, thank you, dear!"

"That isn't a compliment. Tina wants realism."

"You tell her, tiger," Tina growled in his ear.

Ginny saw no alternative but to pry the rhinestone crown from her sticky, sprayed hairdo. "I still can go Broadway if you want," she said hopefully. "A little Liza?"

Tina shook her head. "It has to be your usual for the film."

"Tough to compete with the Beaumont, limited to the usual."

"Don't be so sure." Colby patted her shoulder. "I can almost promise Tina will be filming here." He held a steady smile as both women stared at him in surprise. "For now, Ginny, just show us to a table. We're starving."

Sipping ice water, Tina perused the menu. Colby reached over to put a finger on the left column of the laminated paper.

"This is the house specialty. Sunrise platter. Served all hours."

"I don't eat breakfast at dinnertime."

"Do it just this once."

"I'd rather not."

"Please. For me."

She glanced up at him. Her heart skipped a beat as those amber eyes glimmered. "What are you up to?"

"Something good. I promise."

Twenty minutes later their table was crowded with plates of pancakes, toast, bacon and eggs, as well as condiments and bottles of Pepsi.

"What am I supposed to discover here?" Tina asked as she applied honey to a wedge of toast.

"That honey is made by Violet Avery, for a start." he reported.

Tina took a bit of the toast. "Yum. Can't quite place the flavor."

"She has an hour lecture on her flavors, so you'll find out. But there's something else here of more interest."

She sipped some water. "Okay. Palate is clear. What is it?"

He reached over and sliced a wedge off her stack of pancakes. "Taste this."

"It doesn't even have syrup on it."

"Never mind. Open up."

Tina obeyed, startled as he cupped her chin to better aim the loaded fork at her mouth. She hadn't expected him to touch her face. And certainly not for an intimate feeding. His roughened fingertips grazed her throat as he pulled away, causing a quiver clear to her toes.

"So, how is it?"

She blinked. He meant the pancakes. She quickly tasted them. "Mmm. Not too sweet, not too heavy. The Royal Diner has a good thing going here."

Colby rose from his chair and summoned her along. Easing through the swinging door in the rear, Tina surveyed a bright, clean but rather cramped kitchen. Standing at a stainless-steel commercial stove was young Kaitlyn Schuler from yesterday's brunch, wearing jeans and a white chef's jacket strained over her pregnant stomach, flipping cakes high over the griddle with carefree ease.

"I don't know which is more amazing," Tina marveled, "the preparation or the taste."

"Consider the talent that produces a combination of both."

Kaitlyn became self-conscious when she realized there was company in the kitchen, and totally awkward as Tina spoke to her about her talent. When Ginny budged in for attention, Tina swiftly noted with approval that Colby took a strong role as Kaitlyn's advocate. Proving, she supposed, that his high-handedness had its place at times.

"This whole story is a little like 'Cinderella,'" Colby began.

Tina was rather surprised that Colby was up on his "Cinderella" but didn't comment.

"Kaitlyn started working here at the diner four years ago at age fifteen. At first she was busing tables and doing dishes."

"Until I saw her potential," Ginny put in.

"Kaitlyn eventually was allowed to start cooking," Colby agreed. "She soon emerged as a talented flapjack flipper."

"We always ate pancakes at home," Kaitlyn said shyly. "So I had a lot of practice already."

"Then one day," Colby said, "Ginny ran out of pancake mix during peak lunch hour—"

"Not my oversight," Ginny interjected.

"But it was a good thing, because Kaitlyn pitched in to cover the shortage with a pancake mix she'd concocted at home from scratch. Before long the cakes were a house specialty."

"She gets extra pay for her efforts, of course," Ginny inserted grandly.

Tina could barely contain her excitement. First Little Harve, and now this sweet girl. Two winning subjects for the Four Corners Project. "Kaitlyn, I would very much like to film you in action."

Her hand instantly landed on her stomach. "I don't know. The timing isn't very good...."

"You're beautiful pregnant," Tina said gently, snapping her photo.

Kaitlyn hung her head. But Ginny spoke right up. "She'll be fine. You just let us know when you want to come back to film. And I promise to clear out all the Hollywood stuff."

On the way back to the hotel in the squad car, Tina pondered over Kaitlyn. "It would take nerve to flip those cakes. You'd think she'd be more willing to speak up on her own behalf."

"She's gotten a lot quieter since the pregnancy," Colby admitted. "Lost her self-confidence. I think she can still flip only because she's on automatic pilot and doesn't think about it."

"What about the baby's father?"

"A mystery. Kaitlyn was seduced at a dorm party while visiting a college friend in Alabama. All she ever had was a first name. And somehow nobody down there seems to know the guy."

"How's her family taking it?"

"Badly. The parents are humiliated and disappointed. Kaitlyn is an only child and all their dreams were pinned on her."

"Parents sure know how to muck things up, don't they?" she said with abrupt anger.

Colby glanced at her, startled. "Nobody gets the job perfect, no."

"What is she, all of nineteen?"

"Yeah. Already considered a washout by some."

"Wonder what will happen to the baby."

"The elder Schulers want Kaitlyn to give it up for adoption. And not through any open arrangement in the vicinity, either. They want it shipped across country. But Kaitlyn intends to keep it. Raise it on her own, somehow. Her folks have already eased her into an apartment to give her a taste of what independence is going to feel like, in the hope of changing her mind."

"But she's hanging tough."

"So far. She's six months along."

"What do you think of her situation, Colby?"

"I think if a girl is of legal age, fit to raise her child, she should be allowed to do so."

"So do I. Here is a hardworking mother-to-be who wants to do the right thing. It really ticks me off."

"Yeah."

"I have half a mind to make that girl a star."

"Yeah?"

She watched his profile soften as he maneuvered the hotel's long, winding driveway.

"Just for the record, I know when I'm being led around by the nose."

Colby slanted her a roguish smile as he braked in front of the Beaumont entrance. "You could have pulled away at any time."

"I didn't want to. You were right about her story being of value."

"As I was right about Harvey. The right Harvey, anyway. Stick with me, kid," he said in a mobster gravel. "We won't stop until I've shown you the rest of Sugartown."

She patted his hand on the steering wheel. "Slow down a little."

He glanced at her in sharp disappointment. "Something wrong?"

"No! You've been an enormous help. And so right about my not understanding small-town behavior. Operating out of an anonymous city, I was totally unprepared for the riotous effect I'd have on everyone."

"How long have you been planning that speech?"

Too long, apparently, as he'd easily caught on.

"Talk to me, Tina. What's on your mind?"

So many things. Like the growing temptation to have some harmless fun with this charming guy. But even with that decision, she wouldn't want him hanging on her every move. If she didn't push him off a little, one thing would lead to the next. He would start to notice too much. Ask too many questions. Get in the way of her simple plan to quietly approach Bio Mom.

It was imperative she set some boundaries. For now that meant breathing some air that didn't hold trace of his aftershave.

She inhaled deeply, branding that aftershave to memory. "I don't even know my next move yet. Seems best if you don't just show up here again tomorrow. I'll call when I need you."

"Well," he grumbled proudly, "I wouldn't be able to play hooky all day again tomorrow, anyway."

"I'll be in touch," she said lamely, opening the passenger door.

"And I'll be around, Tina. Count on it."

Tina stood on the walk as he sped away. Feeling thrilled and threatened all at once.

Chapter Seven

The police station was part of the government center on Main Street that housed the mayor's office and license bureau, with an office on the first floor and the jail in the basement. Colby often let himself into the main entrance, on those occasions that he arrived before the maintenance man. He was just plugging in the coffee-pot Tuesday morning when clerk Grace Copeland breezed in.

"Our man about town," she teased.

"Good morning, Grace."

"So, she dump you already?"

"She didn't dump me." He scowled. "Dump...what an idea."

"You have been glued to her so far." She moved over to the windows facing Main Street and cinched up the miniblinds. "A good idea, though, as she would've been squashed without your help."

"So maybe it would have been a good idea for someone here in the office to have told me she was due in town in the first place. So I could have taken advance security measures."

"Sorry. Just got caught in the wave. If you'd wrecked the whole thing, I might never have gotten the chance to audition my cello. If she really hasn't dumped you, Cole, tell her about my cello, huh?"

Colby paused at Grace's reception desk to shuffle through a stack of mail. "Did those new weapon-licensing guidelines arrive yet?"

"Not yet. But there are a couple of FBI most-wanted postings for the bulletin board. I already took copies down the hall to the post office. "

They both turned to the doorway as knuckles rapped jauntily on the threshold wood. "Ah, so you're back from vacation."

Colby exhaled. "What is it, Seth?"

"A moment of your time. In private."

Mayor Seth Husman always smiled when he entered Colby's dinky office, the antithesis of his own, with its crummy gray steel desk and battered file cabinets and row of old school lockers. Colby always pretended not to notice. Though the pompous mayor would never believe it, Colby preferred the worn-in surroundings. Another scuff mark never mattered in here, so the town council never bothered with inspections as they did with the mayor's second-floor digs. Comfort and one less watchdog looking over his shoulder were treasured pluses to Colby.

"I am serious about yesterday being a holiday for you," Seth insisted.

Colby made a face. "It isn't my fault Tina chewed you out for primping the town."

"An honest mistake. Made with the best intentions."

"So tell her." Colby sat down and began to sift through his message slips.

"I tried to tell her last night, but Lizbeth wouldn't put through my calls."

"Multiple calls? How many times did you pester her?"

"That is totally irrelevant!"

Colby tipped back in his creaky chair, trying to look smug. Plainly, Seth was concerned that Colby already had an edge with Tina. He wasn't about to correct this misconception and thus give his rival hope. "It's true you did the worst thing possible, Seth. I mean by tampering with Sugartown's image." He could feel Seth hanging on his every word, so he drew it out. "Any pretense makes her furious. I'm not sure she even likes shiny shoes."

"But she's from New York City. She's very sophisti-cated."

"Yeah, but she isn't attracted to glitter with this project. So for the good of the town, don't try to polish the apple too much."

"What exactly did she say about me?"

"She didn't talk about you specifically, Seth."

"Not at all? All day?"

Colby twirled a pencil with his fingers. "Nope."

Seth sank on the edge of the desk, not even bothering to watch the crease in his dress pants. "She sure is pretty."

"Yup."

Seth leaned over the desk, nearly toppling Colby's SpongeBob bobblehead. "Give it to me straight. Was she with you last night as well?"

The real reason for this visit, of course. Colby leaned forward to meet his earnest gaze. "A gentleman never tells."

Seth sat back up with a grunt. "No, but I thought you might. Always did like to brag."

"You've been the king bragger since your rich pop bought you that fancy two-wheeler with the banana seat and high handlebars."

"Dad and I still wonder who stole that beauty out of our garage."

"Hey, that was the day I decided to become a cop—to stop the harassment of good people like you."

Seth's face crumpled like a child's. "Didn't even take care of it. Left it all mangled in that ditch."

"Too hot to hang on to, I guess."

Colby could feel Seth's accusing eyes burning holes through him, even after all these years. He didn't do it and never heard for sure who did. It was one of the few times he'd felt sorry for Seth. Back then he wasn't yet a pompous know-it-all. And his father, James, made too big a deal out of it. Offered a big reward, just to bring the little miscreant to justice. Over a lousy bike, for Pete's sake.

"So, what's Tina's agenda for today?" Seth demanded.

"Intends to make private visits around town, I think."

"You meeting up with her again? If you are, I want to come along."

Colby's private line jangled loudly, startling Seth to his feet. Colby reached for it, grateful for the interruption. Damned if he'd admit he didn't know Tina's next move. "Chief Evans. Hi, Teresa. He does? No problem. I'll cover it."

"We lose our illustrious crossing guard?"

There was a hint of mocking in Seth's voice. "Timothy has some kind of cough, and Teresa doesn't want him outside today. It is better to use caution at his age."

"Why doesn't the old guy just give it up?"

"You have a replacement in mind, Seth? Somebody who's available every day in all kinds of weather? Brave enough to stop traffic with a red sign, a whistle, a reflective hat and vest?"

"Not offhand," Seth replied. "But do we really need anybody at that corner at all?"

"Until you find funding for a stoplight—"

"Oh, there isn't any money for a stoplight."

"In that case, it's Timothy's job for as long as he's able." Colby launched out of his chair and moved to open the old locker that housed crossing guard equipment. "With me filling in at least for today," he said under his breath as he rooted through the disarray inside.

"You still need to take yesterday as a vacation day, Chief."

Colby slipped into the reflective vest. "Ain't gonna happen, Mayor. I was on duty all day, making sure nobody killed anybody to get to Tina. In fact, I was more accessible to the people than usual. More accessible than you ever are, aside from election time, anyway." Seth opened his mouth again, only to have Colby shove the big red stop sign in his face. "Time to hit the mean streets. Why don't you run back upstairs to your ivory tower."

TINA WAS ACCUSTOMED to walking miles through Manhattan, so opted to hit town the next morning on foot rather than firing up her rental car. Dressed in low-slung black twill slacks, a yellow cotton pullover and comfortable shoes, she set out along the gradually sloped Willow Avenue toward the town proper. She dug into the tote slung from her shoulder for her small recorder to record observations for the final voiceover. "Handy sidewalks, unlike newer suburban sprawl."

As she hiked past streets of old stately homes set in nice yards, she wondered where Colby lived. He hadn't mentioned a street, she was sure. He'd seemed so elusive about his personal life in general, as if he hoped to keep her—or at least her camera—away from it. An attitude so unlike the residents they'd encountered yesterday, who'd pressed hard to give their families a mention. In fact, a group of children with backpacks were heading up an intersecting street right now, calling her by name, like old pals.

Rats. She wasn't comfortable with children up close

like this. It was with great trepidation that she was visiting the grammar school at all before kid-friendly Emmy showed up to run interference. But principal Deedee had been relentless in her calls. The plan was to say the right things, keep her distance, get it over with. A town couldn't be represented without hearing from its youth. She knew that.

The kids were thundering closer now. With a stiff spine she slowed at the street corner to wait for her new friends, if for no other reason than because they might cause themselves injury giving her chase at full gallop on the sloping avenue. There were five in all, and they were younger than she first realized. Bright little faces full of excitement and hope. Those were the days.

"Can we walk with you, Ms. Mills?" asked a girl in pigtails and pink corduroy overalls.

"You may," she said with forced cheer. "And please call me Tina."

They chorused their own names and launched into animated babble. When they discovered she, too, was headed for their school, they went wild.

According to the map in Tina's tote, Lincoln Elementary was located a block short of Main Street on Belmont, across from St. Bartholomew's Church. Belmont Street was easy to recognize along Willow Avenue by the park on the corner.

The kids had to cross Willow and Belmont to reach the school. A stoplight held cars at bay on Willow as they made their way through the crosswalk. Once safely on the other side, the children proceeded along Belmont past the church.

Upon their approach to the street corner fronting the school, Tina was drawn to the crosswalk by the sound of a sharp whistle. A familiar uniformed man, topped with reflective green accessories, was standing in the middle of the street halting traffic in each direction with a red sign. That accomplished, he beckoned a cluster of waiting kids across toward the school.

Once they reached the opposite curb, he stepped off to the side and with a wave and second whistle blow, freed both lanes for travel. With a hop he joined Tina's party on the curb, concentrating hard on the traffic.

Like a student herself, Tina held her tote to her chest and rocked on her heels. "Hi, Colby," she lilted close to his ear.

He stiffly gazed down at her from the shade of his green cap, seeming to enjoy her girlish act. "Morning, Tina."

"How is it you weren't at your post yesterday at this time?"

"'Cause this isn't his job," objected Justin, a self-proclaimed sixth-grader. "Where is Timothy, Chief?"

"Sick," Colby reported briskly. To Tina he said, "What are you doing here?"

"I promised Deedee I'd visit the school this morning."

"Oh? Wonder what she's up to now?"

Tina shrugged. "Getting the school in the footage, of course."

"But how will it inconvenience me?" Colby mused. "How will it cause me irritation?"

Chubby Rachel broke in with a foot stomp and humph. "We like Timothy to cross us better."

Tina surveyed them in disbelief as voices rose in agreement. "But why? Chief Evans is doing a very good job."

"Timothy does the robot."

"Timothy quotes that Shakespeare guy."

"And he wiggles his mustache," squeaked a little redhead wearing a kindergarten badge with the name Eva.

Colby threw his hands toward the sunny blue sky in lament. "Never any mercy for a substitute!" With that he blew his whistle sharply and marched back into the street.

Lagging behind the kids, Tina withdrew her recorder and spoke into it. "For a good time, track down Timothy."

Swallowed up in the sea of flowing children, Tina entered the old red brick building. The broad, tiled corridor held that universal school smell of paper, pencil and disinfectant. Deedee was standing front and center in an impeccable black suit, calling for order, breaking up scuffles. Waving her hands, Tina thought with amusement, sort of like her streetbound brother. When she gestured Tina toward the office door with a no-nonsense thrust, Tina promptly obeyed.

Deedee's office reflected her orderly nature, the furniture and shelving sparse and clean. Even the frames on the walls bearing certificates and photos of children in a wide range of activities were dusted and straight.

"Some of those were taken when this building was a high school," Deedee interjected, closing the door.

"Before the new high school was built," Tina guessed.

"The usual routine in most towns. If we win the hundred grand, it'll go in a new grammar school fund—if I have any say."

"I'd like to see you win," Tina offered.

"Maybe because you haven't been to the other three towns yet."

"Still, this town has a lot of charm."

Deedee joined her at the wall with a knowing look. "You've found Colby in the photos."

"He played varsity football, I see. And hockey."

"And basketball. Mr. Jock. Mr. Homecoming King. Mr. Popular." Smoothing her bob of brown hair, she briskly moved to her desk. "But even his life hasn't turned out perfect."

Tina knew she should be strictly playing producer, getting in and out of this uncomfortable setting with perhaps a segment for the show. But presently she couldn't think beyond how Colby's life might not be perfect.

This was just the kind of pitfall that had her pushing Colby away yesterday. The threat that he might prove too distracting.

Forming a steeple with her hands, Deedee remained thoughtful. "No one's life does, does it? Turn out perfect, I mean."

"No, it certainly doesn't," Tina replied tersely.

Deedee surveyed her speculatively now. "You like him."

"Yes," she admitted carefully. A silence fell between them that Tina was determined not to fill. After all, Deedee started down this road. She did take a chair, though, realizing she needed a breather.

"Well, I know this is none of my business." Deedee halted, color rising in her plain and narrow face. "But Colby's shouldered major disappointments, and presently has a lot of responsibility."

Tina could hardly believe it. "He seems so relaxed, so able to handle himself." *And me,* she was tempted to add.

"Just the same, he's not as resilient as he appears."

"You'll have to be more specific, Deedee, if you want me to respond."

"How much do you know about each another?"

Tina gaped. "Next to nothing. Haven't had time to dig below the surface."

"I would hate to discover you are in any way pretending with him."

"Pretending how!"

"With your flirting. It's all over town after yesterday."

For a moment Tina had feared Deedee was shrewd enough to suspect a bigger agenda. But it was just a case of sibling concern. Tina tried not to look too relieved. "He insisted on escorting me."

"But you enjoyed it."

She sighed. "Yes, Deedee, it was good for me, too."

"It's just that Colby can get too excited about things."

Something Deedee didn't do or understand, Tina surmised. But she did appear to share the Evans trait of overreacting, instantly expressing discontent.

"And it's so hard to pick yourself up after a letdown, if you've gotten too excited." Deedee sighed. "You probably think I'm a meddling nut."

"Where's the harm, Deedee?"

Tina's dismay didn't faze the principal. "I want to be right about your visit being a good thing. The contest being a good experience. I still want to win it. But not at the risk of seeing my brother hurt. He was so against your coming, I didn't see this infatuation…." she muttered half to herself.

Tina spoke slowly. "Excuse me?"

"I do watch *Sex and the City*. I've seen the way those women amuse themselves with men. Colby hasn't a prayer with those ground rules."

She chuckled ruefully. "I'm not quite that glittery. And I don't amuse myself with men. At least not without their consent and encouragement."

Deedee frowned, as if visualizing Colby's consent and encouragement.

"Colby is certainly capable of handling this situation."

"When you get the bigger picture, just let him down easy."

"I hardly think it'll come to that kind of drama!"

"No? I've seen that look in his eye only once before. For his wife."

"Colby's been married?"

Deedee didn't seem to hear her. "You'll be leaving again soon."

Tina wasn't sure if the obvious fact pleased or upset

the woman. "Yes. And surely Colby knows—" She stopped short as the office door swung open to reveal Colby himself.

"Knows what?" Colby watched them intently, hat askew, smile lopsided. "Well, girls?"

Tina met Deedee's new hard look. The woman had remarkable recovery skills. But then again, it was Tina he'd busted in midstream, not his sister. "We were just discussing the contest. That you know the odds."

"On your way to the station, then, Cole?" Deedee prodded.

Plainly not, as he set down his sign and stripped off his reflective gear. "So, what progressive educational techniques do you intend to show Tina?"

"Cole, this is beyond your scope of interest."

His brows winged in menace. "What?"

"Okay, it's beyond your jurisdiction, then. The school is my turf. And I'd like to feature students in the film if possible. It would be a good learning experience."

"Just here to observe." He held up his palms. "See? Nothing up my sleeves."

Deedee rose from her chair with a noticeable snort far beneath her dignity. With a click of sensible pumps, she led Tina and Colby down the empty hall.

"As I tried to warn you over the phone," Tina ventured, "children are more my partner's strength."

"Surely you know what works. Can't hurt to pique your interest." Deedee led them into a room of eighth-graders hovering around a lab table. The teacher was dissecting a frog. Tina dutifully took some Polaroid shots, made some notes in her steno book.

Stepping back into the hall a grueling ten minutes later, Tina struggled for a polite assessment. "Not the kind of eye candy we need, Deedee."

The literal principal looked puzzled. "Eye candy?"

Tina laughed. "Oh, that's what Emmy and I call something snazzy, catchy."

"Eye candy," Colby teased softly, flicking an appreciative eye over Tina.

Deedee scowled. "Are you still here?"

Next stop was an arts and crafts room. Fifth-grade children with smocks over their clothing were standing before large easels copying a landscape print with watercolor sets. Again Tina took shots and notes.

Back out in the hallway, she gave an only slightly warmer review. "Perhaps we can pan all the classrooms in an overview."

"That won't stand out, draw out school character and spirit." Deedee lifted her chin. "Maybe we should wait for your partner."

"Tina is right, sis," Colby interjected. "That stuff is boring. Let's go, Tina."

"Wait! We have one more stop at the third grade." With a wave over her head, Deedee marched them on down the corridor to the rear of the school. Tina gazed ahead to spot a basketball hoop and polished wooden flooring through large double doors, tagging it the entrance to the gymnasium. Music pervaded with a lively, welcoming beat.

A visual wonderland was in store for Tina. Small children twirling around to a square dancer's call in a peewee hoedown!

From an anonymous distance, the threesome watched the group go through the motions. Tina snapped photos with more zest, murmuring good things into her small recorder.

"This has to be more to your liking," Deedee whispered. "Color, motion, sound."

Tina grabbed the photo spitting out of her camera. "This is special. How old are they?"

"Only eight." Deedee beamed like a proud owner next to a Jag.

Colby folded his arms against his broad chest with a frown. "No wonder you wanted to get rid of me."

"Still do." Deedee nudged him with an elbow causing him to grunt.

"What's the matter, Colby?" Tina couldn't help asking. "Don't you want me filming in the school at all?"

"No. I hate to see kids on TV forced to do things."

"Some of the home video shows go way too far with staged antics, but this is a real skill that warrants some attention and respect."

Colby wasn't even listening to her. "You sure won't get my okay, Dizzy."

"Oh, Cole." Deedee shook her head in despair.

Tina watched his darkened profile in confusion. Did he dislike children that much? Did he merely want to tweak Deedee's authority? Did he have something against square dancing?

The music stopped. With a nod from Deedee the teacher directed the dancers off the floor and called in the second bunch of sixteen from the bleachers. Tina watched in fascination as the girls broke off from the boys and formed two adjacent circles, holding hands, facing the center. A lead girl and boy broke free to move toward the front of the dance area, the dual strings of kids following suit. The first couple joined hands as they met, as did the pairs twirling after. A line of couples formed, and the teacher instructed them to form their sets, which brought the children into two groups of four couples. The teacher moved through the groups, adjusting couples shoulder to shoulder. Starting up a recording complete with a booming male caller, the children sprang into action, deftly following the caller's instructions: "Swing 'em boys and do it right. Swing those girls till the middle of the night."

Around in circles they spun. Tina took notice of individual dancers. For instance, a girl she'd walked to school with, wondering if she'd worn a ribbon in her hair today because it would fly during the dance. There was a rather tall girl who was self-conscious about towering over her partner. Another boy stood out due to his slight limp, which he tried to overcome as he twirled his rather impatient partner.

"Will this work?" Deedee asked, close to Tina's ear.

"Without question," Tina said, charging with excitement. "I strongly advise getting ahold of some costumes. Dresses with stiff skirts for the girls. Colorful shirts and denim for the boys."

"How many of them can you use in a shot?" Deedee asked.

"I wouldn't leave out a one. We can choreograph something to bring them in two shifts like this. I even see a camera rigged to catch quick closeups of those excited faces as they twirl by. We're only limited by our imagination—" Tina's breath caught in her throat as the little boy with the limp lost his balance, falling to the hard wooden floor among the swinging legs. The teacher immediately shut down the music to halt the dance.

To Tina's surprise, Colby drew in a sharp breath. Deedee's hand clamped his thick muscular arm. "Steady."

"But I—"

"You can't. You mustn't."

Colby's face twisted in anguish. "He might be hurt."

"It was a mild tumble."

"Kids are laughing at him."

"If you think they're laughing now, rush out there to the rescue. Besides," she said more gently, "it's only the usual suspects. The three bad apples in that whole group of boys."

Colby gritted his teeth. "They make me sick. If only I could fix his situation. Put him in a better place."

"Every class has the creeps. Law of averages. No matter where Jerod might be, they'd be there, too."

Colby responded with a heartfelt sigh.

"He's tough, Cole. Tougher than you." Despite her strong words, Deedee didn't look pleased with herself.

Tina watched them cling to each other in suspense as the teacher offered a hand to Jerod, which he rejected in favor of a classmate's aid. Jerod then had words with the teacher before shuffling away. His female partner was assigned a boy from the other group and the music started up again.

"Here he comes," Deedee said briskly, letting go of Colby. "Act natural."

Colby glanced plaintively to Tina. "Yeah, act natural."

She didn't think she could just yet. There had been a marriage in Colby's past that must have ended sadly and probably produced this little boy with the handicap, blowing her whole image of him being a carefree bachelor up for a little nonsensical love play. Deedee's third degree sure made sense now.

"Dad," Jerod said in utter exasperation. "What are you doing here?"

"Uh, um. I am with her," he blurted out, gesturing to Tina.

"Oh." Jerod's amber eyes twinkled very much like his father's did in lighter moments. "I know all about you, Tina. Dad told us last night. He likes you a lot."

"You okay, Jer?" Deedee asked.

He cringed. "Sure I am. The lift in my shoe slipped."

"Let me—"

"No!" Jerod hissed, pushing Colby away in mid-stoop. "Not here. I was going to the nurse's office to fix it."

"Right on my way," Deedee declared.

"Those back-ordered shoes should arrive any day, Jer," Colby encouraged.

"I'll be in touch about my film schedule, Deedee," Tina said.

"You're putting us in the show?" Jerod demanded in a high squeak.

Tina jumped a little as he grasped her sleeve. "I think so. But don't say anything to anyone yet."

"Doing the do-si-do?"

"Could be."

He couldn't contain his excitement. "I wasn't very good in there today. I can do much better."

"She may not be able to use everyone," Colby cautioned.

"We should have some pull, because you're her good friend, Dad." As Colby reddened, Jerod frowned. "You are her good friend like you said, right?"

"We're friends," Tina assured gently.

"Come on, Jerod," Deedee coaxed.

"Okay, Aunt Dizzy. Oops! Sorry. I mean, Mrs. Littman." He meekly cooperated with Deedee as she guided him along.

"See you, Jerod," Tina said with a wave.

"Come to dinner. Gramps is making his red-hot spaghetti."

Chapter Eight

Tina waited near the entrance while Colby went back to Deedee's office for his crossing gear. Pushing open the double steel doors of the school in unison, they stepped into the sunshine. "Nice boy you have there."

Colby was rueful. "That was more show than I ever intended to let you see."

"You're a good man. A caring father. Nothing to feel funny about."

They went down the short bank of steps to the street. "Kids have a way of keeping you grounded, humble."

"By the looks of you, Jerod still has some work cut out for him."

"Very funny."

She shrugged helplessly. "Just trying to lighten a conversation headed for the waste bin."

"It's a sure bet I'd rather not see my boy tripping around in your show."

"Colby—"

"Or more to the point, I'd rather not see him laughed at by an entire nation." They moved into the crosswalk, Colby blowing his whistle sharply at a single car approaching at a mere creep. The driver was shocked. Colby reluctantly offered an apologetic wave.

Safely on the opposite sidewalk, they stood under a beautiful oak in red autumn flame, a tense silence between them.

"I can only imagine how you feel," she began.

"Not likely," he fired back. "Parenting is a tough job that has to be experienced to be understood. You said you'd never even want to try it."

"I prefer not to discuss that choice."

"Why not? You're digging into all our lives!"

"Yes. But I did call ahead and get the green light to do so."

Colby radiated stress, and it was flowing right through her. Despite a feeble attempt to block the feelings, she too ached for his child, his misery.

To think this fluff piece was originally meant as a mere cover for her mother hunt. She'd been naive to judge small towns as bland territory easily penetrated. She'd been especially foolish to take the carefree Colby at face value. Like it or not, she now had a clearer perspective on the town's police chief. He was an ex-jock hooked on being a bigshot in town, who kept up the carefree facade to escape his troubles.

Everyone would understand where he was coming from, except a stranger like her.

"What will you do about filming at the school?" he finally asked.

"I honestly don't know."

"Those kids painting weren't half-bad," he said with forced enthusiasm. "I just saw a little girl on TV who's considered a mini Monet. Maybe there's a budding master living here."

"Not in that art class." She half smiled. "The grammar school isn't necessarily a priority to me. I only visited because Deedee insisted."

He snapped his fingers. "Right! So far only Deedee

knows what you're considering with the dance number. Maybe I can twist her arm to let it go."

"Possibly. Underneath all that big sister bluster she's a cream puff where you're concerned."

His brows narrowed. "What exactly did she—"

"Never mind. It's inconsequential."

He nodded. "If I can manage her, I'm home free."

"Not entirely. Jerod will want a say in all this."

Colby balked. "He isn't capable of understanding the ramifications."

"As you've so eagerly pointed out, I'm not comfortable with kids. But I do remember being one. You never forget childhood expectations that flop. Crush that boy now when he wants to be part of this project and you'll risk years of resentment."

"It would be to protect him! In time he'd come to see that."

"Fat chance, Daddy-o."

"Would *you* consider telling him it won't work?" he asked hesitantly.

He was asking her to take the fall for him? She reared in disbelief. "He wouldn't buy it even if I tried. He's smart. Sensed my strong interest."

"Oh, how I wish you'd chosen another town," he muttered.

Some choices were made for us, she fumed. And didn't their chemistry count for anything under a little stress? "Look, I don't think we better talk anymore right now. We're both pretty mad. There's nothing to be gained."

He busily shifted the gear in his arms. "I need to get back to the station, anyway." As they both took steps along Belmont Street toward Willow Avenue, somebody's hollering caught their attention. It was coming from St. Bartholomew's a hundred feet away. They moved across the church lawn.

"Hello! Up here!"

"Jeez," Colby muttered. Forming a smile, he looked up to the church's bell tower. "Hello, Pastor Breck. This is Tina Mills."

"Yes. Saw you going into the school, Tina. Dashed right up here to wait."

Tina gazed up, shielding her eyes against the sun, making out the torso of a pleasant-looking bald-headed man. "The juggling, Pastor?"

"Righto. Do you think you'd want to shoot from where you're standing or from another angle?"

"Not sure. Depends on what you've got."

"I got a lot!" Suddenly red, green and yellow balloons bobbed in the air, along with two white bell sleeves. "Splish-splash, I was takin'—"

Impressed with his dexterity, Tina moved a little closer.

"A bath," Colby finished flatly, as a red balloon landed on Tina's head. It broke on impact, spilling cool water over her wavy jet mane and carefully made-up face. Causing her to scream.

"I warned you about him," Colby chided.

"But what are the odds of him hitting me squarely?" she cried, slapping away the handkerchief he offered from his uniform shirt pocket.

He sighed. "I don't know. But thank you, God," he called to the heavens. "For giving Tina a small dose of the trouble she's been dishing out to your humble servant here."

"Oops, sorry, Tina," the pastor called down. "Did you say something, Colby?"

"Just talking to the Lord, Pastor."

"Admirable, son."

"It wouldn't hurt to put some warm water in those balloons," Tina griped.

"Hardly seems necessary, as I seldom lose one."

"Now, Pastor," Colby challenged, "isn't that stretching the truth a bit further than a man of the collar should?"

"This isn't a denominational issue. It's all about Hollywood."

"But I am not from—" Tina broke off in disgust. "I gotta go change." She stalked off without another word.

TINA ARRIVED BACK at the hotel to find Marilyn sitting in the lobby, fringing a yellow-and-white poncho with strands of yellow yarn.

Marilyn gasped at the drenched young woman. "What the blazes happened to you?"

"Pastor Breck's juggling. I can tell you it's a long walk from the church to the hotel in the wind."

Marilyn's concern grew. "You must be chilled to the bone." She rose from her chair just as Lizbeth descended the wide open staircase. "The pastor's audition," she told her.

Exasperated, Lizbeth picked up her pace and rounded the reservations desk. "I have a small bar towel back here somewhere." She found it and closed in to gently pat Tina's face dry. "Hope you don't get sick."

"I'll dig out the blow dryer. It'll be fine."

Lizbeth moved the towel from Tina's face to her hair. "There's a delicious lunch special coming up in the dining room. Ground sirloin and garlic potatoes. Or there's a nice chef's salad."

Tina allowed the solicitous attention to soothe her. "I should keep working."

"You have to eat," Lizbeth clucked.

"I will, in time. Right now I need your help with Violet Avery. Being her friend, you must know her schedule. I was hoping to set up an appointment with her, and I'm wondering how to reach her at this hour."

"You see *her* as an interesting character?" Marilyn hooted.

Lizbeth gave Marilyn a dour look. "Not only is Violet a good friend of mine, Mom, but she loves you to pieces."

"A nutter, I say. Nosy to a fault, full of herself, always bossing people around."

"Well, look who's talking," Lizbeth retorted. She smiled at Tina. "Do not listen to my mother. Violet's a jewel. Like a sister to me."

"Books and bees are her whole life, Tina," Marilyn insisted playfully. "Like I told you during our chat."

Suddenly looking a bit more the regal proprietress, Lizbeth favored each with a guarded glance. "You two already in cahoots behind my back?"

"We met up that first night when I couldn't sleep," Tina explained. "Got to talking about the town. Violet and her interests came up."

"My mother's observations should always be taken with a grain of salt," Lizbeth said tartly.

"Oh, I still know what's going on," Marilyn said in a singsong voice. "A good deal of the time."

Tina waited to see if Marilyn was going to elaborate on the photo albums and their long trip down memory lane, but she didn't. A relief, as Lizbeth plainly didn't trust her mother alone with Tina and certainly wouldn't welcome the news that she already knew about Lizbeth's failed marriage. And Marilyn's shotgun solution.

"So, which of Violet's interests do you want to pursue?" Lizbeth asked. "Her post at the library or her beekeeping operation?"

"The bees."

Lizbeth moved to the desk and tossed off the towel to pick up the phone. "I'll call her at the library for you. See when she can possibly meet you at her place."

Marilyn cackled. "I bet that for a spot in your show, hon, that busybody will buzz right home."

In spite of herself, Lizbeth joined Tina in laughter.

IT WAS CLOSE to the noon hour when Tina pulled her rental car up behind a twenty-year-old red Skylark roaring up a winding dirt driveway. They'd come from different directions on a rural road to close in on the Averys' ten-acre spread. Lizbeth had given her the helpful tip that she'd know the proper driveway by the bee-shaped mailbox.

Violet popped out of her car with a cheery wave, the breeze whipping at her long striped dress. Tina slowly emerged from her rental sedan, surveying the Bio Mom candidate. Violet was tall and thin, like Dad and herself. She also approached with a gait similar to Tina's.

"How nice to see you again!"

"Hello, Violet." Tina responded to the woman's warmth. Knowing that the heat was fueled mostly by the chance to be on the show should keep her grounded. Tina took a closer study of her subject as she shook her hand, noting that Violet could be responsible for the small bump on Tina's nose.

"Let's head right back to the shed to suit up."

Tina inspected the site as they moved, taking some photos. The old farmhouse had character but needed a new coat of white paint. There were four outbuildings.

Violet's tone and carriage exhibited pride. "This place was one of Sugar's first homesteads. Built by my family. Meant to stay in my family."

"You have any young relatives to carry on the tradition?"

She shrugged broad shoulders. "With my single brother long established in New Mexico, and me on my own here, it appears I'm last in the line."

They moved out of the sun into an outbuilding. Violet turned on an overhead light. The interior was neat, full of shelves and cabinets. "I keep my equipment in here. Process the honey in here." She showed off strainers, extractors and something called an uncapping tank. Tina took photos and spoke into her recorder.

"Hate to see it happen, this land passed on to strangers." She paused then and peered anxiously at Tina. "But that probably wouldn't interest the public much, would it?"

"Not the public," Tina agreed. *Only me, if you happen to be my mother.*

"Just as well. I am a rather private person. Always have been. Not to say I don't appreciate your interest in my beekeeping."

"And only the beekeeping will make my documentary," Tina assured.

"Did you wash up like I said?"

"Twice, if you count my water balloon episode with the pastor."

Violet chuckled. "Seriously, bees dislike body odor and any kind of perfume or deodorant scent. Stirs them up in a way we don't want." She provided Tina with a light-colored jumpsuit with the explanation that bees dislike dark colors as well. With unexpected care she helped Tina tuck her pant legs into tall black boots, slide on long leather gloves and adjust a hat and veil combination.

Suited up, they headed back outside. And Violet showed off her gardens, or what she called her wildflower buffet for *her boys'* nectar sources.

"I always tell guests to follow the buzz," Violet chortled, unlocking a gate in a square of chain-link fencing.

Inside the square sat a man-made pond and four rectangular wooden boxes elevated on stands in front of a hemlock windblock. As Violet began a long spiel about sunlight and drainage, Tina simply aimed her recorder at her. By the time Violet had covered production, harvesting and marketing, Tina's chip was full. This segment would indeed be an interesting addition to the show.

Back in their street clothes, Violet led Tina through the rear door into her kitchen. "Sit right down there at the table. I'll get us some toast and honey. And tea if you like."

"Wonderful."

"I intend to treat you to some of my special boneset batch. I swear by its healing properties."

They had their light lunch at an old chrome table with butcher-block-patterned top. Tina admitted to already tasting her honey at the hotel and Royal Diner.

Violet had just sunk her teeth into a wedge of slathered toast so didn't speak until her mouth was empty again. "Ginny is my biggest customer by far."

Tina saw an opening to unwed motherhood. "I intend to film at the diner. I'm very impressed with Kaitlyn Schuler's flapjack technique."

"A dear girl."

"Who got herself into an awkward situation."

"Indeed." Violet shook her head. "When she came into the library looking for books on prenatal care, I advised her to consider handing the child over to a family."

Like Violet had thirty years ago with her baby? "You think that's the best way, then?"

"The father is anonymous. Her own parents are enraged. Seems the practical solution."

"She seems determined to keep it."

Violet didn't appear to be listening anymore as she opened another jar of honey. "You must try this one. Apple blossom."

The phone rang as they cleared the table. A minor problem with the library computer system. While Violet took the call, Tina moved into the living room for a look around. Like the kitchen and outbuilding, this space also had a spartan feel. The only exception was the collection of framed photographs set on every bare surface. There were shots of the property in all kinds of weather through the years. Shots of Violet receiving plaques at library events and beekeeping ones. Violet posing in front of the church with the pastor. Nothing of interest here.

Tina moved to the last frames on an old upright piano, clustered around a metronome. These less formal photos held more promise of social settings. Violet in fancy dress, dancing with a rather plain gentleman. Violet on a picnic with a nice-looking woman. Several shots of Violet with an older couple, who might well be her parents, as it was on the property. Violet in a desert shot with a man most likely her brother. Violet posing with Lizbeth and Brooke Husman at various locations. And a photo of Bill with all three ladies. Not identical to the one Tina brought along, but likely taken the same day, perhaps within minutes. Honey Bee. Dad's nickname fit Violet so perfectly with her hobby. A much better fit than Brooke or Lizbeth.

"Yes, that's me in bell-bottom hip-hugger jeans," Violet admitted, gazing over her shoulder.

"Oh! I didn't hear you come in."

"Hot pants were big back then, too, but I couldn't bring myself to..." She trailed off with a laugh. "I did have a nice shape. But somehow my long legs made those short shorts just a bit too short."

"I share your long legs," she blurted out. "I mean, I understand. I envy my partner, Emmy Snow. She is petite and can wear any fashion well." Tina's eyes strayed to two last photos, of Violet and a masculine female on a picnic someplace, looking rather lovey-dovey. So it appeared Marilyn's observations on Violet's varied tastes were accurate.

"Lots of different experiences in this world," Violet murmured.

"Most definitely," Tina agreed.

"So you and this partner Emmy are…"

"Oh, no. Just platonic friends."

"I only ask because the chief seems so taken with you. Would hate to see him misled about your availability. With the child at stake and all."

Wow. It seemed the whole town was tuned in to their chemistry. Images of their earlier exchange threatened to distract her, but she quickly squashed them. The search for her mother mattered right now.

Tina struggled to imagine what might have transpired between Bill and Violet. For him to discover she was bisexual would likely have been a romance killer, even if she was already pregnant.

But this glitch in their romance wouldn't explain Violet's decision to give up her baby. It had been mentioned that Violet didn't especially care for children. Would that include one of her own?

Maybe she'd softened by now, judging by wistfulness over the family losing this property. Tina would make an easy daughter. In fact, of the three candidates, Tina felt Violet would be the easiest to bond with.

The key was discovering if there was a reason to bond. As much as Violet loved to talk, surely she could be coaxed into letting something useful slip.

"It appears you've led a full life," Tina remarked, still focused on the cluster of framed pictures.

Violet shrugged nonchalantly. "Have had my share of relationships. Oh, I know what my reputation is in town, that of a grumpy old stinker. But I have a fun streak and care about a lot of people. I just like things well run. Quite a normal expectation for a head librarian."

"I've heard something of your fun streak," Tina said,

pointing to the photo of Bill with the trio of females. "From Marilyn."

"Marvelous days back then. The whole lot of us playing around."

"Well, the man pictured here must have liked the odds best of all."

"Bill." Her features softened. "Rarely think of him anymore."

"Appears very handsome in this shot," Tina observed. "Did you like him a great deal, Violet?"

"Very much," she admitted grandly. "Bill was the sort of fella every girl should run with once in her life. You know what I mean, a good-time guy full of delicious trouble."

Tina had always viewed her father as gregarious. She took for granted the fact that other women routinely gave him a second look, laughed too hard at his silly jokes. Never once in all the years, however, had it occurred to her that Bill actively encouraged them. Until now.

"Are you all right?" Violet asked.

Tina drew a strained smile. "Of course. Just considering my own relationships with men, wondering how a woman knows when she's about to cross the line between good-time trouble and the more serious kind."

Violet answered readily. "Gut instinct drives a smart woman. At the first inkling of doubt, she puts on the brakes, assesses the situation and, if necessary, gets the hell out.

"You always been so sure of yourself?"

"Not at all. I was young and stupid once. Or twice."

"What do you regret most, Violet?" Tina asked softly.

Violet stared off into space. "Resisting the temptation to be more unconventional early on, from voicing stronger opinions, to living out my ideals openly and confidently. Back then I was insanely concerned about my career, how my personal choices might affect the library, risk the goodwill of its benefactors. Of course," she added, "taking aggressive action would have involved opening my heart, maybe sharing the old homestead here." She paused and shook her head. "Oh, never mind. Things have turned out okay for me. Probably even in my best interest, as I've never been keen on compromise. I'm perfectly content with my home, my bees and books."

More proof of Bill and Violet's incompatibility. Tina couldn't begin to imagine her father dropping his active life in Brooklyn to come nest up here under this stubborn woman's specific and stifling conditions. Or Violet inviting him in the first place! Just the same, Tina could envision them enjoying a trouble-loaded mating dance.

"All these questions about regrets and relationships don't suit your dynamic personality, your thirst for travel and exploration," Violet observed. "Go full steam ahead with Colby! Worry about the practicalities later."

Tina suppressed a huff of frustration. Violet plainly thought she was asking about her hard choices in order to help with her own. Upon reflection, she figured it was as good a cover for her query as anything else. And Violet's support was flattering, whether she turned out to be her mom or not.

"Have you met the boy yet?"

"Yes. Jerod's delightful."

"I like him better than other youngsters," Violet admitted. "Takes great care with the county's books. Says please and thank you. Not all the kids do. They make me so nervous when they start to run around, yelling and shoving. Though I think Jerod's limp has forced him to be a bit more cautious than he would be otherwise. His dad certainly did his share of roughhous-ing as a boy."

"I can picture it."

Violet's bright-red lips pursed coyly. "I imagine you can."

Chapter Nine

Colby arrived home that evening to find Jerod in the dining nook, setting the table. "Hey, pal!" He scooped the boy into a bear hug. "Is that your gramp's special spaghetti sauce I smell?"

"Sure, Dad. It's Tuesday."

"Right." Colby glanced at the table, then did a double take. "You have an extra setting out. Having a little buddy over?"

"Ha, ha. It's for Tina." Jerod beamed with an innocent joy reserved for eight-year-old boys alert enough to appreciate a pretty woman without knowing the torture they can cause. "You heard me invite her."

"You mean that little thing you said back at school?"

"Yeah." Jerod adjusted two forks beside a plate. "I knew you'd tell her where we live and what time to come. Stuff like that."

Ronny ambled out from the kitchen, dressed in a butcher's apron bearing the slogan If You Can't Stand The Heat. "How did you leave it with her, Cole?"

Colby gritted his teeth. He left it sort of nasty. Insisting she not showcase Jerod's disability. "That wasn't a formal invitation you made, Jer," he hedged.

"I couldn't talk more, Dad. Aunt Dizzy would've gotten mad."

Colby appealed to his father. "You know I have a rule about inviting ladies to the house. So as not to confuse Jerod with my intentions."

"I thought that was only ladies you kiss, Dad," Jerod reasoned. "Have you kissed Tina?"

"Well, no."

"Then it's okay. She's not one of *those* ladies. The ladies of the night."

"Jerod! Don't call any ladies in town ladies of the night."

"But you see them at night."

"Yes. But it has a different meaning to grown-ups."

Jerod exchanged an exasperated look with Ronny.

Colby rubbed his face and shifted nervously. "The thing is, I may have bungled it with Tina. The dinner invitation, I mean. The pastor nailed her with a water balloon and we never got to talking about time or anything."

Ronny sighed. "Then it's a good thing I called her at the hotel."

"You did what!"

"Had to leave a message with Lizbeth, but she promised to pass it along."

Colby remained unhappy. "There is still a chance she may not show up."

Apprehension spread over Jerod's young face. "You didn't make her mad, did you, Dad? Everybody knows you don't want the town to be filmed."

"I just think we all should be cautious. I have made that clear to her."

Jerod slapped his head. "Oh, Dad! She must hate me now."

Panic flashed in Colby's eyes. "No, no, buddy, she doesn't. She likes you very much."

"She say that?"

"Yes."

"Hope you didn't wreck it. All the kids want to dance in that movie. Especially me." Tossing his hands, he did a tromp-limp toward the kitchen.

Colby stared bleakly after him. "All the kids already know?"

"Sure they do," Jerod called from the other room. "I had to tell 'em I know Tina. To make them stop laughing at me for tripping."

"Don't you think, son, that it'll be tough for you to keep up with the steps?"

They could hear the refrigerator door open with a jiggle of bottles. "Maybe I'll have my new shoes by then."

"You probably won't," Colby called back.

"The teacher talked to the class about moving a little slower. Watching out for me. I can do it. I know I can."

Colby rubbed his temples and broke into a frantic whisper. "You should have heard them laughing today, Dad."

"Glad I didn't," Ronny muttered. "But Dizzy tells me it's only a few of the creeps who pick on him."

"Imagine the number of creeps in a nationwide audience."

Ronny frowned. "We'll work it out."

"How?"

"Somehow. It won't be much longer till his surgery next summer. In the meantime, we have to keep his self-esteem high."

"The sauce is bubbling, Gramps!" Jerod shouted.

"Hadn't you better take a quick shower?" Ronny directed quietly. "She might actually show up."

"If she does show," Colby said pointedly, "there's no reason why you two have to tell her any more family business."

"Let's just pray she gets here. For the boy's sake."

Right. To encourage a project that will only make fools of them.

Despite his misgivings, no ring had ever sounded sweeter to Colby than the doorbell did fifteen minutes later. Although it did jar him enough for him to nick himself shaving. He scrambled to dot the bloody spot with some tissue, then refocused on the steamed mirror to finish the job. Standing in his briefs, skin glistening with moisture, he knew it would take some effort to get it together. Hopefully his family wouldn't hand over door keys and diaries in the meantime.

TINA WASN'T ACCUSTOMED to fighting sweaty palms. But she had a bad case of them as she stood on the doorstep of the Evans bungalow. She quickly swiped them dry as the door swung open. A man of approximately sixty stood in the doorway, wearing a jazzy apron.

"I think I can stand the heat," Tina said, offering her hand.

"Oh! The apron. Gift from Jerod. Come right on in, Tina. I'm Ronny Evans. Cole's daddy."

Tina stepped into the tiny foyer, getting a better look at Ronny in the light. He didn't resemble Colby at all, with copper hair, deep-brown eyes and a short, compact body.

Ronny watched her glance into the living room to the right. "Cole is in the shower. Come make yourself comfortable."

The living room was set up more for comfort than fashion. A huge sofa and two chairs were covered in navy corduroy slipcovers. Two large end tables held mismatched lamps. A wooden rack was jammed with magazines. The television was large and set in a wall unit that boasted rows of DVDs and videos, as well as a battered encyclopedia.

"I suppose it's plain only guys live here," Ronny said pleasantly.

Tina nodded in approval. "It's very tidy for guys. You have my respect."

"I like things neat," he admitted. "And have a lot of excess energy I need to use up."

She paused by the wall unit near the set of reference books. "Haven't seen an encyclopedia in a while."

"They belonged to my parents. I still like to read them for fun."

"Oh, Gramps," Jerod burst in. "Dad says those books keep you backward. They don't even talk about going to the moon."

"Some things never change, though," Ronny declared. "Like George Washington, Thomas Edison and the War of 1812."

"All the new stuff is right at the library," Jerod persisted. "On computers."

"That's not all there is at the library," Ronny grumbled. "That Violet Avery has more rules than a jailer." He lifted his chin. "I don't care enough about the moon to tangle with her."

Jerod smiled shyly at Tina. "Hi."

"Hi, Jerod." Tina looked down into the sweet young face so much like Colby's. The amber eyes full of worship, free of suspicion. She wondered if Colby's similar eyes ever reflected that kind of magic anymore. "You helping out with dinner?"

"Gramps did all the work," Jerod said.

"He helps out," Ronny insisted. "Sets the table. Adds the secret spice to the sauce."

"It's Coumadin," Jerod eagerly confided.

"That's my blood thinner. You mean cumin." Ronny released an exaggerated sigh. "There goes my secret."

Jerod hardly looked worried. "She won't tell, will you, Tina."

"Of course I won't," Tina promised, raising her palm in oath. She was startled when Jerod snatched her hand in midair and squeezed it close to him.

"I'll show you where to sit. Gramps has the food all ready."

Colby entered the dining nook just as Jerod was tucking a large paper napkin in the neck of Tina's clingy blue sweater. "Jer," he gently chided, "ladies put their own napkins in their laps."

"Even for spaghetti?"

"It's fine." Tina gave the boy's head a single pat, making contact with Colby's tense, observant eyes. If only she hadn't blurted out her misgivings about kids. The protective parent would be watching for mistakes.

The food was served home style. Pasta, sauce, salad and bread, passed from the right, giving first honors to Tina.

"When I was exploring the church and school this morning," Tina observed, "I had no idea you lived so close, right on Belmont."

Ronny smiled sympathetically as he took the pasta bowl from her. "Had you known, you could have stopped in here for a towel after the pastor's flub."

"You weren't home, Dad," Colby reminded him.

"True. I meant you should've brought her."

"I dashed off before Colby had the chance," Tina interjected. "All for the best, really. I needed a word with Lizbeth. Help with contacting Violet."

"Check out her beehives?" Jerod asked excitedly.

"I sure did. Pretty cool."

"She's always inviting me over. But nobody will take me."

"I won't be trapped in her chain-link cage!" Ronny proclaimed.

"Dad's afraid he might get stung," Colby deadpanned.

"I tell you, Cole, the woman has a major crush on me. But this is one wild stallion that won't be housebroken!"

Colby's eye roll signaled the unlikelihood of this threat.

Jerod beamed at Tina. "Maybe you'll take me sometime."

"Maybe," Tina said, faltering.

Everyone concentrated on twirling spaghetti around their forks.

"This is wonderful, Ronny," Tina praised. "The sauce is so unique."

"A secret ingredient," Colby hinted. "Not oregano, like it always is on TV."

"She already knows," Ronny reported.

Colby shook his head. "Another family secret out."

"She won't tell," Jerod insisted.

Tina pierced some of the greens on her salad plate. "I should have brought a nice wine to accompany the meal. I was a little too rushed when I got back and found your message. Perhaps next time."

"Wine is never necessary," Colby rumbled evenly, concentrating on buttering his bread.

"Oh." Feeling a sudden tension in the air, Tina measured each man at the opposite ends of the table. Both avoided her gaze, making her fairly certain she'd committed a faux pas. Dipping her head, she sipped her water.

"You're fine, Tina," Ronny soothed. "I am an alcoholic. There is never any booze in this house. Some people with the ailment can handle watching others imbibe. I can't be within a hundred feet of the stuff. It takes three trips a week to AA for me to stay clean. But I go." He thrust a finger at sulky Colby. "There's no harm in telling her about that, either."

"It's not even a secret," Jerod piped up. "Like the Coumadin."

"You can relax with your secrets, Colby," Tina said patiently, "I am not doing a reality show on the Evans family. For starters, I think you're too darn boring. Except maybe for Jerod," she added, winking at the boy across the table.

"You're right, Tina," Jerod said without pretense. "I am pretty interesting."

The ice was completely broken with common laughter.

"What's your life like in New York, Tina?" Ronny asked.

"Well, I live in Manhattan with my friend and business partner Emmy Snow. She'll be coming with the mobile unit."

"You got a boyfriend?" Jerod asked sweetly.

Tina was startled. "Nobody special."

"I want a girlfriend just like you someday."

Tina blushed under his adoring gaze. It was proving tougher to keep her cool professional perspective with this child. Not only was he a chip off the old Colby, in looks and personality, he was vulnerable and so anxious to connect. It was getting easier to understand Colby's scramble to make his life just right.

While Colby helped his father clean up the kitchen, Jerod took over as host. He served Tina a slice of apple pie in the living room, picked her brain about Violet's bee operation and explained that he might end up in the movie business himself. Tina soon forgot her discomfort with children, seeing Jerod solely as an interesting individual.

A clever individual, it seemed, as he steered her to his bedroom for a look at his plastic dinosaur collection. "Some of the kids say dinosaurs are a dumb hobby, but I love them," he announced rather defensively, closing the door after her.

Tina picked one of the ugly creatures from a card table covered with papier-mâché terrain. "This is a cool setup."

"Me and Dad did the board. We used newspaper and flour and water. Made the shapes. Let it dry. Then painted all of it."

"Very nice, Jerod."

"Call me Jer."

"Okay, Jer." She set the toy back in place. "Maybe you'd like to show this collection in the show?"

"Heck, no. This is just for Dad and me to have fun with." He sat on his bed and patted the mattress. "Come sit here."

Tina complied. "You want to tell me something in private?"

His eyes widened. "How'd you know?"

"You shut your door and you keep looking back at it. And you're sort of whispering a lot."

Jerod took her hand. "You are so pretty."

She eyed him in amused speculation. "What do you want, kid?"

In a mix of exuberance and desperation, he told her.

TINA FIGURED IT WAS TIME TO LEAVE when they returned to the living room to find Colby pacing, glancing at his watch. And promptly announced as much.

"Don't mean to rush you," Colby said hurriedly, "but it is bedtime—" He broke off as his son glared. "For Ronny."

At the sound of his name, Ronny's head jerked up from the newspaper. Jerod walked over to pat his head. "Yeah, Gramps has to take it easy."

Ronny looked around, plainly disoriented.

"I'm walking Tina back to the hotel, Dad." Colby dug into the front closet, slipped on his leather jacket. He produced an old red-and-white letter jacket as well, which he held open to her. "It's a little chilly for your light sweater. Sorry, I don't have much of a selection."

"I can get her something from my room," Ronny offered. "I have a nice suede number the ladies seem to like."

Colby frowned. "It's back in Ronny's room because it smells like cigarettes."

Tina pushed her arms into the sleeves. "This is fine. I've always wanted to wear one of these. Bye and thanks," Tina sang out as Colby urged her outside.

Jerod called after them through the screen door. "It's okay to kiss her, Dad. We can make a new rule about the ladies of the night."

Tina skipped down the walk to the sidewalk and whirled with a teasing smile. "Care to explain that?"

Colby took her arm with determination. "I'm gonna give it a try."

They strolled down Belmont Street, Colby relating how he long felt it his duty to shield Jerod from his casual dates. "I just don't want him to pin his hopes on any particular lady. Seems best if I do the sorting on my own. If something ever gets serious, I can always draw her closer."

"Haven't he and Ronny ever brought someone in under the wire, like they did me?"

"Never. We respect each other too much to sneak around."

"So they broke the house rule just this time with me."

"Well, show folk do have a way of corrupting normal people."

"Oh, Colby, really!"

He chuckled. "I'm kidding. Your nose crinkles so cute when you get mad."

"You're half-serious. And even that's too much. I had such a nice time tonight, I don't want you to distrust me anymore, even a little bit."

"You really had a nice time?" He was pleased. "I

hope Jerod didn't bore you too much. Didn't have the heart to cut in on him."

"Like the average male, he was working an ulterior motive. Gave me the old have-a-look-at-my-dinosaur-collection line."

Colby was plainly amused. "Did he want you to film the collection?"

"No, Colby. All he wanted to do was get me alone to make certain the square dancing was a go."

Colby grimaced. "The little pirate. I called him from the station after school to tell him not to get his hopes too high. He seemed to accept it."

"Please don't blame me for your little pirate's mutiny. You know that Deedee would never have let me off the hook in viewing the school."

"True." Colby expelled a breath. "I gotta sit down before you tell me what you said to him. Come on."

Tina trailed him into the park she'd passed earlier in the day on the corner of Belmont and Willow Avenue. He passed by a merry-go-round, slide and monkey bars in favor an old steel swing set with six battered swings. "Welcome to my comfort zone. The place I've always come to think."

They slipped onto adjoining swings and began to pump their legs for momentum. Neither one went very high, they were so intent on one another.

"Give me the worst," he finally said.

"I told him the dance would depend upon a lot of things. Deedee's final approval over other school activities. My partner, Emmy, agreeing that it is entertainment. And even if we do the shoot, there is no guarantee it'll make the final cut."

Colby brightened. "Lots of loopholes there."

"Would it be so bad if he tripped a little?"

"Yes! Don't you see? I have to protect him until he

can protect himself! He's scheduled for surgery to lengthen his leg next summer. Even then, it'll be some time before he can mend, hold his own."

"I realize it isn't my place to argue."

"You wouldn't come up with any new points, if you tried. I've heard them all from Dizzy. It just kills me watching him struggle. It's so unfair, him already missing a mother."

"What happened to your wife, Colby?"

"Diana died in an accident several years ago. She was my perfect match," he said gently. "Grew up here like me. Loved this town like I do, with no desire to ever leave it. Crazy the way it worked out. She felt lucky to win a national baking contest for her lemon pie. Flew off to a Miami convention to accept her prize. The result was insanely unlucky. She went out on some sightseeing cruiser, and the craft was struck by a speeding cigarette boat." He gripped the swing chains tighter. "Some people were rescued from the water, but she was already gone, due to a massive head injury."

"I am so sorry."

"I didn't spend much time sulking about being a widower. Jerod being left without a mother concerned me much more. Losing my own mother way too prematurely gave me a full understanding of his fragile state. Ronny was always a drinker, but really went heavy on it after Mom died. He literally fell apart when Deedee and I needed him most. And we tumbled into the nightmare right along with him. I didn't want that fate for Jerod."

"Didn't the town care about you and Deedee?"

"The whole town grieved our loss at first. But with Ronny shooting his mouth off everyplace, we soon lost that edge. Ronny became a joke, the town's most tenacious drunk. Deedee and I went on the defensive, hating Dad's problem, but feeling like we had to protect him.

Ladies like Lizbeth and Ginny Royal hung on through the roughest times, nagging Dad to keep the measly janitor job he had, coming over to the house to help us clean up and organize the bills for Dad to pay. Deedee and I owe them and some others our lives."

Tina smiled faintly. "I can see why you two are so hardheaded."

"To his credit, Dad got his act together and we moved on. He was long sober when Diana and I decided to marry. But I will always remember that dark span of time. As I made a fresh start with my own family, I vowed nobody would ever laugh at us, that no child of mine would ever have to run to the playground to swing away his troubles. I would see to his happiness, his needs. Understand?"

"There is no missing your devotion to your son. And I've already admitted I don't know a thing about parenting," she said softly. "What else can I say?"

"Nothing." He slipped out of his swing and held out a hand to her. When she stood, he tugged her close. "I'm stumbling around, trying to apologize for being a jerk outside the school. You stomping off drenched and upset left me more miserable than I can say. I don't want to spend any more time arguing. We have something great between us, and I want to enjoy it. So in that spirit, I'm going to trust you to take care of all of us on your show."

"I do want you on my side," she said softly. "I can already see this as a wonderful showcase for Sugartown. I absolutely promise you'll be pleased."

"As for Jerod…"

"I will handle him with the care he needs and deserves."

"Thanks, Tina." His finger skimmed her cheek, moving to the tender skin of her throat. She put her hands to his chest and quivered a little. With that crooked smile she liked so much, Colby kissed her. "You look so cute drowning in my old jacket."

Standing on tiptoe, she kissed him back. Then they walked along the quiet streets in a comfortable silence.

Tina rarely allowed anyone to take the romantic lead with her. But she would let Colby do it. He had a son to raise. A job to do. This was his town and he had to live on here after she was gone.

Chapter Ten

All too soon Tina and Colby reached Hotel Beaumont property. She pushed some hair from his forehead. "We can say good-night here, if you like."

"No, I'll take you all the way."

They ascended the winding driveway, the huge white stone building looming in the moonlight like a castle.

Moving across the wide, shadowed porch, Colby grasped her shoulders with his large hands.

"So this is more than a simple drop-off," she teased.

"Aren't you glad?" Crowding her against the door frame of the wide front door, he kissed her more wildly than he had at the park, with the heated pressure of his tongue. She could feel the solid wood against her back as he moved his hands underneath the front of the jacket, then underneath her sweater. She looped her arms around his neck and moaned into his mouth as the rough pads of his fingers deliciously skimmed her sides and belly, working their way up to her skimpy bra.

Just as his hands cupped the weight of her breasts, the door swung open.

There stood Marilyn, gray hair looped in a messy topknot, dressed in some flowing lime-green number. With a gasp, Tina fell limp.

"You want something, Marilyn?" Colby asked eloquently.

"I want you to quit ringing the damn doorbell!"

"Oh!" Colby swiftly pulled Tina off the door frame.

"It's a slow time for us, but we do have some guests who might wonder if this is a loony bin."

Colby was properly chastened. "It won't happen again."

She surveyed Tina, who was busy tugging her top into place beneath her borrowed jacket. "Just what are you wearing?"

She gaped helplessly. "Didn't bring my own jacket. Cold outside."

"Huh." She bared crooked teeth at Colby. "I thought you'd be able to keep it simple. But, oh, no, it's gotta be a game. New talent in town, a relapse of high school testosterone.'

Colby scowled. "Excuse me?"

"Next that dopey Mayor Husman will be rushing over here to wrap her up in his old sweater for the sock hop. Our phone will be jangling off the hook. The doorbell will be ringing all hours. Cars will be tearing up the driveway. Horns will be honking."

"You encouraged me with Colby," Tina blurted out.

Marilyn gave Colby a wily stare. "That was before I knew the rivalry was already underway. We won't tolerate your old shenanigans under this roof."

"We are two grown men, Marilyn. That's kid stuff from the past."

Her eyes crunched in her withered face. "You sayin' that you haven't discussed Tina, jock to twit?"

He squared his shoulders. "Can I assume I'm the jock?"

"Don't get smart. And don't try to lie. Seth skulked around our lobby for an hour tonight, popping Tic Tacs, waiting for this little miss to show. And your name was mentioned a few times, Colby, in mutters about abuse of power, dereliction of duty and brainless brawn."

Colby hovered over Tina. "You encourage him?"

"I haven't even seen him."

Marilyn scoffed. "It's bad for business, him roosting here. Can't have it."

"I'd gladly arrest him for loitering next time," Colby offered.

"Just set him straight."

"Sure," Colby promised. "So can we drop it now?"

Marilyn continued to doubt his veracity. "Are you heading straight home from here?"

"Yes, ma'am."

"Then I'd like you to tell Ronny I need a ride to AA again. I know it's my turn to drive but Lizbeth's car needs a wheel alignment."

"I'll tell him."

She thrust a bony finger in his face. "You won't forget."

"I won't forget."

"Because I can call him."

"He's probably settling Jerod down for the night. I'll tell him."

Marilyn pulled the door wider. "You coming in now, Tina?"

Tina gasped at her nerve. "No, Marilyn."

"Well, lay off that bell!" she huffed before shoving the door closed.

Colby shifted from one foot to another, staring up at the dark and starry sky. "The jacket doesn't mean anything weird, honestly."

"Hey, I like it." She drew a white leather sleeve to her nose. "It smells like Mennon."

"Well, I was on a budget back then." He leaned against a concrete pillar. "So what to do about Seth…."

"How bad is this rivalry between you? And don't try

to tell me it's long over. I watched you go at it the minute I arrived in town."

"It's always been the clueless rich kid with a pedigree versus the poor kid from the house of dysfunction. Nothing serious. Just life as we know it."

"I can't really do anything until he puts a move on me," Tina reasoned. "He may not ever even do that."

"But you aren't interested in him, are you?" he asked worriedly.

She tried not to hesitate under his watchful gaze. But Seth could very well be her relation, as Brooke might. "Seth isn't my type. But I don't dislike him for any reason. And I do have an appointment with his mother tomorrow."

"What for!"

"I've decided she'd be ideal to cover the shoot for your newspaper."

"How'd you hook up with her in particular?"

"Met her at the brunch, remember? Seemed pleasant."

"There are other reporters. I can introduce you."

"I don't want another reporter! Oh, forget about it," she said in a lighter tone. "Come up to my room for a…Pepsi or something."

"Not tonight," he said, removing the hand from inside the jacket she wore. "So far I only have the family's permission to kiss you."

"Then I only imagined those hands in my sweater."

He tapped her nose. "I really should head back, give Ronny Marilyn's message before he dozes in front of the TV. Marilyn deserves the courtesy. It was her influence alone that got Ronny to his first Alcoholics Anonymous meeting and back on track."

"Somehow I wouldn't have imagined them pals."

"You won't notice any magic between them. There is the big age difference and nothing much in common. Long sober by the time Ronny was at his worst, Marilyn merely saw him as a pity case who needed a boost into sobriety."

She touched his collar as he turned to leave. "Guess I'll see you."

"When..." Clearly, he wanted an exact time.

"Tomorrow's bound to be hectic right up until night-time, when I visit the Think Tank."

"Dad's dating pool?"

"I need a narrator for the film and thought I might find someone with a powerful presence at the poetry club."

"I will gladly run you over there."

"Who will watch Jerod?"

"Deedee's kids are a bit older and love to have him over." With one last kiss, he was gone.

Tina stepped inside, still wearing the jacket. Lizbeth was hovering behind the desk, trying to look busy with fluttering hands.

"Have a nice time tonight, Tina?"

"Very nice. I like the Evanses."

"Marilyn thinks you like Colby the best." Lizbeth surveyed her. "Judging from that jacket, she's right."

Tina pulled the jacket closer to her body, inhaling Mennon. "I like the way it makes me feel, all warm and wanted."

"I'd forgotten how much static those two guys can cause."

"We're both sorry about the doorbell and Seth."

"Must say, you've managed to liven things up around here fast." Her indulgent smile suggested that wasn't such a bad thing.

"THE MOON HUNG LOW in a velvet sky. A drop of dew—No, no, make that rain. A drop of rain." Ronny was pacing around Colby's office at the police station the next morning, composing poetry on a legal pad. Colby was seated at his desk going over a report from the night shift. "What do you say, Cole?"

Colby glanced up from his work with a huff. "The moon hung low in a velvet sky. A drop of rain fell in my eye. Made me blink and order pie."

"Fine! Don't help me win the narrator position."

"You already have an edge knowing tonight's Think Tank meeting is sort of an audition. None of the other Tankers are likely to have a clue. Just relax and write the best poem you can."

"Okay. Guess it's really the delivery that matters most."

"Right, Dad."

"So, she really had a good time last night."

"Yes, Dad."

"Then why do you look grumpy?"

"She's getting entangled with Brooke Husman."

"Got to expect it. That family's the closest thing we've got to ritzy, with James the bank president and Seth the mayor. What exactly bothers you? The idea that she might go for Seth?"

"He has stolen girls away from me."

"Not this one. She likes you too much."

"It's more than that," he admitted, going on to explain the circle of names in Tina's notebook. "She claims to hit town with no agenda, then suddenly has Brooke, Lizbeth and Violet tagged for hot pursuit."

"Well, you saw her notebook after the brunch and they were all there, right?"

"Yes." Colby slid a pen between his fingers. "That might have been enough exposure to set them apart. But none of them are particularly flashy or memorable. Somehow I just don't buy it."

"Is it necessary for you to buy it?"

Colby sat up with inflated dignity. "I continue to feel responsible for the contents of this TV show."

Ronny placed a hand on his heart. "My multitalented son, Colby B. DeMille."

He scowled. "I mean as a representative of the law."

"You still can't be trying to compare her agenda to the orange-grove guy. He was all over town collecting goodies he didn't deserve. Tina's hardly done that." His expression grew wily. "Nobody's given her anything much. Jer and I are out a little pasta. You're out a letter jacket. And maybe a few kisses, judging by the lipstick on your face last night."

Colby grimaced. The only disadvantage to the old boy being sober was that he missed nothing!

"You never could hang on to that jacket for long," Ronny said wistfully. "Must say, nobody's ever looked cuter in it. And she seemed so happy over your fussing. She really likes you, Cole. Overlook all the rest or you'll flub it up."

"Seems so unfair, though. Somehow she wheedled my whole life story outta me. I'd like the same courtesy."

"Give her a little time. We hit her with a lot last night. You gave her the big death scene with Diana. I gave her the recovering-drunk lowdown. Jerod went behind your back to get in his bid for the square-dancing segment. Can you think of a moment when she might have even had a chance to respond?"

"Not offhand."

There was a rap on the glass door and the station's office gal Grace Copeland peered inside. "Better get a move on, Ronny, if you hope to make your AA meeting."

Ronny glanced at the clock on the wall with a yelp. "Thanks, Grace. I bet Marilyn is already down the hotel driveway." He barreled out the door, shoving his pad and paper into Grace's hands. "Lock this in the gun case or somewhere else safe until I get back."

Grace glanced down at the top sheet. "The moon hung over a velvet sky. He had that much when he came in."

Colby smiled. "Any ideas for line two?"

"Well, how about Silver clouds scudded by."

"Write it down. Who knows?"

THE *SUGARTOWN GAZETTE* had its own building at the end of Main Street. Tina entered the reception area dressed in the most elegant clothes she'd brought with her, a slim tan skirt topped by a navy cotton blazer and white polo top. Her black hair was done in a single smooth braid. Her pearl jewelry was trendy faux, her handbag and shoes the real deal. She'd prepared with extreme care today, wanting to meet Brooke Husman on her own terms and impress this third and last Bio Mom candidate.

It was frustrating to Tina that she was no closer to pointing out the woman Bill referred to as Honey Bee than she had been back in her Tribeca loft last week. She was so grateful her friend and partner was coming to town. She would gather information from Brooke just as she had from Lizbeth and Violet and together she and Emmy could tear through it.

Brooke was leaning at the reception counter, not bothering to disguise the fact that she was waiting to spring on Tina, much in the way her son the mayor had done upon her arrival in Sugartown.

"How nice to see you again!" Brooke sang out. There were a few people milling around the front office, and Brooke introduced each of them with complimentary observations. But she couldn't resist distinguishing her exclusive affiliation with the filmmaker. "We must push on. Confer."

When Tina met Brooke at Lizbeth's welcome brunch she didn't realize that she was a Bio Mom candidate.

But now she was aware and totally prepared to make educated comparisons between Seth, this woman and herself. Mother and son were fair-haired and friendly, with balanced facial features best described as handsome. Both were of average height for their sex. Both were overconfident, a trait probably due more to being affluent and powerful around town than to genetics. Tina was in many ways a physical opposite to the pair, being tall for a female, with hair as dark as coal. All three shared dark-blue eyes, though.

They were on the move now. Brooke, noting Tina's spiked heels, passed the stairs for the elevator.

"Those are lovely Prada shoes," Brooke said as they entered the car. Her eyes narrowed for a more frank inspection. "That outfit must be Tommy Hilfiger. The tote Vuitton?"

"Yes, yes and yes," Tina replied brightly, observing that she also shared Brooke's nerve for firing out direct questions!

Brooke punched the button marked two and suddenly grew girlish. "I just love nice clothes, don't you? I mean, nobody around here appreciates mine, but *I* know they're quality. And that's enough for me really, just knowing. This is Anne Klein," she intimated, doing an awkward pirouette in her teal suit just as the car lurched into motion.

Tina tried to envision her father with this exuberant and intelligent woman. Not the sophisticated pillar of society she was today, but as she was years ago, per Marilyn's description. Young and restless, still hanging around the Beaumont Hotel with Lizbeth and Violet, despite her husband. Judging strictly by appearances, Brooke would likely have caught Bill's eye first.

But would Bill have seduced a married woman? Well, why not, she thought ruefully. He was married and breaking his own vows. Maybe he liked that Brooke was married, knowing she'd never expect commitment from him. If Bill had gotten Brooke pregnant under her husband's nose, he worked a rare kind of trick getting the baby for himself. But it could be that Brooke had admitted to James that the baby was not his and James might be the sort of man who'd have insisted the baby be passed on. Rumor had it the whole family was big on appearances.

By now they'd exited the elevator on the second floor, Tina stalled in the corridor with her musings.

"Tina?" Brooke said a trifle impatiently. "This way."

"Yes. Coming." Tina walked through the office door Brooke held open, surprised to find the room rather sterile, with the regulation steel and vinyl and glass furniture common to office space.

Brooke was swift to read her thoughts. "I prefer to keep the place uncluttered, with minimum distraction. I don't spend all that much time here, running around town to track stories. And when people visit, I generally like to keep the interviews brief and on track."

Just the same, there were a few framed photos on one open wall, as well as some media awards and articles by her and about her. Tina made for them before Brooke had a chance to direct her to a chair. "You've sure achieved a lot," she said. "Forged an impressive career, raised a child, made lifelong friends."

Brooke pulled a smug smile. "Oh, yes. I'm very satisfied with how things have turned out. There were times when I wondered if I could do it all. When time and energy get short, it's traditionally expected the woman's career will be the first to go. But I decided not to compromise too much in that area. Now, all these years later, my husband and son are so proud of my position here at the paper." She squeezed Tina's hand. "You'll get there, too. It involves being tough and ambitious. While looking after your emotional needs, of course."

Tina complimented some awards, then pointed to some photographs of strangers, whom Brooke identified as relatives, most of whom had moved on to larger cities. Trying to pace herself in a casual way, she moved on to point out the photos of the three women taken over the years. "You, Violet and Lizbeth sure go way back. It's nice to keep old friends, isn't it? I have a few from grammar school, a few from college. They know you like nobody else. Accept you warts and all."

"Violet and Lizbeth are like sisters through thick and thin. I keep the photos here because James…" She shifted uncomfortably from one sandal to the other. "Well, James doesn't want them displayed in the house. He's long been a little jealous, claims my time spent with them is time robbed from him. All in all, the girls just annoy him."

Maybe he especially didn't he like to be reminded of Brooke's wilder days with her friends. Perhaps even the unwanted pregnancy that resulted when Bill joined the girls club.

"There I go again," Brooke chirped, "talking too much to someone I like."

"It's sort of like shop talk," Tina hastened to encourage. "Between two pros who see the world through curious eyes."

Brooke nervously patted her cap of light-blond hair. "James wouldn't want any part of our personal life broadcast."

"Of course not."

"I'm eager to hear how you see me fitting into your project," she said with more ambition.

"It's simple. I want to give you a chance to report step

by step our documentary process. Sort of a follow-the-show series of articles."

"Brilliant girl!" Brooke pounced on Tina with a kiss to her cheek.

"That a yes?"

"Jeepers, I've left a lip print." With a huff Brooke took a tissue from a box, dipped it in a glass of water on her desk, reached up to grasp Tina's chin and busily rubbed her cheek in motherly fashion. "Something like this could be picked up by all sorts of media once you hit television with the contest. Maybe even one of the big magazines!"

"Never know. But it will take a lot of your time. We'll have to prepare, get our work schedules in order." Tina paused, pretending to think. "Is there any way we can talk at length, off the clock, in privacy?"

"Of course!" Brooke tossed the tissue away and rounded the desk for a look at her appointment book. "We have plans tonight. But how about lunch at the house tomorrow?"

"Perfect."

"Confidentially, Seth has been pestering me to have you over to the house, anyway, so this will get me off the hook there, too."

"Seth still lives at your home?" Tina said with some surprise.

"Our house is a mansion, dear," she said with the mild condescension probably allowed any possessive mother who happens to be rich. "He has his own space, *for guests,* for all intents and purposes really. Why, it would be silly for him to even consider living anywhere else. The house is fully staffed to see to all our needs. And in another ten years, James and I will be retiring from our respective jobs and wintering in milder climes. Gradually, Seth will take over everything."

Certainly more explanation than Tina desired. She was only concerned with Colby's reaction to her paying a visit to the lair of his nemesis. But it had been her intent all along to get inside Brooke's home as she had Lizbeth's and Violet's for any clues to her heritage. It couldn't be helped if Seth would be on hand. She'd be foolish not to welcome him, in fact. A big talker just like his mother, it doubled Tina's chances of learning something valuable.

She reaffirmed that her search had to come before any romantic feelings for Colby. She longed for his trust and support, but since her beloved father's betrayal of her mother, Tina was having a terrible time taking anyone at face value. As sincere as Colby seemed, he might well mishandle the truth. Especially burdened with his cop mentality. His mission was seeing to the good of the town, rooting out threats and cons. He might spout off any number of concerns over invading her potential mother's privacy. The embarrassment factor. The pain factor, not only for her, but any current family members. The right that her mother had to keep the baby she called Natalie a memory of the past.

He was sworn to serve and protect Sugartown, and in her own defense, Tina believed he'd put that before any feelings for her. At least in these early stages of their relationship.

If for any reason Colby didn't like her game and chose to reveal her, this whole setup would be for nothing.

Chapter Eleven

The Think Tank meeting was set to begin as Colby hurried into the American Legion hall that evening. He scanned the rows of folding chairs arranged in front of the podium, relieved to discover average attendance of about thirty.

Apparently, news of Tina's search for a narrator hadn't hit Sugartown's informal newswire.

Colby had been held up at the station by a crisis and had sent Ronny to pick up Tina. Though still dressed in full uniform, down to the gun he seldom wore, Colby allowed the stress of the day to ebb as he spotted them together on the left side of the aisle near the front, reserving an empty chair between them. He eagerly edged by the row of knees to take the only open spot.

Was it his imagination that Tina's back stiffened slightly as his shoulder grazed hers?

"Sorry I'm late," he said. "Get Jerod to Dizzy's all right, Dad?"

"She couldn't watch him," Ronny replied. "Some last-minute thing with John's family. They're on the way to Stone Ridge."

Colby grew plaintive. "So where is my boy?"

"He's out at the water fountain."

Colby was nonplussed. "You brought him here?"

"No choice."

"Bet he's mad."

Ronny chuckled. "The minute he heard we were collecting Tina, he was hopping into the car."

Tina leaned over to join their chat. "You're sitting in my friend's seat, by the way."

"That's right, Dad." Jerod was back, staring him down man-to-man.

That likely explained Tina's tension. She was looking out for Jerod. How well they all fit together, he realized with pleasure. Or would do so, if they had a spare chair. Intent on making room for all of them, Colby glanced down at his lap, giving his knee a welcome pat.

"In your dreams," Jerod said in mortification.

Ronny rose from his seat. "It's okay. I'll go sit in back."

Colby flashed his father an appreciative look.

"Dad," Jerod prodded, "you're still in my seat."

When had his child gotten so savvy? Sighing deeply, Colby rose and gave Jerod the chair between Tina and himself.

Jerod got comfortable and glanced over to find Tina arranging her recorder for best reception. "I heard about what you're doing," he whispered. "Looking for an announcer, right?"

"Right. But that's our secret." Tina squeezed his hand, causing Jerod to beam in unadulterated wonder.

Colby watched in equal wonder. Any apprehension Tina felt for kids was truly blown way out of proportion.

"Do you like poems?" Jerod asked her.

"Very much. How about you?"

His bright young face soured. "I think this show is gonna be pretty boring."

"Shush," Colby chided. "You'll get us in trouble."

Tina laughed, giving him a look that would be better served if she were wearing her catwoman costume. "I think we can take 'em if things get hot."

"Sure," Jerod piped up. "We'll use Dad as a body shield."

"I know I'll be sliding in right behind him if necessary," Tina said silkily, winking at Colby over Jerod's head.

Colby's heart began to pound unmercifully in his chest. If he wasn't mistaken, this beautiful woman was suddenly giving him the green light in a big way! As if she too had reviewed last night's incident with the doorbell and liked it.

Each poet had upon arrival signed in on a blackboard resting on an easel up front and would perform in that order. Poetry flowed for the next two hours. Highlights were diverse. Chamber of commerce president and nurse Jessie Miller recited a poem she had composed about a patient in the emergency room. Both the young and the old Harvey Beyers took turns, respectable and randy in turn. Ginny Royal expounded on the joys of window shopping. Lizbeth, being precise in all things, clocked in with her usual fourteen-line sonnet, this week about the intricacy of a bird's nest. Ronny gave them his moon limerick.

There were many, many others that Colby chose to tune out.

He actually allowed his eyelids to droop, eventually feeling a small elbow in his gut. He blinked to find Jerod grinning at him. "Is it over?"

"Almost. I'm next."

"You, Jer?"

"Sure."

"You mean you've got a poem of your own?"

Jerod shrugged. "Wrote it on the way over. No big deal."

Sure enough, his name was printed at the very bottom of the blackboard.

"Oh, if one could bottle a child's fearless muse," Tina said, only to have Colby nod in mutual lament.

Jerod rose, digging a folded sheet of paper out of his jeans pocket. "Don't get too excited. It's only about how I want a dog."

Colby moved his legs so his son could inch by. "A refrain I've already heard many times afore," he said in *Masterpiece Theatre* loftiness.

Jerod moved up the aisle. The podium was too high for the boy so Lizbeth produced a stool for him to stand on. Clearing his throat, he began:

"The Dog
I want a dog to hug real tight
Who only bites when I say, Bite!
I'll feed him food and give him a bath
Even when I don't want one
A bath, I mean."

Laughter and a burst of applause followed his recitation. A pleased Jerod returned to his seat.

Colby patted his shoulder. "That was great, Jer."

"So, can I have a dog now?" he asked eagerly.

"No."

The boy scowled. "Maybe I'll come back next week and write about how you *don't* want a dog."

"Hey, you said this poetry deal was boring," Colby objected. "Besides, this whole thing runs past your bedtime."

Jerod laughed. "I'm kidding, Dad. I'd rather be watching TV. With my dog."

A small reception boasting coffee and pastries followed. Colby and Tina watched in amusement as a few ladies fluttered around a very composed Ronny.

"He does know how to work a room," Tina observed, nibbling on a cookie the size of a pancake.

Colby was matter-of-fact. "Told you so."

She offered him a bite of her cookie. "That sort of charm seems to run in your family."

He closed his hand over hers and drew the sweet to his mouth, giving her finger a quick lick. "Oh, it does."

"You any easier to catch than old Ronny seems to be?"

He murmured close to her ear. "The girl who has my letter jacket shouldn't even have to ask."

She gaped. "Oops. I should have brought that along. To return."

"No rush."

She met his gaze with eyes shimmering with promise. "It has been a long while since I enjoyed anybody's…jacket so much."

"You ever going to invite me to your room again?"

"Last night's invitation still stands."

With some reluctance, Ronny agreed to take the yawning Jerod home at about nine. "This is usually when things heat up for me around here," he informed Colby on the side as he slipped his smoky biker jacket off a hanger near the exit.

"Dad, you can see any of them anytime."

"Ginny Royal's sister isn't in town for long."

"She's in town until Thanksgiving," Colby corrected him dourly. "Weeks longer than Tina."

"So bring Tina along home, too. Pop some corn. Watch the news."

"Dad, I want to *make* some news."

The older man lit up. "Ah, so that's how it is."

Five minutes after Ronny and Jerod departed,

Colby extracted Tina from a band of well-wishers out into the crisp night air. She looked around at the parking lot on the side of the building. "I see you brought the squad car."

"No time for anything else. Thought I'd drop it and my gun back at the station. Walk you back to the hotel like a regular citizen."

"Hoping to stop the gossipers from seeing your car, catching on to our *friendship?*" she teased. "Wary cop consorting with possible con artist?"

He would undoubtedly catch some flak for crawling into bed with the visitor he'd so opposed. But it would be worth it. And certainly not the issue of the moment. He was determined to shut work out for a change. Felt he deserved to. "I'm not afraid to advertise our friendship," he corrected. "I'd just prefer that anybody needing a cop call my night man at the station. Understand?"

She gave him a jaunty salute. "Roger and out, Chief."

Marilyn was behind the reservations desk when they arrived at the hotel. Her face was set grumpily. "Was the meeting as dull as I think?"

"It was fun," Tina objected. "You ever been?"

"No." Marilyn grew hopeful. "Is it really fun? Lizbeth having a good time?"

Colby shrugged. "When we left, she and Ginny were discussing which produce supplier offers the best broccoli."

"Just as I thought. Another trumped-up activity Lizbeth pretends is fun."

"Lizbeth appeared perfectly happy," Tina insisted.

"I keep telling that kid she needs a life!" Marilyn smacked a tablet of paper on the desktop. "It was all wrong for me to allow her to hide out here in this old tomb. Look what she's become. Old before her time, quibbling with that hussy over things that don't amount to a hill of beans. Ginny's almost as big a dud, but at least she has a husband to go home to."

"Why the sudden concern over Lizbeth's lifestyle?" Colby wondered.

Marilyn opened her mouth and closed it again. Unusual for her, Colby thought. She rarely censored herself. "I dunno," she grumbled. "Old people just get to thinking things over. If they've done right by their kids. Helped 'em enough."

Tina watched her sympathetically. "Lizbeth seems perfectly content. Don't upset yourself this way."

"Or your guests," Colby added, tipping his head at some cute newlyweds passing through the lobby rather hurriedly. Marilyn wagged a crooked finger after them. "Lizbeth used to smile just like that new bride does."

Colby couldn't recall such a time. Must have been before his. "If you don't mind, we'd like to finish off the night happy."

"By all means, don't let me stop you."

"Any messages for me, Marilyn?" Tina asked.

Marilyn slid a stack of clipped pink slips at her. "Just the usual suck-ups. Oh, and this, too." She reached under the desk and produced a large basket full of fruit, nuts, candy and a bottle of Zinfandel, which she set down with a thump.

Tina reared in surprise. "From whom?"

"Couldn't say. Must be a card somewhere." She surveyed Colby as he grasped the basket. "Hey, how about a tip?"

"Sure thing, Marilyn." He leaned into the polished wood desk. "Try and lighten up a little." With that he urged Tina to the staircase.

Inside Tina's room, they dissolved in laughter. "Is Marilyn always so volatile, Cole?"

He set the basket on the dresser and took her in his arms. "I love it when you call me that."

"About Marilyn..."

"She is a total nut who gets her kicks spouting off." He kissed her nose. "But it's usually about national politics and local irritants. Wonder what's got her so cranked up about Lizbeth?"

Tina shrugged. "People tend to examine their lives more closely when a documentary is in progress. See it all the time."

He caressed the wispy hair at her temples. "Makes sense, I guess."

"A little scrutiny always seems to jar people."

"Hope nobody becomes too unglued."

"Relax. Leave it all in my hands." With that she looped her arms around his neck and pulled him down to her level.

He took her kiss eagerly, pushing his tongue deep into her mouth. He rubbed her back to win a pleased moan. He cupped her bottom to feel her soften against him.

It was a repeat of last night's passion. She was giving in to him. Opening up to him. With no doorbell in sight. He moved his mouth over her face, down her throat, fully aware that her hands were tugging his uniform shirt out of his waistband, methodically working open the small, stubborn buttons clear up to his collar. Shucking his shirt, he pulled her red sweater over her head.

He groaned at the plunging red lace bra underneath. "This looks like company's-coming underwear to me."

Her coy smile confirmed as much. "You had much exposure to company's-coming underwear, Chief?"

"Not lately...."

She put his hands over her breasts and pushed into him. His palms filled with soft flesh, hard nipples, restrained by stiff lace. Pulling her up his thigh he leaned over to suckle one mound only to feel his erection crowding his pants.

She must have felt it, too, for she slid off his leg, worked free his belt and zipper and shoved the works to the floor. He went for her zipper and soon they'd undressed each other.

He took the time to scan her body with appreciation, then crushed her against him. Running a hand down her back, he molded her close, groaning as her soft feminine curves melted into his length. Grabbing a handful of her hair, he tilted her mouth up for a consuming kiss. Then he picked her up and took the few short steps to the bed.

Setting her flat on her back, he poised overhead with a discontented growl. "Wait! I don't have any protection."

She touched his thigh. "It's fine, Cole. I'm protected."

His growl took on a hunger as he climbed over her. For the first time since they'd met, he felt on top, in control. And for the first time she didn't look the least bit wary or apprehensive. Her dark-blue eyes shimmered with pure desire.

The crush of body and lock of lips jolted Colby with a sharp electrical spark. Fascinated with the sensation, he glided his hair-dusted skin over her silken length, swiftly building up an electrical charge between them. He eventually shifted position to explore. His mouth moved over her breasts to draw her nipples to hard cores, then down her belly to plant tiny kisses inside her thighs. Resting up on his knees, he opened her legs to expose her soft, inviting core. He took deep, even breaths, going dizzy as her primal scent intermingled with her sweet perfume.

Tina cried out as his tongue teased and probed her center for the longest time. Finally shifting position on the mattress, she took the initiative to guide his penis inside her.

He paused after taking one hot plunge. "Oh, baby..."

"Keep going," she panted.

Cradling her bottom with his large hands, he drove inside her over and over again with searing friction until they both exploded in release. He lay over her then, anxious to remain close but careful not to squash her with his weight. As their hearts pounded together, he felt they were a single entity. He'd only felt this kind of total consummation once before, and he'd married the girl.

But it had been different with Diana. She'd been open, available and predictable.

He and Tina were connecting strongly on a basic level but struggling with distance in the form of miles, agendas and career choices. Suddenly frustrated by it all, he rolled off her. "That was fantastic," he admitted softly. "It's not like I never get any sex. I just don't get it like that!"

She leaned over to kiss his damp forehead. "Stay the night. We'll do it again."

"Can't," he said simply. "I need to get home. After I catch my breath, anyway." He wasn't about to tell her it would take time to digest what had just happened here before he went at it again.

"I understand," she said softly. "Go ahead and use the bathroom first, while I catch *my* breath."

By the time Tina exited the bathroom in a sleep shirt, Colby had calmed down. Standing in his briefs, he was tugging at the cork in the bottle of wine.

"Where did you ever find a corkscrew?" she asked.

"I have one on my pocket knife." With a pop of cork, he filled two stout water glasses. "Lots of great snacks in this basket. Funny, I couldn't find any card."

"I'm sure the sender will check back for a thank-you. But I wish they hadn't done it. I'm not much for snacking. And that bounty is overkill for one person."

He lifted the glasses in the air. "What do you say we take this lying down."

They both eagerly climbed back into bed. Lounging against the headboard, Tina took a sip. "Why can't Jerod have a dog?"

"That's all you have to say to me? Not something like, 'Masterful moves'?"

Her black brows narrowed. "Answer me, Daddy."

Colby propped several pillows on the headboard and sank back. "I feel we already have enough going on at the house. My hours are strange. Ronny works some evenings. Jerod frequently ends up in Deedee's care, sometimes overnight. The dog would always need to be covered. I just don't want the added pressure."

"You feel that pressured?"

"I worry most about overloading Ronny," he admitted, "making it tougher for him to stay on the wagon. I go out of my way to make him comfortable."

"Have you ever asked Ronny how he'd feel about a dog?"

"Well, no."

"He might not mind."

"Of course he wouldn't! He's got the emotional intelligence of his grandson, a bit hazy about consequences when he gets excited. I have to do all the heavy thinking."

She regarded him in loving exasperation. "Oh, Cole, how can you possibly always know what's best for everyone?"

"Look, it takes a lot of nerve to be police chief. I have to step forward, make decisions all the time and hope they're the right ones. Hesitating at all would be far worse than making a few mistakes."

"Lots of families have dogs. They manage."

He gazed over her wryly. "You had one as a kid."

"A collie named Buzz." Her smile was fond. "Buzz

gave me a lot of companionship when I was Jerod's age, Cole. Lots of comfort when I felt nobody else understood me."

"But if it doesn't work out, then what? Another loss for Jerod." He shook his head. "Seems like such a great risk."

To his relief, Tina changed focus. They finished the bottle of wine, talked about the poets and potential narrators. Tina seemed in no hurry to choose one.

"I wish I had that session on film. It's not only the voice at stake, but the person delivering it."

"Ronny is really hoping for a break."

"I'm sure. But we may go for someone apart from the Think Tank. Luckily, nobody outside your family even knows I'm looking."

He caught her message. "I'll remind the boys to keep quiet. Can't have people making speeches to you on the street."

"Thank you." Tina's cell phone rang on the night stand. She glanced at the Caller ID. "It's Emmy."

"At midnight?"

She hit the talk button with an indulgent smile. "Midnight isn't very late in Manhattan. Hey, Em. Oh. I was speaking to Sugartown's chief of police."

Colby tried to make out what Emmy Snow was saying but could only catch the odd word. He was sure, however, that she was asking if they were in bed and was gleeful with Tina's affirmation. Apparently, the other woman knew about him and had seen this coming. This was a welcome insight into Tina's head. He tried not to be too obvious in eavesdropping or too content with the result. But he wanted feedback, payback for her stripping his own soul so bare.

"By the way, Warren tells me you've been visiting the nursing home nearly as often as he and Myrna. Thanks so much for going. I call every day, but it isn't the same as being there. Absolutely, come as planned. The sooner you help me wrap this up, the sooner I can return and take over. Perfect. See you tomorrow."

Her last gush of words held an urgency that startled and interested Colby. He shifted on the bed as she disconnected and set the phone aside, intent on cornering her physically. He did it with suspects sometimes, with more clothes on, of course. "Everything all right?"

Tina sighed in resignation. "My mother, Angela, is in a nursing home. Emmy and the family lawyer have been standing in for me."

Colby allowed the huge development to sink in. "That explains why you always frantically check your Caller ID with every ring. What happened to her? I'm guessing she isn't all that old."

"She's barely sixty. Had a severe stroke. A neighbor found her several hours after it happened, so any chance of getting her immediate relief from emergency services or even an aspirin were long lost." She waved a hand in a helpless gesture. "In all ways that matter, she's already gone."

"Do you have any family helping you with this?"

She shook her head. "I have no siblings. Dad died years ago in a car crash."

"There are no relatives at all?"

"Mom has two sisters who would like nothing better than to take over her affairs—push me out! But I won't allow it, Cole. I'm Mom's executor and intend to see things through."

"Wow." He captured her hand to find it trembling. "Why didn't you tell me sooner, Tina?"

"Because…"

He could feel her mind working, and desperately wished she wouldn't calculate so much.

"A lot of reasons, I suppose. I don't want this

problem to overshadow my project. And I don't want you or anyone else to treat me awkwardly! I've had some time to process this tragedy. I've managed to accept that Mom is terminal." She faltered. "Finally accepted that my connection to her has always been terminal. There was never any magical connection between us, like you have with Jerod. Not that I didn't try my best, as kids do. But she was determined not to open her heart. A basic rule of human nature is that it takes two to make a loving relationship. Without her participation, we were doomed from the start."

"Oh, honey." Colby pulled her against him and squeezed tight. Again he felt that intimate tug that belonged in a real, extended relationship. Wanted nothing more than to help her through her trials. To understand everything.

For starters, it certainly was no wonder that she felt so awkward on the subject of child rearing. "You can do it, you know," he murmured. "Move beyond your own childhood, skillfully raise a pack of kids."

Nestling her cheek against his chest, she gently patted his ribs with a long, slender hand, as if humoring him.

"It's all about love and good intentions," he went on, stroking her hair. "Jerod's a kid and he senses those qualities in you already."

"I like him, too. But he still makes me a little nervous, like all the others. I don't want to ever damage a child by saying or doing the wrong thing."

"Mistakes are made by all adults, Tina. I've already told you that. Whatever your mother's problem…" He stalled briefly, hoping she'd jump in with that problem, if she knew it. But no such luck. "Whatever it's been, it mustn't cripple you forever. It's all about making the effort."

She sniffed. "No man's ever encouraged me this way before."

"Then you've been hanging with the wrong kind of man. Till now...."

"Maybe in time I will feel I can manage a family of my own."

Her refusal to instantly melt under pressure grazed his ego. "I say this out of affection, Tina, but you are a little too intense about everything."

She glared at him. "Takes one to know one, Chief Father Knows Best."

"I suppose I deserve that." But he clearly didn't think so.

She smacked his arm. "Oh, don't be pouty."

"Well..." With mouth twitching, he stared off into space.

"Tomorrow will be exciting, with my crew coming."

"Maybe..."

She gestured to the brimming basket on the dresser. "And you can have the goodie basket. That should keep your little troop fed for hours."

Colby cupped her cheek. "Now you're talking a deal."

Chapter Twelve

"You must have one of these shrimp canapés, Tina."
Brooke Husman made the offer as a uniformed maid
stood by with a silver platter.

Tina had kept her date at the Husman mansion the
next afternoon and was in the process of admiring a
Lichtenstein print. Steadying her daiquiri, she reached
for a small pink-and-white puff. "You've gone to way
too much trouble."

Brooke dismissed the maid with crisp instructions.
"Can't let you starve. Seth and James are both running
behind with morning appointments, so we'll be having
lunch a little later than planned."

"Your home is lovely." Tina wandered closer to an
ancient-looking chair on casters with a shaped rush
back, paneled arms and a board seat.

"Oh, Tina! Please don't sit in that chair. It's a nine-
teenth-century Orkney!"

Tina hopped back a little. "I didn't realize."

"A three-thousand-dollar investment." Brooke ex-
pansively waved her hand. "This room is full of precious
antiques. The closest Sugar will ever come to a
museum." She eagerly gestured to an old desk that
looked as if it had seen better days. "This Federal inlaid

mahogany piece, also which nobody uses, is worth six grand. It belonged to my grandmother, who, like you, lived in Manhattan. She even resembled you slightly, I think, with a nice long frame, large eyes and beautiful black hair."

Interesting aside. Brooke may not look like Tina but there was a resemblance somewhere on the family tree. Tina drained her daiquiri and pondered the possible implications. Being Brooke's daughter would mean she was wealthy. She could have a servant at her beck and call all the time. Tina gave the hovering maid her empty glass, declining a refill. She suspected the novelty of a lot of money might wear off fast, however, as one became consumed with appearances, both social and physical. Emmy Snow had grown up in this atmosphere and chosen to abandon it for their more bohemian lifestyle.

Just the same, Tina could see how a person could become addicted to all this. Seth must be, for he'd never left the nest.

Tina listened politely as Brooke went on in fevered antique-dealer mode. On view was the collection of Baccarat paperweights from the mid 1800s, collected by a French uncle who was a famed painter back then. The Regency rosewood eight-day bracket clock with brass inlay, done by a London craftsman who was great friends with James's family. Not to mention an assortment of lusterware jugs, which Brooke couldn't help but mention.

The only thing in the room left unaddressed was a rocker holding a large doll in a faded white dress. Always a doll lover, Tina was drawn to it.

"The chair is a rod-back Windsor," Brooke said wistfully, her face suddenly looking older behind its layer of artful makeup.

"She's gorgeous." Tina almost instinctively reached

for it, as she would any doll anywhere, but held back as she remembered the no-touch rule of the room.

"By all means, hold her," Brooke invited softly. In fact, she picked up the doll herself and handed it to Tina. "It's an original Steiner. Fixed blue eyes, mohair wig. Circa 1870."

"Mother!" Seth strode in and gave Brooke a kiss on the cheek. He then took the doll from Tina, set it back in the chair. "Giving Tina the tour, I see."

"Hello, dear." Brooke exchanged a strained look with her son.

"Dad's here, too. So it's time to eat." Seth put his arms around both women and steered them toward the arched doorway.

The dining room was every bit as opulent as the Hotel Beaumont's, featuring twin chandeliers, satiny cream wallpaper and an impressive wooden table with pedestal, surrounded by comb-back chairs.

"Relax, Tina," Seth said with amusement. "The table is refectory but it's one antique Mother lets us use."

"Under careful watch, of course!" A distinguished middle-aged man with silver hair and tanned skin entered. His pinstripe suit was a perfect fit for his trim figure and his shoes were made of soft leather. The look, finished by the heavy-looking Rolex on his wrist, well fit the image of a bank president. He extended his hand to Tina. "I'm James Husman. Pleased to meet you."

Tina shook his hand and allowed him to pull out a chair for her.

Brooke delicately eased into the chair her son pulled back for her. "Seth has no respect for the family treasures."

Seth snapped open his napkin and placed it on his lap. "I only hope to live long enough to see your Tupperware skyrocket in value."

"Oh, really," Brooke scoffed, but the dig brought back her cheer.

"She honestly does have Tupperware, always kept hidden from guests," Seth persisted. "Along with some Corningware. The little bowls with the handles are my favorite for heating up all the little fancy bits she serves her scrawny friends—who never eat anything anyway."

"Hush up or that will be the total of your dowry!" Brooke scolded.

"Girls have the dowry, Mother."

"To compensate for your wicked humor, we will be forced to give your future bride hazard pay."

Tina suspected this skit had grown well rehearsed with other young women brought here to dine. She wished Seth didn't look at her with such interest.

"How is your project going, Tina?" James asked jovially, leaning back as a server set a salad before him. "I noticed you haven't visited the bank yet."

Tina chuckled, thanking the server when a plate appeared in front of her. "I don't intend to highlight banks in any of the four towns. Seems unwise to give away your floor plan and location, make a national invitation to robbery." She gazed to Brooke, seated on her right. "The same goes for your beautiful things. No sense in bringing a camera in here to advertise your treasures."

"It wouldn't be smart to show off, Mother."

"But I want to call the right kind of attention to our family," Brooke objected.

"You'll be covering the film for the newspaper," Tina reminded her. "We already discussed how that may lead places."

"But my pieces would cinch recognition. And we do have a fine security system."

Seth shook his head. "Say the alarm system goes off. It would take the security company time to make sure it's a legit break-in. Time to alert the county sheriff. More time for the sheriff's department to respond. It's a hazard of living in the boondocks."

"I'm not necessarily in favor of opening our home to the camera," James interjected. "But I think it's only fair to mention our own police chief as a security asset. Wouldn't want the film to reflect anything but our respect for Chief Evans."

"I don't see any reason to give any special attention to that hothead," Seth grumbled.

James frowned. "I like Colby. Always have. And before you go on, I have to say that Tina's mention of robbery strikes a big nerve. Colby really showed his stuff late yesterday at the bank, personally rescued me from a huge mess."

Everyone glanced up sharply at James, no one more quickly than Tina.

"We had a ruckus with those work-release road laborers staying out at the trailer park. A few of them created a diversion in the lobby while one tried to pass a stolen paycheck. They were clever, choosing our extended weekday hours so it would be getting dark, waiting until the last minute so tellers would be anxious to close. Luckily, I had the chance to quietly call the station to report it. Colby arrived with a couple of his men to take control, tossed the lot in jail for the night and it's my understanding they're all headed to the big house today."

Seth sat back in his chair. "This is the first I've heard of it."

Tina took a minute to find her voice. "Same here."

"Funny there hasn't been more talk," Seth said.

"I asked my employees not to discuss it in order to

keep gawkers away. Luckily the bank was empty at the time, as most people are home at that hour."

"A share of adults were at the Think Tank meeting, too. Like me." Tina sipped water from her crystal goblet, trying not to tremble over the potential danger Colby had faced. No wonder he was barely on time for the poetry reading. And he never said a word about it. But listening to him talk last night about duty and family and trying not to pressure Ronny, she guessed it had a lot to do with compartmentalizing his different worlds.

"I'm surprised he didn't try and capitalize on it right off, make himself the hero of the film," Seth observed.

"He doesn't care much about being in the film," Tina said quietly.

"He was against the whole thing," Brooke interjected.

Brooke and James begged off after lunch to discuss how the newspaper would cover the incident at the bank. From his expression, it was clear to Tina that James wished his wife wasn't a reporter.

Tina was left alone with Seth and didn't mind at all. Maybe she'd learn more about the Husman family from the son than she had from the mother. Standing up, she walked out of the dining room in the direction of the living room, relieved as he trailed after her. Oozing with self-involved charm, he was going on about how often he traveled to Manhattan to shop, see shows.

"I suppose you take your mother sometimes," she ventured, feigning interest in the Lichtenstein.

"Sometimes. She has friends there and connections at some of the papers."

"What do her friends call her? I mean, any nicknames?"

He screwed up his face. "I don't think so."

"What about your father, for instance?"

"He sometimes calls her Lois Lane. You know, after the reporter."

"Yeah." She grinned. "I get it."

"Sorry. I'm just a little nervous." He adjusted the knot of his tie.

"Please, don't be. Any other names come to mind?"

"I've noticed that people with one syllable don't have a lot of nicknames. I mean, you can't shorten a single syllable, can you?"

"Sometimes nicknames pop up in other ways," she persisted. "Like Sweetie Pie. Or even Honey Bee."

He looked more perplexed than ever. "No, I've never heard her called anything like that. You have any nicknames?"

"Some people call me Tee."

"I like Tina much better. It's such a pretty name." He leaned toward her and brushed her hair from her forehead. "Feminine and lyrical. Just right for you."

She faltered. "Thanks."

"I hope there will be a small place for me in the show."

"I think the mayor of each town should do the closing. And that reminds me." She moved to the sofa holding her tote bag and extracted her camera. "Let me just snap your picture for my storyboard."

He went to the mantel, moving one way and then another. "Let me find a good pose. I like my right profile better, don't you?" She needed a simple head shot but didn't discourage him.

With a click and a flash it was done. She stowed the camera away again. This time when she whirled and straightened, he was there to block her, reaching to touch her face and kiss her forehead.

"Don't, Seth." She eased out of his reach with as much grace as possible.

"I thought you'd call me last night. I waited up quite a while." He paused. "You did hear I came round, didn't you?"

"Yes, I did."

"Sent a basket, too. You get that?"

"Yes, Seth." So that little mystery was finally solved. "I do thank you for the attention—"

"I only want a chance with you," he said hopefully.

"Sorry, no."

"Colby beat me to it, didn't he?"

"I am involved with him. Would you mind so much being friends instead?"

"Good enough for now. I'll just wait until he screws up, move in then."

She laughed. And so did he.

Relaxed and relieved, Tina prepared to follow up on the only promising lead of the day, the old porcelain doll on the antique chair.

"This is such a lovely piece," she remarked as he hovered behind her. "May I hold her again?"

"Of course. It's only when Mother's around that the thing is a problem."

Tina gingerly cradled the doll. "How so?"

He glanced back at the wide doorway and lowered his voice. "Mother lost a baby before me. At nearly full term, I understand. The details are sketchy even now. I only know what Father's been willing to reveal. All seemed well with the pregnancy at first...." He trailed off, looking years younger all of a sudden. "The whole thing is so sad, angers Father to this day. Anyway, Mother went kind of crazy after it happened and brought home that doll. Sort of a standoff between my parents all these years, Mother insisting upon displaying the doll, Father wanting it put aside."

"Funny a powerful man like your father lets a doll bother him."

"It's obvious that he wishes Mother would put those memories behind her."

Perhaps it was James Husman who didn't want a reminder of the baby he forced his wife to give up, presumably upon learning that it wasn't his. And while Brooke had done the necessary thing to fix her marriage, she wasn't totally healed, even now.

Seth shoved his hands in his trouser pockets and stared at his shoes. "It would've been nice having a sister all this time."

"So the baby was a girl for sure, then?"

"Oh, yes."

Tina desperately wanted to ask if Brooke had named the baby—Natalie, for instance. But she didn't dare. She'd already asked her limit of questions on the subject. It wouldn't be fair to alert Seth to anything his mother had chosen to keep from him. She was trying to respect the privacy of her birth mother, after all. This meant more to Tina than ever, now that she'd met all three Honey Bee contenders. She wouldn't want to hurt any of them for the world.

COLBY WAS AT THE STATION near the day's end, in the process of unloading the three miscreants from yesterday's bank incident to the county authorities. It had been a long afternoon, waiting for the county to send transport. He stood out in the alley behind the government center, helping the two deputies settle the cuffed trio into the caged back seat of the transport van when Grace Copeland showed up at the rear steel door. "Phone call from home, Chief."

Ronny had been pestering him about everything from what he could eat from Tina's food basket to the broken CD player. "Take a message."

"It's the little guy this time."

Colby's face lit up, and he shook hands with the deputies. "Guess that wraps it up." With one last thank-you between them, Colby dipped back through the door Grace was holding open.

Striding over to Grace's desk, he snagged the phone receiver. "Jer?"

"Hi, Daddy."

"How was school, buddy?"

"Good. We practiced our square dance over and over."

"Oh." Colby's spirits fell. It seemed his son was dead set on dancing on camera. "Any problems today?"

"No. Why do you always think that?"

"I don't."

"I'm calling about that cool basket from Tina."

"I told Ronny you could dig in."

"Sure. But I found a card under a box of cookies. I don't get it."

So there was a card, after all. Colby was brimming with curiosity. "Can you read all the words?"

"Sure. That's why I don't get it."

"Well, son," he prodded. "What does it say?"

There was a slight pause, then he began, "'Can't wait for our date, good-looking. Warmly, Seth.' Is that the mayor, Dad? Is this his food?"

"Finders keepers. Just eat what you want."

"Hey, did you catch some bad guys yesterday? Why didn't you tell me?"

"Yes, at the bank. I didn't want to worry you, son."

"You do some shootin'?"

"Not yet." He grimaced at a sudden vision of Seth. "I mean, no. I took them into custody without firing a single shot."

"But you must've pulled your gun to get 'em to jail."

"I raised my gun and yelled a lot. That's all it took."

"Oh."

"I've told you before, I don't like to pull my gun. So I don't want a big deal made of it around town."

Jerod sighed in childish exasperation. "I don't get it."

"You will when you get older." Colby smacked the receiver down. Tina had a date set with that zero and hadn't said a word! What had their time together meant to her, anyway?

Grace was sinking into her chair, watching him rub hands over his face. "Everything all right?"

He stared at her for a long time trying to regain his composure. "News leaked out about the bank thing yesterday," he finally offered.

She rolled her chair closer to her computer. "Naturally. There are no secrets in Sugar."

"There are a few, I promise you," he snapped.

"Cole, you're too reluctant a hero."

"I do feel successful for not having to fire a shot," he conceded. "And I look forward to the day Jerod understands that."

"Don't expect that kind of progress until high school. Maybe later."

Grabbing his jacket, Colby said with a wave, "I'll be around town if you need me."

On automatic pilot, he steered his squad car to the Hotel Beaumont and stalked through the lobby. Lizbeth was at her post behind the front desk. "Good job yesterday—"

"*She* in?"

"Tina, you mean? Yes, I think—"

With a nod, he was taking the wide stairs two at a time. With a single knock to her door, Colby burst inside. Only to come face-to-face with an unfamiliar beauty.

He blinked back his shock, keeping a sharp focus on his anger. "Who are you?"

"The best friend." Feline eyes skimmed him with unabashed appreciation. "And you must be the yummy Chief Evans."

Chapter Thirteen

The woman reminded him of a small tigress, moving with speed and grace across the room despite clingy black clothes. Colby flinched when she picked up a Polaroid camera from the dresser and snapped his photo, out of which came an undeveloped square.

"Why'd you do that?"

His growl only urged her smile wider. "I can actually feel your passion. Wanted to try and capture it on film."

Colby arched a brow. "Always so shy?"

"A shy documentarian. Not likely." She extended her hand. "I'm Emmy Snow, by the way."

"Figured. The whole crew here?"

"Not yet. I drove up on my own." She paced in a circle around him. "I can assure you I'd have no trouble arranging your fifteen minutes of fame. Just give me the word."

"The word is Tina. Where is she?"

"Just stepped out."

To see Seth? Colby's blood was simmering. He wondered if Emmy Snow could feel *that*, too!

Emmy sauntered closer to the bed. It looked so ordinary now from a distance, made up in its frilly skirting with the sham-covered pillows propped against the headboard. There was no sign of last night's fevered passion. Except in his mind, along with visions of Tina with Seth.

Emmy tapped the photo of him with her thumbnail. "Come over here. Just looking for a spot for you."

Moving to her side, Colby discovered a collage of Polaroids on the mattress, snapped during Tina's tour through town. He zeroed in on a photo of Seth. He'd seen Seth earlier from across the street and Seth's ugly aqua shirt suggested the photo was taken today. Presumably, they'd already had their "date." During the daytime. That settled him. Slightly. "I'm not a participant in any of this," he informed her.

"You were in my best friend's bedroom last night, hardly a mere observer."

"How do you know that? I mean, I have no place on the *storyboard*."

Just the same, she wedged his photo in next to Jerod's, taken at the school the other day. "Your kid is really cute," she remarked. "Nice family already in the making. Very inviting story in itself, strictly off the storyboard, I mean."

It appeared Tina had already confided a lot to Emmy. If Emmy saw a future for Tina with him, Tina must have intimated the possibility. The very idea jolted him with a strange, forbidden hope. He'd long ago decided he wouldn't try to replace Diana. And for five years he hadn't, choosing to tell his dates when they asked that his family was complete, thank you very much. It kept life neat and safe. But since last night, when Tina had rocked his world making love, he couldn't stop replaying the time they'd shared. The way she'd fit so nicely into their home. The way her shell continued to crack under his boy's worshipping eyes. The feelings she drew out of him made risks seem necessary again.

But that was the positive side. There were plenty of

cons. Tina didn't live in Sugartown, wouldn't be here for much longer. And she did seem to be holding something back from him. Most recently her prearranged date with Seth, which she'd kept from him all evening long. The thought of them together drove him crazy!

"Where did you say Tina was?" he asked.

Emmy beamed with amusement. "I didn't."

Colby began to pace.

"She's at the store, Colby, picking up some things I forgot to bring. Gee, to think she's landed somebody even more serious than she is."

Tina popped through the door moments later. "Hey, Cole." She stood on tiptoe to kiss his jaw. "You're just the guy I want to talk to."

"You find everything?" Emmy asked.

"Yeah, the dime store had all our favorite toys, bulletin boards, paper, easels, markers and tacks. The mobile unit just arrived, too. I left the crew downstairs in the dining room with the stuff."

Emmy collected the photos and a walkie-talkie with haste but took time to pause at the door to watch them. "I'd tell you two to get a room, but you've already got one."

"We'll be right along," Tina promised.

"Hope so. The crew's on the clock." She closed the door firmly behind her.

"EXPLAIN!"

"We gotta talk!"

Colby and Tina spoke in unison, startling each other. He flicked a finger under her chin. "Ladies first."

"You almost got shot yesterday!"

He was flabbergasted. "That's what you have to say?"

"Imagine me having to hear it from someone else. Everyone else! You handling it okay?"

"I came out of it without a scratch. And the jailbirds are off the work program, back on a bus headed to jail."

"What a relief!" She patted her heart. "You in danger often?"

"No."

"You sure you don't want mention of it on camera? We could use you and witnesses to recount events, with some bank security camera footage. Small-town-hero stuff."

"Never! I've made it clear I don't want any media attention."

She pushed out her bottom lip. "Well, you've softened on other issues. Thought I'd give it a try. So what did you want to say?"

He grasped her by the forearms. "You ever find out who sent the basket?"

She grew wary but smiled at him. "Am I being investigated?"

"Of course not! I found out by accident. That it was from our pal Seth."

"How?"

"Jerod found a card confirming your *date*. So what's up?"

"We had no date. I had another meeting with his mother—the reporter set to cover my project," she reminded him. "He and his father simply showed up."

"Have lunch?"

"We did eat some food around midday. Yes. It was nothing."

"If it was nothing, why didn't you mention it ahead of time?"

"Because it *was* nothing. It's plain we have different views about what *nothing* means."

"I don't understand you. I don't understand what you want."

She moved her hands to his uniform collar. "I clearly want only you." Wrapping her long fingers around the back of his head, she pulled him down for a kiss. The wet heat of her mouth sent his brain spinning. But only for a minute. Gently he pried her loose.

"I wish you'd tell me more about yourself, Tina."

"Ditto. Bank buster."

He grimaced. He'd withheld one thing and now she was putting their secretiveness on the same level. Was this conversation just a little dirty dueling to keep him from prying into her filming, or was she scrambling to keep something much bigger hidden? As reasonable as she appeared, as much as he believed in her affection for him, his instincts persisted in sending out warning signals.

"Look, I need to continue to follow the job where it leads," she asserted. "Today that happened to be at the Husmans'."

But was her trail random or a plotted course? Guess it depended upon what, if anything, that circle with Lizbeth, Violet and Brooke written in it meant.

"It isn't my fault Seth joined us," she pressed on. "Or that Brooke showed him off like a prized pony." He couldn't help twitching his mouth at the pony part, which she obviously caught. "James sure respects you. He's the one who told me about the bank incident."

"You were eating their food, talking about me?"

"That's right, Cole."

That appeased him a little. "Did Seth try and kiss you?"

"He only made it to the forehead. I told him about us and that was the end of it." She paused. "He's willing to wait until you screw up."

That made him laugh. "Guess I should let you get to work."

"I'll get there." She pushed a single finger into the center of his chest. "When we're finished talking."

He could feel himself slipping into her soft smile and huge vulnerable eyes.

"What did last night mean to you, exactly?"

"You want to know that now?" Colby asked. "But don't you want to—"

"Right now."

He deflated slightly. "It's not easy to put into words. From the minute I laid eyes on you, I felt *something*. Suspected you might have stumbled into town mostly for me. Last night went far in confirming that. After Diana died, I sort of lost all feeling around the heart. But you've mended me so effortlessly. Given me new hope."

She grew shy. "Can we... Should we go ahead and be exclusive?"

"I'm all for trying it." His voice grew hoarse. "But I am boxed in here with a certain lifestyle. At least for the foreseeable future. And you seem pretty set in the city, as well."

She bit her lip. "We do have separate lives."

"I hate to say it, but the biggest change would have to come from you." She wasn't fazed by his nerve.

"I'll give it thought," she promised.

He crooked a finger under her chin. "So, officially, you are out of circulation."

A crackling sound disrupted them. Colby noted for the first time that she had a walkie-talkie identical to Emmy's clipped to the belt of her low-slung jeans. And wasn't too happy with the "oops" sound she made. Or the fact that she spoke into the thing without pressing a button. "I'll be right down."

"That was on the whole time, wasn't it?"

"Afraid so. But look at the bright side. Introductions to the crew won't take so long."

TINA HAD ARRANGED with Lizbeth to use the dining room between four and five for their meeting. Emmy and three members of their crew were milling around two corkboards when Tina entered with Colby. She gave Colby a lot of credit for accompanying her into the den of jaded New Yorkers who'd just heard his innermost feelings. They must have admired his guts, too, for they barely gave him a glance.

"Okay, people!" Tina whooped and clapped her hands like a cheerleader. "We've got a great thing going on. A lot more fun than usual. So let's get in the spirit." She paused briefly at the sight of Marilyn, dressed in a beaded shirt and bell-bottoms, seated off at a table knitting. "This is Colby, the police chief. He's provided me with some surprisingly necessary security. Colby, the skinny guy with red hair and goatee is our cameraman, Michael. The tall blond guy with the crew cut is the sound recordist, Alan. The kid here who catches all our mistakes is the production assistant, Stacy," Tina concluded, pointing at a young woman who had brown hair.

"Who's the old hippie?" Stacy asked in a loud voice.

Tina thought Marilyn winced at Stacy's tone, even though she kept on knitting. "That is the marvelous Marilyn, a subject for the film." Nobody looked impressed.

Alan raised a finger in query. "Which boss lady is going to direct?"

Tina glanced to Emmy who waved her off. "You've already got your teeth into this first town," Emmy said with a smirk for Colby. "I'll stay back here and take orders."

Tina nodded and advanced on the two boards propped up on easels. One had the Polaroids posted to it and the other held a large sheet of paper. She grabbed a marker off the table and scribbled "Four Corners" across the top of the blank paper. "As you know, Emmy and I started preproduction planning back in the city. And I trust she has clued you in on the ground rules. Four towns contending for top honors as best town. To be broadcast on cable. Voted on by the public. I've already done the scouting, as you can see." She glanced at Colby, who had taken a seat at a nearby table, and spoke directly to him. "Next we'll review what each photo stands for, sketch out a rough outline of what is to be shot and why. I'll draft a potential storyboard. Tonight we'll take a quick spin by specific locations. Tomorrow, we'll visit our subjects, rough out some kind of shooting schedule, check sites for light and sound."

"It'll be odd," Michael complained, "repeating this gig four times in a row. We usually do something once. And I bore easily."

"It won't be totally the same in each place," Tina objected.

Michael continued to scowl. "But it will be disgustingly cheery. This isn't like you at all. Tell me there's a surprise ending," he said anxiously. "Like that missing person case in Cincinnati."

"No, Mike," Tina said sharply. "This job is cut-and-dried simple life. If you feel like suffering, you can go home and wait for something meaner to come your way." A tense silence followed.

"I think I can replace you myself," Emmy purred.

"Oh, I'll do it, girls," the cameraman lamented. "Just don't go Thelma and Louise on me."

"Then don't give us the haughty Bette Davis routine," Emmy retorted. "People in small towns actually smile when they're out on the street. Give it a shot."

Tina shrugged at her two guests. "Artists. We're weird." She began bouncing between the boards, explaining the photos, drafting a possible storyboard. To her disappointment, Marilyn and Cole departed soon after, within minutes of each other.

COLBY GRABBED some Chinese takeout on his way home, getting extra chow mein so they'd have leftovers.

He could hear blaring square dance music even before he opened the back door.

Setting the sacks of steaming food on the kitchen counter, he moved into the living room. All the furniture was pushed back and Dizzy, Ronny, Jerod and Dizzy's fourteen-year-old daughter, Ashley, were spinning and gliding round the floor, following the caller's instructions. Jerod was the last to notice him, he was concentrating so hard on his every step. Colby abruptly shut off the CD player.

Ronny shot him a warning look, so Colby forced a smile. "Time for a break. I brought home some takeout!"

Dinner wasn't much fun. Colby could barely get a bite in, answering all the questions his family raised about the film crew. "Don't expect them to relate," he finally said. "They're a very slick bunch."

"Forgive us for keeping an open mind," Dizzy replied.

"They are what I say, sis," Colby said firmly, leveling his fork at her.

"Doesn't matter," Ronny interjected. "Tina said *we* are the film, so all they have to do is aim the camera."

"She say when she's coming to the school again?" Jerod asked, his voice high and excited.

"No. They were ironing out the details at the Beaumont when I left." Colby watched his pretty, serious-minded niece intently. "Hey, Ash, maybe you'd like to be Jer's partner for the film. What do you think?"

Ashley regarded Colby in abject pity. "I am fourteen years old."

"But you look much younger," he persisted hopefully.

"Thanks a lot, Uncle Cole."

"Hey, you're the cutest girl in town!"

"Get real. I'm not dancing with third-graders."

"Besides, Dad," Jerod complained, "we end up switching kids."

"But you do have a main partner—"

Jerod pounded the table. "I'm no crybaby! I don't need my cousin's help."

"I didn't mean it like that."

"Let me alone. I want to be in the show." Pushing back his chair, Jerod scrambled back into the living room and turned on the music. With chilly looks for Colby, the rest of the group followed.

Changing into worn Levi's and a long-sleeved plaid shirt, Colby wandered over to Main Street. It was around seven, past normal closing time for many shops. But tonight everything was open and owners were busy sprucing up their properties inside and out. Word was the crew had already walked through town. He heard people talking about how one crew member wore an earring in his snoot and the other had a lopsided haircut. The younger girl wore a giant diamond on her right hand and winked at both Harveys over at the pharmacy! They'd roared out of town not ten minutes ago with Tina to find somewhere to eat.

Colby headed into Tuggle's Bar on a side street off Main for his dessert. The small, dim tavern always smelled like smoke, popcorn and beer. He leaned into the bar and nodded at owner Ben Tuggle, who was re-filling some popcorn bowls.

"Hey, Chief."

"Ben."

"Pull up a stool," Ben invited. "I'll pull you an ale and you can tell me all about the movie people."

Colby was about to oblige when he spied a dejected-looking lady seated alone in a back booth, staring at a cocktail. "How long she been here?"

"An hour. Barely moved a muscle."

"Hold up on my order." It took all of Colby's self-control to advance on her table slowly, casually. "Penny for your thoughts, ma'am."

Marilyn Beaumont's crafty eyes lifted to meet his. "You always were a nosy cuss. Even as a kid."

Colby slid onto the bench opposite her.

Marilyn swatted the air, clinking her tin bracelets. "Go on back, get a damn beer."

"Guess I'm overtrained. Ronny just can't stand temptation this close."

"I s'pose you're wondering why I'm in here making life worse for myself?"

Colby studied the salted-crusted tumbler full of green liquid before her on the shiny scratched table. "Guess I do."

"Some people just keep on punishing themselves for no good reason," Marilyn muttered. "And just for the record, I haven't touched this drink yet."

People have reasons for everything. Colby knew that much from his years on the job. "You still stewing about Lizbeth's happiness?"

There was a noticeable hesitation. "Mostly. Wondering if I was a good mother."

"It's hardly over. You're still her mother."

Her stare labeled him a fool. "I mean, back when we were both a lot younger. Back when she really needed me."

"I couldn't say, of course. But the relationship has endured."

"Not due to me. I wasn't there for her or Dad or any of them when I was a lush."

"You mean Brooke and Violet, too?" he dared to suggest.

She paused and blinked, leading him to believe she was impressed by his insight. "Not only was I a poor influence for them when they were in school, but later on as well. I allowed them to hang around the hotel long after they should've been up to other things. I mean, Brooke was already married to a Husman. Violet was building a reputation at the library. Lizbeth was representing the hotel. And I was the one who gave them the place and permission to party the nights away. I feel responsible for everything that went on under my roof at that time. Right down to mixing margaritas like this one by the gallon."

"Don't be silly. They were all over twenty-one."

"I will never understand why that is the designated age of maturity."

"There has to be a cutoff someplace."

She shrugged. "So, care to buy a dame a cup of coffee?"

"I'd love to." Colby tried not to trip over his own feet as he took her full glass back to the bar. With measurable relief he slid back into the booth with two mugs of steaming coffee. He wouldn't have to worry about Marilyn's sobriety anymore tonight.

Marilyn promptly loaded her brew with two bags of sugar. "So what did you make of that film crew?"

"Not impressed."

"Me, neither."

"I figured they'd be just like Tina."

"We sure what she's like, Cole? I only ask because you've gotten the closest look."

"You think?"

She cackled over the brim of her cup. "By law you should've registered as a guest last night."

"I didn't stay the whole night!"

"Whatever. So, you still have faith in her after seeing her mingle with that crowd? Discussing shock value? Surprise endings? Boring old hippies?"

Nobody said Marilyn was boring, but he had to admit it was implied. "I plan to give Tina the benefit of the doubt." He went on to tell her about Jerod's square dancing. "For both their sakes, I'm trying to like this project. But somehow the idea of my kid being the laughingstock of a nation upsets me."

"That dancing thing is more Deedee's fault than Tina's though, right?"

"Oh, it's all Dizzy's fault. But placing blame doesn't help."

Ben strolled by and filled their mugs from his glass pot. Colby told him to put Marilyn's drink on his tab.

Ben smiled. "Already done."

"It was happy hour," Marilyn pointed out. "So don't you try and gyp him."

"Don't *you* bring that charm back in here for another year," Ben replied before moving off.

Colby was set back. She hadn't been in here for a whole year and suddenly she was. He was so glad he'd found her in time.

"Jerod probably isn't dedicated to dance, is he? He mostly just wants to be on camera, right?"

"Right." Colby watched her curiously. "So…"

"I'm thinking that if you are set on supporting this thing, there might be another answer. Maybe he could be given another job, on the other side of the camera."

It was Colby's turn to pause and blink. "That never even occurred to me."

She tapped her temple. "All it takes is a sober head."

Colby grasped her withered hand. "Thanks."

Colby walked Marilyn to the Beaumont to discover a familiar after-hours sign propped on the hotel reservations desk near an old brass bell that read Ring For Service.

Lizbeth proved to have a clear view of the lobby from her seat in the dining room, however. She was easily spotted at a round table, immersed in a weekly game of hearts with Violet and Brooke. As shrill laughter rose, Colby tried to imagine them as young women. It wasn't all that difficult. They were only in their midfifties and all still vital women.

Spotting him, they chorused his name.

Marilyn had disappeared to her room, so he made a solo voyage through the doorway. To face their merry, sly smiles.

"What's new on the street?" Violet asked, shuffling the deck.

"Found Marilyn at Tuggle's," he muttered to Lizbeth.

Lizbeth sighed. "Ben called me to report the cocktail and again to report the coffee. Thanks for stepping in. I know better than to rush down there myself anymore. It only makes Marilyn mad. And she falters so infrequently now. I don't think she'd ever really take the dive."

"Glad you're so faithful," Colby said with a note of disapproval.

"It's not what you think. I made a deal with Tuggle years ago. He doesn't coddle her or deny her. But the drinks are virgin. I can't pull that trick all over town and hope to get away with it, but that is her favorite place. It's the very best I can do short of locking her up."

Faced with a clearer picture, Colby showed instant remorse. "Of course it is. Don't mean to sound self-righteous."

Lizbeth smiled up at him. "You're the kid of an alcoholic, just like me. We're comparing notes, is all."

Colby sat down in the last empty chair. To think Marilyn was still blaming herself for their corruption. He had the feeling that no matter what, all they'd ever had to do was join forces to be trouble.

"Mom confide whatever's bothering her?" Lizbeth asked.

"That's not for me to say."

"Give it a try," Lizbeth coaxed. "We're all friends here."

Suddenly the three of them were cornering him with fused energy. This was proving more traumatic than the bank skirmish! He placed his palms flat on the table. "Why don't you deal her in on a game or two? Never takes much to get her talking."

"She doesn't like talking to us."

"She's ready to now," Colby protested. "Get to the bottom of her problem, Beth, so I don't have to haul her out of Tuggle's again."

With that, Colby walked out.

Chapter Fourteen

The film crew moved through the hotel lobby at about midnight. Tina stopped dead near the dining room doorway, marveling at her dumb luck. The three Bio Mom candidates were actually seated together in one spot. On perfect display for Emmy's perusal. Keeping her excitement in check, Tina led her crew forward with a tentative wave. "Hey. Hope you weren't keeping things open for us."

Their crescendo of protest sounded rather tinny and strained.

"I generally lock up about twelve thirty," Lizbeth said. "But all your room keys fit the front door. So you and the others should feel free to move about." She surveyed their unconventional appearance. "Quietly."

Tina made careful introductions, waiting for, and finding, a glimmer of recognition in Emmy's eyes.

"Did you have a nice evening?" Brooke asked politely.

"Yes. We ate at a little Italian place by the county line. Talked about the project."

Violet was openly scrutinizing Michael. "That nose ring get in the way of...blowing, or anything?"

Throwing his hands up in what had to be total exasperation, the sound man stalked off.

"We'll just say good-night," Tina said.

Leaving Stacy and Alan at their doors, Tina and Emmy closed themselves off in Tina's bedroom.

"What a lucky break, catching them together," Tina enthused.

"They didn't seem too friendly, Tee. Do you think that somehow they may be on to you?"

"I don't see how. My name is different from Dad's. Thirty years have passed. I've been careful."

"You had to feel the tension."

"I imagine they're reacting to the startling impression you guys made around town. A lot of people seemed slightly put out."

"We already discussed that among ourselves. The guys don't know why this project is important to you, but they're willing to play ball. After all, it's a job. Michael was first to say he'd temper the culture shock by taking out his nose ring. For a few hundred bucks."

"He's on," Tina said promptly. "I'll give Alan the same if he gets a real haircut."

Discussion quickly moved to the Bio Mom candidates and the woman Tina's father called Honey Bee. Emmy settled into the room's only chair and eagerly encouraged Tina to give her an official presentation, as they did on the job, to help sort through her discoveries, pinpoint opportunity and motive.

Fueled on Diet Pepsi, Tina put fresh poster paper on a bulletin board and proceeded to write each candidate's name in a different-colored marker.

Tina had determined, through photographs and a talk with Marilyn, that all three had mingled with Bill and had opportunity to fall for him, give birth to his baby.

Lizbeth. Honey Bee could refer to the short form Beth or maybe even Beaumont. She had an abusive husband some time back then. Unfortunately, Tina hadn't yet been able to pinpoint the time frame of her marriage. But it might be that she didn't want her baby to be subjected to her husband's abuse. The husband might have even realized he wasn't responsible for her pregnancy. Or the husband could have been long gone by then, already leaving young Lizbeth soured on marriage—to Bill or anyone else. The normally sensible Lizbeth may have measured her limitations and decided she couldn't raise a baby while running the hotel and looking after Marilyn.

Violet. Honey Bee could be a reference to the very bees she raised! She appeared content, if not determined, to live alone. It was possible her sexual appetites were confused back then, making her reluctant to accept any life with Bill—in the unlikely event it was offered. Add to that her disinterest in children, and it was reasonable to envision her giving up a baby that was the result of a tryst. Keeping it all a secret, of course, to maintain her respectable reputation at the library.

Brooke. Honey Bee could also stand for *B* as in Brooke. She was married back then, but perhaps wild enough to break her vows. There had been a pregnancy before Seth. A baby girl who might not have died as claimed, but may have been given up because James was on to the baby's true paternity. It could be Brooke regretted the decision from the start and kept the doll around to punish herself and James for the loss.

All three women had reasons to forgo motherhood at that time. And in the background there was always the persuasive Bill Mildenderger, wheedling the baby out of its mother's hands, preferring to keep his marriage intact than retreat to a life in Sugartown. It might be because the small-town life didn't interest him enough or because the relationship was never meant to last.

Emmy frowned in the face of the overabundance of

evidence that pointed nowhere. "Have any gut feelings?" she asked.

"Too many. How about you?"

"Not a clue."

"I'm dying to move in closer, ask direct questions."

"Whether you were to confront them individually or as a group, it would be a risk to her privacy. And this whole setup was intended to protect that privacy."

"But my sensitive approach has gotten me nowhere fast. Without more aggressive questioning, it seems impossible to figure out who knows what. But I still won't consider hurting anyone for the sake of the truth." Tina sighed. "It wouldn't be fair to spread my pain to these women who have been so kind to me."

"I'm so sorry. But you knew this hunt was a risk."

"Yes. Knowing that I tried to sort out the truth may have to be my consolation. Along with finding Colby, of course," she said on a brighter note. "He's wonderful, isn't he?"

"I really like him, too. Just keep in mind that you're unusually vulnerable. And he's been very supportive at a time when you need it most."

"First off, he hasn't been all that supportive. He's only recently resigned himself to this project."

"Just the same, your relationship seems a little too convenient."

"Convenient? With miles between our homes and careers? A little boy in need of a mother stuck in the middle?"

"Okay, it seems a little sudden."

"Hey, it's called spontaneous combustion. I didn't choose to love him. I just do. Can't you relax, be happy for me?"

"Be reasonable, Tee. Look at this objectively. You've come to discover your precious father had some shortcomings that did serious long-term damage to your family. While you finally understand what scarred your mother, it is too late to reach her for a candid discussion. Which means she is about to die without ever admitting what a fine daughter you are. It's natural you should feel cheated. Natural," she said in a lower voice, "to reach out to the first interested party."

"Interested party? You can be so insulting sometimes, Emmy."

"I am being brutally honest. Because I've earned that right, through years of loyal friendship. We're always a team after the dust falls, you know that. Whether the same can be said of you and Colby remains to be seen."

"Not his fault he hasn't been severely tested."

"At the rate things are going, shouldn't be long now."

An irate Tina unpinned the poster paper from the cork board, folded it into a neat square and slipped it in the top drawer of a fine old walnut dresser. The jangle of the telephone on the nightstand cut through the quiet room. She scooped up the receiver.

"Hey, it's me."

"Hi, Cole."

"I know it's almost one," he said with hesitation.

She glanced at her watch. "Oh. I hadn't noticed. Emmy and I were just going over some tactics."

"Look, I have something really important to ask you."

"Something really important to ask me?" she repeated for the sake of a skeptical Emmy.

"If you're not too tired."

"I'm never too tired for something important."

"I had a talk with Marilyn tonight. About Jerod."

Tina drooped a bit. "I already told you, it's wrong to force him out of the square dancing bit."

"I don't intend to force him out. I hope to bribe him out."

Tina listened while he made a case for making Jerod the narrator of the film. "What does Ronny say to that?"

"He sees it as a good compromise. Naturally, he'll gladly step out of the way and nobody else in the Think Tank even knows they had a chance at it. Tina, are you there?"

"Yes," she said in a small voice.

What had she expected? A rash plan for an elopement? Maybe a small part of her had. It would be comforting to have the assurance that Colby would love her no matter what. She was sure he would take his vows as seriously as he did everything else. And in doing so, make her feel safe and desired.

But as it was, they were still doing the wary mating dance around each other. And he'd revealed a lot more of himself than she had. Been a lot more aggressive in the chase. He was only waiting for her to come clean now, propose a rational plan for the future. In the meantime, he was busy interfering once again in her project.

"I'm not sold, Colby," she finally admitted. "I think Jerod should dance if he wants to dance."

"All I'm doing is tempting him with a better option. With your permission, that is. Of course, I want to tell him *you* asked, so he doesn't think I'm butting in too much."

"I'm more than willing to give him a chance at playing host, see if he has a knack. But he might not be old enough to manage it, to blend with the crew. They aren't accustomed to children."

"Don't worry, I'll be there to help you manage."

Of course you will. "We're meeting in the dining room at six," she said. "Lizbeth is closing for breakfast until noon to accommodate." With his confirmation, she dropped the receiver back in the cradle.

"That wasn't a proposal, was it?"

"Certainly not the one I'd hoped for." Tina told her

what Colby had said. "Bottom line, I want to do whatever it takes to protect Jared. Even from his own father's good intentions!"

"Think the kid has the nerve and charisma to narrate effectively?"

"Probably, if he's given a supportive environment." Tina raked a hand through her thick black mane. "It's down to the unruly bunch we've hired."

"I expect at the very least it will cost us a few extra hundred in bribes. Including Stacy, who has never forgiven us for making her go into that monkey cage at the British zoo."

"The little monkey that chased her was harmless. She overreacted."

"I reckon kids and monkeys are all the same to her. She's barely out of college, Tee. Goes to clubs most of her free nights. Skips meals to splurge on new shoes. Dates on a merry-go-round system. Not a patient girl."

"Why can't we adapt to people like everybody else?"

Emmy smirked. "Because we've had too close a look at them."

COLBY APPEARED AT THE HOTEL early the following morning with Jerod in tow. Both were dressed up, Colby in his uniform, his son in pressed black pants, white shirt and a red bow tie, which was presently getting a tug from small, antsy fingers.

"Way to get outta school, Jer," Tina congratulated with a high five.

"Deedee's given him some time off, as long as he gets his work done," Colby said. "We figure this is an education in itself."

Colby frowned at the crew lounging around in some very sloppy outfits, more discontented with them than he was yesterday. They just didn't reflect Tina's high-class style, her openness and friendliness, all the things that drew Jerod in. In short, he couldn't imagine them treating his son with any mercy.

Tina must have noted his apprehension because she put a protective arm around Jerod. "So you want to audition for a bigger role, huh?"

"Sure!" He gazed up at her with adoring eyes. "Thanks for asking me."

She ruffled his hair. "You are so welcome. Let me introduce you around."

An anxious Jerod broke free of her and, straining to control his limp, went around to shake hands with the crew. They looked surprised and even a little wary.

"Can you read, little monkey?" Stacy asked with a single pump to his hand.

Jerod snatched his hand back. "Sure I can! Since I was a child."

Colby watched Jerod stiffen a little bit as the three strangers stared at his son. Emmy saved the day by tugging Jerod close to tweak his chin. "I have two nephews about your age. Seeing you makes me miss them."

"We'll start the audition soon, Jer. But first I want to give you an idea of how we do things." Tina drew him to the twin corkboards on easels. "Here you can see the photos I took around town of possible movie subjects. I've put them in a shooting sequence. That doesn't necessarily mean they will appear on film in that order. I've grouped them by how much time they'll probably take to film, if we need daylight or not. On the storyboard you'll see I've sketched out a sequence for the shots as they will appear to the audience."

Jerod studied the crude sketches and scribbles. "You draw funny."

The entire crew broke up. "Knock it off," Tina said. "I may draw funny but I am the boss."

"I'm only teasing," Jerod whispered loudly.

"We're all teasing," she whispered back with a gentle pat on his shoulder.

With lingering concern, Colby hovered close enough to scan the photos.

Tina made an effort to include him. "We've got the pastor's balloon juggling, Kaitlyn's pancake flipping, Violet's beekeeping, Harvey's birdhouses and the square dancing. Then on to Lizbeth and Marilyn right here."

He pointed to the last photo. "Why is Seth bringing up the end?"

Tina tried to not be defensive. "It's good public relations to give an official like the mayor the last word."

"Hope you have miles of film. He can get long-winded."

The crew exchanged nervous looks. Tina hastily intervened. "He cleans up nice. And we'll maintain control, like always."

Michael favored Colby with a grateful smile. "Thanks for the warning, Sheriff. I've been known to shut off my camera on tedious politicians. Or make them disappear on the cutting room floor."

Colby didn't correct the title error. All things considered, he had a mind to rethink his nose ring prejudice.

Tina broke away and glanced into the lobby. "We need Lizbeth for our practice run. Funny, I left her a voice mail asking her to show."

It was several minutes before Lizbeth was spotted on the open staircase. "Good morning!" Tina called out. "We can use you now."

"At your meeting?" Lizbeth hesitated by the archway, clearly apprehensive and looking surprised to discover the Evanses. If Colby didn't know better, he'd have thought she was getting cold feet over her participation.

"Jerod's getting a shot at the narrator job," Colby encouraged. "He needs you as his test subject."

Lizbeth's face softened slightly. "Oh, I see." She joined them then.

The crew went into action. Emmy unloaded the lighting kit from a large canvas sack, set up three halogen lights on collapsible stands and hung a reflective umbrella. Michael picked up a compact camcorder resting on the floor. Alan adjusted a microphone on a long boom. Stacy brought out a black-and-white clapper board on which she wrote Audition. Tina circled the group, giving narrative to their actions for Jerod's sake, allowing him to spy through her small viewfinder, explaining how it helped her visualize a scene through a particular lens. Even though they called themselves filmmakers, she told him they no longer used film on the job, but rather a digital cinema camcorder that emulated the look of film. Jerod looked overwhelmed until she pointed out that George Lucas did the same thing in some later *Star Wars* movies, with all the special effects.

"You gonna add some monsters to Sugartown with a computer?" he asked.

"Not this time," Michael put in, pausing to gently cuff the boy's chin. "But I like your creativity."

Jerod threw his shoulders back with the compliment.

"I'm not really dressed for filming," Lizbeth blurted out nervously.

"Nobody but present company will ever see this audition," Tina soothed.

Colby watched Lizbeth swim in her own silent quandary and wondered what had changed her attitude. The sudden talk with Marilyn? Had he inadvertently triggered trouble by instigating it? He turned to the equally stressed Tina, presently combing his son's hair.

Was there another storyboard behind the one Tina had sitting on the easel that told a different tale?

Eventually, the shot was set up near a large buffet against the wall with Lizbeth seated in a chair and Jerod standing beside her. Lights blazed, Alan held the boom over the set and Michael lifted the camera to take aim. Kneeling in front of Jerod, adjusting his little bow tie, Tina encouraged him to welcome viewers to Sugartown, say his name and introduce Lizbeth. She rose and stepped back, cuing everyone.

Stacy stepped up with the clapper board, held it in front of the camera, clapped down and said, "Monkey audition. Take one," before dipping away.

Tina nodded to Jerod in encouragement. He cleared his throat, blinked against the lights and stammered. Michael glanced at the director for instructions. Tina twirled her finger to keep going. "Come on, buddy," she murmured. "Plenty of time. Just start over."

They worked two hours, cuing Jerod to say different things to a rather wooden Lizbeth.

Finally Tina yelled, "Cut! That's good for now."

Lizbeth promptly excused herself.

Colby had stayed away, but now approached as Tina conferred with Stacy. "I expected the process to be more choppy."

"We don't stop recording very often in documentaries if we can help it," Tina explained. "Any interruptions halt the flow of realism. And I figured the clapper hitting over and over would upset Jerod too much." She gestured to him. "He's held up very well for his first time."

"Guess that's a monkey for you," Stacy lilted, walking off.

"Does Stacy have to call him a monkey?" Colby complained.

"It's nothing personal. She's just at that awkward age, too into herself, too intolerant. But I will speak to her," Tina vowed in his shadowed look.

He shifted uneasily. "What happens next?"

"We need to clear out of the dining room," she admitted. "Emmy and I will go to my room and have a look at the footage, decide how to proceed." She reached up and smoothed his uniform shirt over his chest. The unexpected intimacy made his shudder. "Seems a waste of your time, sitting around here looking so official. I advise you to go kick butt at the station."

"And Jerod?"

"I want him to stay. Use this downtime to interact with the crew."

"That might get his hopes too high," Colby argued.

"He's in, Cole. We just need to measure what he's capable of." She linked her arm with his and steered him toward the lobby. "Give him space. Let me take care of him." Dropping her voice lower, she said, "You know Lizbeth better than I. Why is she acting so strangely? *Is* she acting strangely?"

So she had noticed, too. "I'd say she isn't herself," he admitted.

"Maybe it's stage fright." She stood on tiptoe and gave him a quick kiss. "Here's the plan. Emmy and I will go off and get critical in private. We'll come back down, feed everybody right here. Then we'll have a coaching session with Jerod. Haul our stuff over to the church for a session with your pastor juggler."

"Call me when you get there. I'd hate to miss it." Colby turned to see if Jerod would mind if he left, but the boy barely glanced up from the camera's viewfinder as he said goodbye.

When Colby pulled the squad car around on the hotel's parking lot, he just happened to look up at the giant brick hotel. In a sitting room window opposite the dining room stood Lizbeth, staring straight at him, with the telephone at her ear.

Chapter Fifteen

Grace Copeland was pacing the station like an expectant father when Colby entered the police station. "Cole! How did things go?"

"Good, I think. It's actually pretty fascinating to see how something is filmed. And it looks like Jerod will be narrating the piece." He followed her to the reception desk. "Anything happening?"

"Mrs. Fitzsimmons called an hour ago to say her cat was up a tree again. I called her son to go take care of it. That's a job for him, not us."

"In a perfect world, it's his job. Still, better call back to make sure he did it."

"The state police called about the bank skirmish. They'd like you and James Husman to drive over to Stamford tomorrow to give formal reports. I said you'd be there unless notified."

"When things are so busy here?"

Her eyes twinkled. "That's showbiz."

"Cute."

"Oh, and Violet called only two minutes ago. Said she'd be—" Grace halted in midstream as Violet Avery entered in a huff, the hem of her regulation library shirtwaist dress flying in her wake. "Colby, I must speak to you!"

He was taken aback. "Sure, Ms. Avery."

Violet breezed by Grace's desk, slowing long enough to inspect its disarray. "Neatness counts on any job, Gracie. And I want that overdue paperback returned at once to the library." She leaned over the clutter almost brushing Grace's nose with her own. "The one with the scantily dressed girl humping the Indian chief's thigh," she muttered. "Not my cup of tea, but it is community property under my jurisdiction."

"How on earth do you know the Indian is a chief?" Grace challenged. "If it isn't your cup of tea?"

"It's all in the feathers, young lady. I'd know that sort of headdress anywhere." With that she flounced into Colby's connecting office. Once Colby entered, Violet closed the door firmly.

"I'm glad you stopped by, Ms. Avery," he said.

Her eyes bulged. "You are?"

"I'm curious about Marilyn. Did you ladies speak to her as I asked?"

"Well, yes."

"And…"

"You should have stayed if you wanted to know. As it is, I have a more pressing problem that needs your attention."

"An overdue book epidemic?" he asked hopefully.

"No." She smacked her large leather purse on his desk and flopped into a guest chair. "Come sit." Once Colby eased back in his chair she leaned over his desk. "It's this TV show."

He gritted his teeth. "What's the matter?"

"I've had serious second thoughts about my participation."

"Why? You're so proud of your beekeeping."

"It's the honey angle I hadn't considered. Allow me to explain pollination. The bees pollinate my blossoms.

They have pollen baskets behind their hind legs to hold the pollen, transport it back to the hive."

"I have a general idea of the process, Ms. Avery."

"Honey bees have the unique habit of going for the same kind of blooms time after time," she said. "The honey they produce from a certain nectar takes on the unique flavor characteristics of a certain flower. That's how I get my special honey flavors."

Having been up since five this morning, Colby couldn't help putting his head in his hands. "What are you getting at?"

"The issue of my secret flavors, of course. I can't allow my trees and wildflowers to be filmed for a nation to pick up on, to duplicate. We are talking about my clover honey, apple blossom honey. But most important, it is my boneset flavor at issue. I ship that all over, as a healing honey. In hindsight, it seems a hazard to display my *Eupatorium perfoliatum* for all to see."

Colby highly doubted her flavors were all that special, just as he doubted she was being sincere. He set out to tweak her. "Your trees and flowers can remain a secret. The crew can do close-ups of you and the hives. Tina can demonstrate shots for you through her viewfinder."

"Already have the lingo down, I see. The man who so sorely objected to this project in the first place."

"But I was overruled by people like you. Saw no choice but to go along."

"Yes, those beds are comfy over at the hotel," she sniped.

"Ms. Avery!" Colby was flabbergasted by her liberty.

"Oh, grow up. I'm just saying you were right."

"Yeah," he marveled. "I was, wasn't I?"

His reaction didn't affect her. "I am seldom wrong, as everyone knows. But the whole town has been wrong this time. It would be in our best interest to send this crew packing."

"In exactly whose best interest, other than the honeybees'?"

She avoided the question with a tightening of lips. "In any case, you can count me out of the shooting. And tell as much to your little girlfriend."

He lifted a brow. "Did you sign a release form?"

"Well, er, ah, yes."

"Then just do the darn thing, will ya?" he pleaded. "It's already gone so far. So many people are involved."

She stood, smoothing her dress. "Don't play helpless. You could pull the plug on the whole project this instant. Single-handed."

He stared at her. "I don't see how."

"Let's just say that Indian chief on Grace's overdue book has nothing on Sugartown's chief. You could take a firm grip on that girl."

This was not a conversation he'd ever expected to have with the uptight librarian.

Violet glided to the door like royalty. "The fate of my boneset is in your hands. Be careful how you treat it."

Colby tipped back in his creaky spring chair, recalling the image of Lizbeth on the phone when he'd left the hotel. What were the odds that it was she who had set Violet on him to start a loud protest against the project? Again, he thought of the trio circled in a steno notebook that linked them to Tina. And he thought of Marilyn's distress of late. Something definitely was brewing under his nose, degrees hotter than Ronny's sauces. But what? Why wouldn't anyone tell him?

On so many levels he considered Sugartown his responsibility. Only briefly did he entertain the idea that he had no place in the female brouhaha.

In a perfect world, Tina would be the one to clue him in.

Grace peered into his office. "Afraid the world isn't perfect."

"What?" He snapped to attention, startled by her apparent mind reading.

"The cat is still up the tree."

FOLLOWING A BRIEF STOP to rescue the stray feline, Colby headed for Main Street and the bank to speak to James Husman about the trip to Stamford. When James heard Colby was out in the lobby, he swiftly appeared, dignified as usual in a black pinstripe suit but ready with a warm welcome. Colby followed James to the banker's private office of golden-hued wood and fixtures, where Brooke was already ensconced in a plaid wool dress, well-shaped legs crossed.

Another member of the mystery trio. And, by her sharp expression, anxious to pounce.

James listened intently to Colby's message. "I'll be glad to oblige the state authorities. Want me to drive?"

"No, we'll take the squad. I'd like to get an early start…get it done."

James nodded and shook his hand. "I'll be on my doorstep at seven."

"Imagine running into you in particular, Cole," Brooke said suddenly.

Here it comes.

"I want to treat you to lunch. For rescuing my man here the other day."

"Just part of the job."

"Nonsense."

"Go ahead, Cole," James said with a laugh. "Nobody says no to Brooke."

To Colby's surprise, she steered him to Tuggle's Bar on the side street.

"This is bound to be quieter than other places, don't you think?" she asked.

"Yeah, it's bound to be dead. But the sandwiches aren't so good. You especially won't..."

"Oh, I love it. Come here all the time."

Brooke chose a booth in the rear with a full view of the place. When the waitress appeared, Cole ordered an Italian sub and iced tea. Brooke ordered lemonade.

She carefully placed her manicured talons on the scarred wood table. "I want to do a story on your heroism."

"A brief account was already written up by Corbin Saunders," he pointed out.

"Oh, I am thinking of a huge feature, with a personal slant on the man behind the badge."

"Not necessary."

"Could be good for your career. Help assure you another term by the city council." Their drinks arrived along with his sandwich. She nervously dumped two sacks of artificial sweetener in it.

"I think they sweeten it with sugar at the soda fountain."

"Oh?" She gave the glass a nervous stir with a spoon. Then tasted it with a funny look. "You're right."

So much for being a regular. She just didn't want to be seen anywhere with him, having this weird conversation. Colby unwrapped the sandwich and frowned at the small wilted lettuce leaf, pale tomato slice and fatty meat.

"Just as you're right about a lot of things," she quickly went on. "I mean, you were on the mark about wanting to block the film project."

"You think?" He took a bite of his sandwich, watching her intently.

She looked around in a manner more fitting a fugitive than a tough socialite reporter. There was no one remotely close to their rear booth. "I would like to speak to you in confidence on that, if I may."

"Guess so." His voice was flat, but his pulse had quickened. Maybe she would let something of value slip. She was higher strung than Violet.

"I know you and Seth aren't best friends. But you can be trusted with a secret about him, can't you?" She stared at him. "Why are you making that sour face?"

"Because this sandwich is pretty bad."

"Shall I have someone do a bad review on Tuggle's for the paper?"

"No, Brooke. You're the only one who's in the dark about this place. Ben Tuggle has a right to make a living. Now what do you want to tell me?"

"You remember that whole thing about how Seth was pushed up a grade when he was a child."

"Yes, Brooke." He drank half his cold tea.

"Well, it was all due to special coaching he had that summer beforehand."

"Common knowledge."

"Really?"

"Yes. Nobody gives a damn."

She gasped. "Everybody gives a *d-a-m* about our family."

"All I mean is, don't worry about it making the film. Isn't likely to."

"If only that were the end of it. There is another little educational snafu on his town résumé that must remain covered up." She paused as the waitress brought pitchers of lemonade and tea for refills. Colby accepted more tea. Brooke set a hand over her glass. "None for me. It's just too sweet." The waitress frowned at the empty sweetener bags by Brooke's purse and drifted off. Brooke spoke softer. "Seth never actually finished college. He only has a two-year associate degree."

"No scandal there, either, Brooke. That's what I have."

Brooke's eyes glinted hard at his easily made comparison. "Oh. Yes."

"Look, I already know about his education," he admitted quietly. "A background check through the department for any new public official is routine."

"You've known this all the while and said nothing?"

"It's nobody's business. And in his favor he always glosses over that imaginary Ivy League stint."

"He just took off to tour Europe after a couple years! We were horrified. But what do you do with children?"

"Beats me."

"We just continued to brag as though nothing had changed. Then when he returned, ready to settle down, we decided there was no harm in hiding the truth."

"This film threat must mean a lot to you to bring out this laundry."

"I figured by confiding in you alone, maybe I could protect the secret from everyone else. Even if it meant, well, handing you a bonus," she said slyly.

His patience was suddenly worn dangerously thin. "C'mon, Brooke. I can't believe you're all that worried about this secret."

"Sure I am! Real, real worried. If someone spots Seth on camera and decides he's capable of higher office, the secret could harm him." She drew a courageous breath. "I'd rather he just stay put than suffer any humiliation."

"Any political spin doctor could turn it around. Seth could even take classes over the Internet, get his four-year degree in a snap."

The pert little woman was scooting her bottom off the wooden bench. "I am deeply disappointed in your attitude."

"Same here!" he called after her, causing Ben Tuggle, stationed behind the bar, to guffaw.

THE AFTERNOON was a sunny sixty degrees. A decent temperature for perilous water-balloon juggling, Colby thought as he approached the churchyard. The Reality Flicks crew was setting up their equipment in busy disorder. Tina was on her cell phone, sexily disheveled with her sunglasses lodged at the tip of her nose, her wild mane of hair flying everywhere. She jabbed the off button when Colby sidled up. He cupped her chin and gave her a long, warm kiss.

"That call about your mom?"

"No. Just trying to reach Brooke at the newspaper for the fourth time today. I keep getting her voice mail."

"How is everything else going?"

"Fine."

He glanced at the small crowd, standing a respectable distance away. "Town behavior has improved some, I see."

"Don't pride yourself too much on your warning bark. I think they're more afraid of Michael's bite. I paid him two hundred bucks to lose the nose ring and goatee but he wanted triple that for attitude." She hooked her phone back to the belt of her jeans. "The weather is perfect for this." She grasped the viewfinder hanging round her neck, held it up to her eye.

Tina addressed Michael as he joined them. "I see the pastor's hands as an important focus, Mike. The jolly face is worth a close-up too, I bet. Especially when a balloon gets away."

Michael held up his own viewfinder. "I also want to catch the balloons against the sky, too. We'll need a few takes. With balloons of the same color and number."

"I'll tell Stacy to have a word with the pastor."

"No, let the kid do it. Then we can watch the pair interact, figure out Jerod's best approach." Michael walked off, calling for Jerod.

Colby scanned the church yard. "Wonder where Jerod is?"

"Last I saw he was eating candy out of Stacy's purse." Tina pointed to the grounds' twin oaks just as Jerod popped into sight. Spotting Colby, he waved.

"He's even gotten to her?"

"Yes, Cole. We all think Jerod is such a doll."

"He likes to be the tough guy, so don't tell him that."

"I already did. And he kissed me." She tapped her cheek. "Right here."

Colby stared into the sky. "I won't even know him after this."

"Sure you will. He's just maturing into a fake tough guy like his dad."

When Pastor Breck appeared in his black cassock, Michael urged Jerod his way. In careless exuberance, Jerod tripped on an exposed tree root and went sprawling. Colby noted that none of them rushed to help him. And Jerod bounced back up, with only a quick sharp glance to Colby. Colby would have acted, given time, but it all happened too fast. He had to let it go as Tina tugged at his sleeve.

"Who is that guy strolling across the street taking notes?"

Colby frowned behind his wraparound shades. "He's Corbin Saunders. From the paper. You suppose Brooke sent him over in her place? Wonder why she'd do that, Tina?"

Tina's smile was plainly forced. "Maybe she knows about the pastor's poor juggling record. You'd never catch Brooke under one of those missiles."

"Tina—"

"I can't talk right now. And look, here comes Ronny." With that, Tina scooted off.

In short order the crew and Evans men were filling

up water balloons at the church building's outside spigot. The pastor was encouraged to practice for them on street level. Jerod's brief opening narrative was agreed upon and they began shooting.

The sun was setting when they finally wrapped. An unremorseful Pastor Breck had managed to nail just about everybody from the steeple during the shoot, so the nondenominational crew felt no guilt over soaking him to the cassock the instant he hit the ground again. All hell broke loose then for a wild water-fight finale—caught on film thanks to a sharp Michael.

When Colby gave Tina a hug goodbye, the soggy couple literally smacked together. "Want to dry off and come over?" he murmured in her ear.

"We need to head back and view our work," Tina said apologetically. "Make sure we have what we need."

"You'd actually come back for more?"

"Not if we can help it." She pointed to the gleeful pastor high-fiving Jerod. She stood on tiptoe to kiss him. "It's good-night, I'm afraid. We're bound to work late."

He in turn explained his early trip to Stamford with James Husman. "Ronny is covering somebody at work tomorrow, so Jerod will be in Dizzy's hands first thing in the morning."

"I'll call her tonight to set up Jerod's day." She impetuously squeezed him tight and murmured in his ear. "Can't wait to make love to you again."

"I'd be satisfied with a talk," he admitted.

If that appealed to her, she didn't show it.

COLBY'S DOORBELL RANG that night around eight. His heart rose with hope, only to deflate when he saw who was on the doorstep.

"I suppose you expected Tina," Lizbeth Beaumont greeted him crisply.

"She did warn me she'd be working."

"They were still hard at it when I dropped by with some sandwiches. Seemed like the perfect opportunity to speak to you myself."

Colby ushered her inside and closed the door against the evening chill. He wouldn't give her the satisfaction of looking shocked or curious. After all, he was half expecting her, too. Three friends, three excuses to boot out Tina. Like the others, he didn't expect her to spill anything straight or helpful. "Sure cools down fast now after sundown."

The remark seemed to break Lizbeth's concentration. "Why, yes. I always know to dress warmly at this time of year, though." She touched her heavy blue cable cardigan and patted her golden red hair, slightly ruffled by the wind.

Colby set his mouth tightly. Cool, controlled, prepared—that was Lizbeth Beaumont. He'd always liked her, but he wasn't inclined to make this charade any too easy for her. He gestured to the living room suite. "Have a seat."

She chose a compact rocker and stiffly looked around. "We alone?"

Colby closed the *Sports Illustrated* magazine he'd left open on the sofa and sat close by on the end cushion. "Jerod's asleep. Ronny's at the movies."

"Good."

"So, what will it be, Lizbeth?"

"You may not know it, but I have an ex-husband," she blurted out.

"Guess I've heard mention of him. Not recently...."

"Well, it was before your time. Anyway, there have been uncomfortable times when he's made contact by phone and letters. Some of the contact wasn't very pleasant."

"You should have filed a complaint," he pointed out.

She gasped at the idea. "Never considered telling anyone. A foolish mistake. A private mistake."

"But you have decided to tell me," he replied.

"Yes. After over a year of silence, this latest missive came today." She reached into the pocket of her cardigan and produced an odd-shaped postcard, which she handed over. Colby examined it. One side held a photo of a tropical island, the other block lettering which read: This Could Be You.

"How did the postmark get smudged?"

She averted her eyes. "I don't know! Must've gotten wet. I believe this is a veiled threat. That he would like to trap me on an island!"

This leap of logic would have been enormous for a woman half as sensible as this one. It took an extraordinary amount of willpower to erase a cartoon image of Lizbeth racing around the sand in a bikini with false cries for help.

"There isn't even a signature."

"Of course there isn't. Would you sign a threat?"

"What is his name?"

She cleared her throat. "Arthur Porter."

He crunched his features and hardened his tone. "Leave it to me. I'll dust this card for prints, try to track this nut down for a little talk."

"No! That's not what I want." She tried to reach for the card but he kept it out of reach between his legs— a place she would never invade. "I've simply decided I don't want to be in the documentary anymore. I fear that publicity for the hotel may entice this jerk back to town. We were struggling to get by when he left, so he might come after my money, the hotel, now."

"You gotta admit the card and message are both pretty ambiguous."

"I have to be careful. Marilyn drove him off with a shotgun! He may never have forgiven either one of us for that indignity."

This caught Colby by surprise. "Marilyn did that? Thought she was a pacifist."

"She's always gone through maternal phases, making awkward attempts to mother me, bail me out of jams. Of course, those phases were less frequent during her boozing years."

"Too bad she was nearly pushed to drink again so recently," he prompted.

"I must insist you keep this an absolute secret, too, Cole," she finally said. "But that near slip also had to do with the film project."

His mouth curled in cynicism. *Oh, gee. What are the odds?*

"It's all about keeping her past in the past, too," Lizbeth claimed. "A bit of a scandal surrounding her thirty-day stint in the county workhouse."

"Marilyn did time?"

Lizbeth blushed. "Don't make it sound so juicy. There was some kind of ruckus at a county tavern, property was damaged. She didn't even remember it the next day when the state police showed up!" She thrust a finger at Colby. "In light of the film, she's fretting about a public rehash of the whole sorry mess."

"Why didn't she speak up sooner?" Colby challenged.

"It sometimes takes Marilyn a while to pull out of her self-centered shell."

Colby sighed. Here sat a woman who'd been a friend to his own late mother. Who, despite the fact that she hadn't had much nurturing, always went out of her way to comfort Deedee and himself. Who'd always been meticulously honest about the perils of dealing with an alcoholic parent. As much as he hated to believe it, she was at least to some degree leading him around in circles. Tossing away her good nature and sense of fair play to dispose of Tina Mills. Colby had noticed Tina's name was never once uttered by Lizbeth. An attack of conscience, maybe? Not having the heart to personalize her campaign?

Lizbeth was rising to her feet now on some lame excuse. It was frustrating, as he realized he'd just struck out with the third member of the trio.

Lizbeth gave Colby a last once-over, no doubt looking for the threatening postcard. But Colby had long ago wedged it out of sight between the sofa cushions. After she'd left, he took the card out for another look, tapping it with his thumb. There was something about that photo....

On impulse Colby went to the small desk in the kitchen where he paid the bills. There sat a stack of junk from the past couple months. He flipped through it and came across a postcard identical to Lizbeth's, except for a wider shoreline. It was from a travel agency and postmarked six weeks back. Lizbeth must have smudged the date on hers and trimmed the agency name off the bottom of the back, giving her less sandy beach on the front. The message was even the same: This Could Be You.

So the whole ex-husband threat was totally bogus. He had half a mind to track down this Porter fella just to bust Lizbeth for lying to an officer! But Violet was no better with fake concerns about honey, nor Brooke offering up her son's imagined shortcomings.

Something mighty big had to be driving them. But they were crazy to think he'd tamper with Tina's plans now based on their silly whims! He was too deeply involved with Tina. And, even more importantly, she was too deeply involved with Jerod. If only they'd given him a clue to the problem, he might have a way of fixing it. He liked to fix things around town. Everybody knew that. But apparently, he wasn't going to get the free pass into the girls' club. For the first time ever in his career he felt out of his depth in Sugartown.

Ronny entered through the back door minutes later to find Colby deep in thought. "You gonna treat us to a trip?" he asked rather excitedly.

It took Colby a minute to realize Ronny was referring to the travel agency postcard. "Dad, was Marilyn ever in the workhouse?"

"Yeah." He grew thoughtful. "Things got a little out of hand at Big Sky Tavern one night. She was chosen as an example because the owner had the hots for her and she didn't tumble for him." He stroked his jaw. "We didn't call it the hots back then, I don't s'pose."

"Was she guilty?" Colby asked impatiently.

"Guess there was no denying some glass got broken and she was in on it."

"Did you actually witness any of it?"

"Nope. Your mother never liked those smoky dives. And that was mostly an older crowd, played mostly country-western music. Why do you care?"

Colby held up a hand to stall the question. "Marilyn ever run off Lizbeth's hubby, Arthur Porter, with a shotgun?"

"Probably happened that way. There was a hole in a wall someplace in the private wing once. My uncle Victor was paid well to patch it up and keep his mouth shut. Why the interest? You weren't even born yet."

"Just trying to sort through a very thick smoke screen. And amazed that one of the stories told me today is true. Must be a fluke."

"Huh?"

"I'll tell you everything once I figure it out." Colby

put a hand on Ronny's shoulder. "When you get off work tomorrow morning, would you hunt down Tina and Jerod on site? Make sure they're all right?"

"Already plan to. Now about that travel agency. Let's have a nice cup of cocoa and talk about it."

TINA BARELY HAD her teeth brushed the next morning when Deedee showed up at her hotel room door with Jerod. "I just spoke to your husband," Tina said, inviting them in. "Couldn't believe I already missed you."

"There a snafu?" Deedee demanded with a fretful look to her nephew.

"Nothing to do with Jerod's position," Tina murmured, forcing a smile. "We're soon off to the Royal Diner to film Kaitlyn flipping her cakes. But Violet has begged off for this afternoon, so I would like to fill that open slot with one of tomorrow's shoots, either Harvey's birdhouse hobby or the square dancing. Must say I would feel kind of bad if Colby weren't here to see Jerod introducing his classmates. But Harvey might not be able to handle the last-minute change, with his hours at the drugstore."

Deedee slowly brightened. "I insist you come over to the school today." She pointed at Jerod, who was now standing in front of the TV. "It will go much easier with you-know-who out of the way."

"Shouldn't that be you-know-whom, Aunt Dizzy?" Jerod asked sweetly.

"No, it shouldn't." Deedee blew him a kiss then headed out. "I have the costumes ready at the school. Just call ahead and give me a time."

WHEN COLBY RETURNED that evening, he had a surprise waiting for him in the living room. Tina was cuddled up in a recliner with Jerod, reading a story. She nodded to him but didn't interrupt her narrative. Colby's throat constricted as he witnessed a dream scene he'd played over in his head many times. Tina in his home. With his child in her arms. Any trace of apprehension she might have felt with the boy was long gone. All part of the dream.

"Tom Sawyer?" Colby said in mock fear. "You'll have this kid pulling all sorts of pranks."

Jerod giggled. "Oh, Daddy."

Colby noted then that the boy was in his Western costume meant for the square-dance segment. Even though Jerod was now working as the narrator, it was decided that he'd wear the jeans and red shirt with white piping and pearl buttons anyway. "Showing off your gear for tomorrow?" Colby asked. "Please don't wrinkle it. I have enough ironing as it is."

"It's all over!" Jerod reported excitedly, scrambling off Tina.

"You mean I missed it?" Colby gaped over the news, glad Tina had the courtesy to wince in regret.

"Sorry, Cole," she said. "Violet pulled out and Deedee wanted her slot." She reached out to ruffle the boy's dark hair. "I'll send you a video copy the minute we edit it. It was the best segment yet, with Jerod giving us a brief unscripted tour of the school, explaining what the dancers were doing. He's so good at this stuff. I think he has a future as a host."

"He's going to be a doctor!"

"Not for sure. I might be a truck driver or a barber." He turned back to Tina. "Trucks are awesome and barbers always have good candy."

Ronny burst in the room then, also in full Western gear. "Did you tell him yet? You promised I could!"

Jerod shook his head. "We waited, Gramps."

A beaming Ronny tugged at his string tie. "I got to be the caller."

"The what?" Colby asked.

"The square dance caller," he explained in a rather patronizing tone. "They usually use the one on the record, but then Deedee thought, why not me?"

"How did that ham get herself into the film?" Colby asked wryly.

Jerod sighed. "She danced up and down between the rows of kids. It was pretty embarrassing. She was clapping and skipping in a big poofy dress."

Tina erupted in laughter. "She flashed her undies once with a swish of skirt, but I'll edit it out."

"Not in my copy, I hope. We always watch home videos on Christmas."

Ronny took Jerod off to bed with a promise not to return and Colby snuggled into the chair with Tina. "That darn Dizzy," he grumbled. "With me out of the way she saw her chance to bring the Evanses to the screen in full force and glitter."

Tina nibbled at his neck. "So much talent in one family."

He fought the urge to give in. "What's the story with Violet pulling out?" he demanded suddenly.

Tina studied his jaw. "Something about honey flavor security."

"You buy that reason?"

Her voice rose. "You know something I don't?"

"Don't think so," he said slowly. "But she was gung-ho till now. Wondered how you felt about it."

"I think she's an eccentric," she said. "Kaitlyn did beautifully in the diner segment, by the way," she added quickly. "I meant it when I said I was going to help her if this town can't accept her as a single mother. So how was your trip with James Husman?"

"Good. We get on well together."

"Really? Even with the friction between you and Seth?"

His eyes twinkled with humor. "This is a small town, Tina, where people rub shoulders all the time, often too much. Rubs are bound to cause irritation. It's nothing serious."

"That's a nice way to live."

"I highly recommend it." On the subject of the Husmans, Colby wondered if Tina knew that Brooke was also out of the project. "You finally hear from Madam Husman today?"

"No. Corbin formally introduced himself. He's taking over the coverage. Apparently Brooke is too busy."

"You believe it?"

"Shouldn't I?"

More questions to his questions! But he had to admit she seemed concerned rather than angry.

"I need Jerod early again tomorrow, by the way. He own any corduroy pants? Flannel shirts?"

"Uh, no."

"He'll need them for the outdoorsy feel of Harvey Beyer's carpentry workshop." She waved. "Never mind. I'll buy him the right outfit. For the hotel segment he can wear his original outfit of formal white shirt, bow tie, et cetera."

"Those are the two shoots for tomorrow?"

"The only ones left. Harvey first and at least a start on Hotel Beaumont sometime after lunch."

"The hotel will take longer than an afternoon?"

"I am looking for ways to make it longer, due to Violet's bailout. Shouldn't be hard, with Marilyn's knitting sideline. That lady can gab."

But would she still be willing to gab? Unlike Violet and Brooke, the Beaumont team apparently hadn't officially dumped Tina yet. Thank God. "I won't have time for Harvey's shoot, but I will swing by the hotel," he promised.

She looped her arms around his neck and planted kisses all over his face. "I love you so much, Cole. And I love your family, your town. I think I even love the dog Jerod should have."

"I love you too, honey," he whispered hoarsely. "Don't love that crew of yours yet. But I'm workin' on it."

"You think Ronny meant it about leaving us alone?"

"I think he'll try. It's best we keep our clothes on, though. There is usually the random request for water or hot cocoa, not to mention the threat of fire."

She seared his mouth against his. "Oh, there's gonna be a fire."

With a soft growl he slipped his hand under her sweater and grazed her belly. She moved over him and moved a thigh over his groin. "This is a neighborly rub you're gonna like, Chief."

"Sex isn't going to work out here." He said it as his hands were pushing her sweater high enough to expose her tiny push-up bra. A sweet little pink one. He licked the rough lace shielding her nipple.

She gave a soft wanton cry, driving her hands through his hair. "Come back to my bed then."

"Let's just go for a drive. I know all the good places the kids go. An advantage of chasing them off with my searchlight."

She eyed him with a kittenish look. "Getting inventive."

By necessity. He didn't have the patience to see Lizbeth again after the stunt she'd tried to pull last night. He would figure out what was going on tomorrow. If it was the last thing he did.

Chapter Sixteen

Tina woke up the next morning with a rough shake to her shoulder. She blinked a few times to focus on Emmy. "What…"

"You've overslept!"

"Oops. Never heard my alarm."

"Because you never set it!"

"Oh." Yawning, Tina sat up.

"You were awfully late last night. Thought you were just reading the kid a story."

"Colby came home," she mumbled.

"Oh! So what happened?"

Tina flicked back the covers with a sly smile. "We made it in the squad car. Cuffed ourselves together the second go-round."

Emmy waved her off. "Like I need this distraction with such a full schedule. But now that you mention it, neither of you seem quite reckless enough for that trick."

"Well, first I made sure he had the right key to spring the lock. And he insisted on driving deep into a field that had to be on the edge of civilization. That settled, we went for it." She padded into the bathroom.

Emmy rifled through the paperwork on the table. "Sounds like you're closer than ever."

She popped into the doorway, brush in hand. "I'd say so. It'll be hard to put him out of my mind today."

"You better try. We need to wrap up a program about three tough hens, two of whom have already flown the coop."

"Oh, c'mon. Violet really may be worried about her honey flavors. And Brooke may have too many obligations to report on the project."

"They know you're up to something, Tee. Their bailout is obviously a protest."

Tina shook her head. "I've decided we can't be a hundred percent sure of that."

"This sour turn can't be easy to take—"

"It's impossible to take! They're three kind and sensible women who wouldn't turn mean without good reason. And I've given them no reason. Look, I thought this through last night. This whole town appears to run on an amazing support system." Tina rushed closer, her face flushed. "Sugar's energy flows in an endless circle, connecting everything and everyone, in a big crazy family way. It finally hit me that my mother hunt doesn't have to end with the shoot after all. It's a sure bet Colby and I will be planning out some kind of future, so I can go on working inside the circle with these people. I, too, can become part of the family. And in turn, eventually find my mother and win her over. It's a matter of patience, persistence."

"That's a fine plan for tomorrow, Tee," Emmy said patiently. "But today has to be all about the program, making sure we hang on to Lizbeth. The bees and the byline aren't crucial, but the hotel footage is. Okay?"

"You're right, of course. One more day will mean everything to the program."

Emmy grimaced. "In the meantime, let's just hope whatever fuse you managed to light in those women doesn't sizzle its way to an explosion."

THE CREW WAS SETTING UP equipment at the Beaumont when Colby caught up with them. Tina was going over possible opening scenarios with Jerod when he came up between them. She automatically kissed Colby on the cheek, then stared back at her clipboard.

"How'd the shoot with Harvey go?" Colby asked.

Jerod grinned. "Really cool, Dad. He went through all the steps of making a birdhouse."

Tina smiled, too. "It was really great. He had everything set up on an assembly line with wood and saws and sandpaper and paint. We filmed about three hours. It'll be a breeze to edit."

"Old Harvey showed up wanting to talk about his herbal wrap, but little Harvey locked him out," Jerod added. "What's that about, Dad?"

"I'll explain later."

Alan interrupted. "I think we need lapel microphones for the shoot in the lobby. If you're going to have Lizbeth descend the staircase."

Tina nodded. "I see her making that kind of entrance. A 'welcome to my hotel' sort of thing. I want Jerod's intro outside, though. We really need to start coaching him on what he's going to say about the general history and exterior." She looked around. "Emmy! How is that script going?"

Emmy was at the front desk with a dour Lizbeth. "Nearly there. Short and sweet. Jerod will have it in a snap."

Colby's face clouded. "Sounds kind of tough, Jer."

"Don't worry," Tina said. "We condense the info into

short lines. Then we feed the lines to Jer." Tina patted the boy's head. "He's a natural."

Jerod rocked on his heels. "Yeah, Dad. That's my job." Emmy crooked her finger at him and he scooted to the desk.

Nearly an hour later the segment was blocked out on Tina's clipboard and Jerod was outside doing his bit on the hotel steps. Colby was close by near a large oak tree, and Tina couldn't resist standing near him to watch the scene unfold from his perspective. This was his boy, doing a wonderful job. Finding himself, due in a big part to Tina. The Sugar family circle was closing more tightly around her by the minute, and it was the sweetest feeling imaginable.

Tina hated to shout "Cut" and end the magic. But there was no choice. Jerod had gotten it perfect in one take.

More time passed as they went back inside to set up. So busy with her notes, Tina hadn't noticed Emmy's nudge at first.

"They're here, Tee."

"Huh?"

"Violet and Brooke."

"That's great!" Tina's enthusiasm faded at Emmy's obvious distress.

"Isn't it?" Tina followed her friend's line of vision to the hallway where the trio was conspiring.

"Judging by their fierce expressions and stiff spines, I'd say they're primed for battle. Which means Lizbeth may be on the way out, too."

Tina could no longer deny Lizbeth had been in ill-concealed misery all day. "I don't deserve this," she choked. "I've done nothing to hurt them."

"Just the same, they must see you as a threat. People are unpredictable under stress. You knew going into this search that the results might be as disappointing as your dealings with Angela. Sweetie, you *knew* it."

Colby, who had been combing Jerod's hair, approached with concern. "What's the matter?"

Tina had to work to find her voice. "Not now, Cole."

"Then when, dammit?" He tried to hold her, but she pushed him off. "If we don't get this segment now, the project will be down the tubes. And that would cost you the most, Cole, as Jerod would be crushed. So...so, let me be."

With a dark look he backed away.

With enormous self-control, Tina called for attention. "I think we'll save Lizbeth's staircase descent for later, when the sun is angling through those high windows." She tore a sheet off her clipboard. "Here are lines Jerod can use to introduce Lizbeth. Lizbeth, start walking from the base of the stairs over to the reservations desk. Stacy, position Jerod near the desk. Emmy, help me with the lights."

The next three hours took them through the rooms on the main level. Tina gave Jerod a continuing role, his presence seeming to keep Lizbeth grounded. As the sun streamed through the windows and over the staircase, the crew began to set up Lizbeth's final shoot. Tina moved over to the stairs with Michael, conferring with their viewfinders and posing Lizbeth in different ways.

Michael expelled a heavy breath. "This lady's dress is wrinkled. Again."

"Linen wrinkles," Lizbeth said briskly.

"My daddy irons," Jerod piped up.

Alan snapped his fingers. "The perfect catch for our grubby director. Snatch him up now, Tee!"

There was a mild rumble of laughter, but there was no breaking the tense spell that had settled over the shoot. Tina felt closed in with stony Lizbeth barely cooperating, Violet and Brooke huddled together, Colby pacing around. Marilyn was seated on the lobby settee like a sentinel, knitting a bright-yellow poncho. Dressed in a purple tunic and shiny black pants, gray hair flowing over her shoulders, she waited for her turn on camera.

Lizbeth folded her arms against her chest as Stacy crawled around the lobby floor, pulling a hot steamer over the rumpled dress.

"Ouch!" Lizbeth jumped back. "You burned my legs."

"Only because you moved," Stacy snapped.

"I'm glad I escaped this torture." Violet stood nearby, obviously unable to curb her snippy comments.

"Maybe I should be reporting some of this," Brooke added. "Colby is way too smitten with Tina to see the truth."

"What truth?" Colby demanded, closing in on the women.

Lizbeth threw her hands up. "That's it. I can't do it anymore."

Colby's eyes narrowed. "Can't do what?"

"Can't pretend that any of us are comfortable." Lizbeth's gaze swung to Tina, standing by with her clipboard against her chest. "That any of us appreciate Tina showing up here after all these years. That we can trust her with Sugartown."

Tina's hollow, stricken eyes swung to take in each of the trio. "Is it all that horrible being my mother? Do you have to continue to hide? Try to crush me? My film?"

Marilyn rose slowly from the settee. "I told you this was the wrong way."

"Oh, Mother!" Lizbeth lamented. "It's agreed we will handle this."

"The three of you are bunglers. No. I'm doing what I should've done the minute I knew this was Natalie." She took Tina's clipboard, handed it to Emmy and guided Tina to the staircase. "Come along, child."

Tina followed, but thought to stop her ascent midway to glance back to spot Colby. He met her look with twin eyes of stone and bowed his head. She was torn for a brief moment, wishing he could somehow know it all. But there was no turning back now. She'd put this mission first and had to see it through.

Marilyn took Tina to her bedroom and closed the door. She settled on a wide sateen-covered love seat and motioned for Tina to join her. Cupping Tina's face in her hands, she studied her. "Nobody was expecting you after all this time. There were those uncertain months after Bill's obituary appeared in the city newspaper, but that was years ago."

"So when did you figure me out, Marilyn?"

"You looked so much like Bill at first sight," she marveled. "But when none of the ditzy trio noticed, I thought maybe I was overreacting. I got my rock-solid proof soon after, though, when we sat down to look at the photo albums. We had no copy of the photo you brought out, the one of Bill and the girls, so it had to be a plant. Then you started asking all those questions about the trio. It was plain you'd deduced that one of them was likely your mother."

"Oh. Guess I wasn't very smooth."

"You were too anxious. Understandably so."

"Why didn't you just give it to me straight right there and then?"

"Because I wanted to figure out your intentions first. I know better than to trust anyone at face value. And it troubled me that you didn't fess up to me, either, when I admitted to knowing Bill."

"That wasn't enough reason to spill my guts. For all I knew, you might not have even known there was ever a baby."

Marilyn frowned. "Hadn't considered that excuse."

"I've been working undercover solely to protect my biological mother from pain and embarrassment!"

"That seemed most likely. I was just taking my time to make sure."

"Then how did all this go so wrong? Why did Lizbeth, Violet and Brooke suddenly turn on me?"

"All my fault," Marilyn lamented. "I took one look at your hard-edged crew and panicked. Decided you might be up to no good after all, intending to pull a long-lost mother stunt during filming."

Tina gasped at the implication. "You thought I intended to expose my mother on camera with no warning?"

"Yes. You have to admit it was possible, due to your covert moves and past projects. That's when I finally told the trio who you really are, what you might have in mind. I advised caution and an open mind. But, concerned that I was nearly driven to drink over your intentions, they panicked." Marilyn went on to explain how each one approached Colby with an excuse to bow out of the project and thus discourage it from being completed.

"He didn't say anything," she grumbled.

"He was way out of his league, I think, between their bull and his infatuation with you. I am furious that they bothered him at all."

"I've come here with the best intentions. To connect with my mother, figure out my father. Now I insist you get my real mother up here now. To explain all this away!"

Marilyn sat back, coy and exasperated. "Haven't you really guessed? Dear girl, *I* am your mother."

"But—" Tina stared at her, flabbergasted "—you're old!"

"But I wasn't thirty years ago, in my forties."

Tina shook her head, dazed. "So much older than Dad."

"Yes. But I was a real looker. And experienced in what men like."

"You weren't even in the photo."

"But I was there, *behind* the camera. Funny that's the photo you found. There were so many others taken of the two of us."

Tina frowned. "I hadn't even considered the photographer. Just found the photo, jumped to some conclusions and ran with them." Under Marilyn's encouragement, Tina explained about Angela's stroke and her aunt's rude hint that she wasn't a blood relative. The family lawyer cracking. The film project thrown together as a cover.

"Those Winston bitches," Marilyn seethed. "Bill couldn't stand them."

Tina rubbed her temples, reeling with shock. "What exactly happened back then?"

"Bill started staying here at the hotel on his pharmaceutical route, and being a fun-loving guy, started joining in the parties held by Lizbeth and her friends. Nothing big, mind you. The girls just liked to hang around, mingle with the guests and a few select locals. Gradually Bill and I became infatuated. I was at the height of my irresponsible lifestyle, roaring drunk most of the time. My husband, Lizbeth's father, was long gone. My father dead a couple years. Lizbeth was already in the driver's seat, managing everything with ability and ambition. I'll never know where she got the guts so young, just out of her six-month marriage-from-hell."

"So you and Bill fell in love."

"Fell in lust. Just so happened we connected at a time when we both were feeling let down by life—after a little fun. And we found it for a time. Anyways, I got pregnant. That sobered me up pretty fast."

"Didn't you want me?" Tina asked bleakly.

Marilyn was plainly taken aback. "Why, ah, I didn't know what to do. I didn't feel up to raising another kid.

Lizbeth only turned out because my father helped rear her. Also, I was facing thirty days in jail for a barroom ruckus, a sentence to be served after I gave birth. I was never so trapped or confused."

"Did you two even consider getting together?"

Plainly, Marilyn was thrown by her line of questioning. "It was discussed. Bill was convinced by then he had married the wrong person. But he would have lost the Brooklyn house and much of his savings in a divorce and would have been banished to life here in poky Sugartown. Besides, his wanting a divorce was only half his battle. It was unlikely that Angela would have agreed. It went against her religion and sense of pride. As for me, I'd long ago decided I would never marry again. In short, we were two self-absorbed people who weren't willing to make the necessary sacrifices on a bet with very poor odds. But once the dust settled, Bill made it clear that he desperately wanted you."

"Came up with the story of a pregnant girl on his route, just dying to give her baby to a nice couple," Tina finished.

"So you know that much. Apparently, Angela bought the story whole. Even accepted the terms, the shady handover, pretending to be pregnant. But we all know how persuasive Bill could be. Still, I was a little worried that such a cool-hearted frump could raise a kid with warmth. But Bill reassured me that you would have a fine life. Eventually I gave birth, met Bill and Angela at a café and went off to serve my delayed sentence."

"Didn't you even check up on me?"

"Did so as soon as I got out of jail. First thing out of Bill's mouth was that Angela had noticed chemistry between us and wormed the truth out of him about our affair. The stupid fool! I was horrified at how Angela might react. Talked of taking you back. But he claimed she was fine with it. They had an agreement that she would raise you like her own if Bill put me and Sugartown behind him. He held to the deal fairly well. We never spoke again. But he did send me written updates and photos on the sly, on the condition that I didn't reply."

"I found a draft of a letter, naming me Natalie."

"You like it?" Marilyn asked hopefully.

"Yes. But I'll always be Tina."

"As could be expected, the letters stopped coming. Bill's attention span was pretty short, though, so it was no surprise. Can you understand that I stayed away for your own good? Angela's continued goodwill?"

"Angela's goodwill?" Tina shrilled. "That was gone the second she cracked Bill about my origin. She couldn't stand the sight of me. Ever! But she was trapped, you see. She'd pretended to be pregnant. People had seen me. She had to go on living the lie."

Marilyn looked as though she'd been slapped. "Dear Lord, if only I'd known. Bill should have said something. Done something."

"Bill always looked after himself first, though," Tina conceded. "He must have been satisfied with the setup as it was."

"Yeah, he did cherish his respectable image. Wouldn't have wanted me messing up his life again, even if it was in your best interest."

Marilyn embraced her. "You sorry little runt. If I'd known, I'd have pounded your door down. I could have managed it, too, as I sobered up for good after jail. Stopped partying and dating indiscriminately. It took some time but I eventually came to realize that it was wrong to give you up. But by then it seemed wrong to upset your family. I truly believed you were better off." Marilyn released her with an adoring look. "Please forgive me and Lizbeth. Please, let us start over."

"Yes, Marilyn. Let's try and do that."

"For now you better shoo, get on to Colby for a quick word."

Tina's heart tripped. Colby. There would be hell to pay there. She hoped she could break all this to him in some way he could understand.

Lizbeth showed up at the door as Tina prepared to open it.

"I've already made your apologies," Marilyn proclaimed.

Lizbeth's mouth tightened in disapproval. "What else have I missed?'

Marilyn told her everything. Lizbeth was markedly relieved. "I, too, am sorry under the circumstances. But this isn't all hearts and roses. I hope you understand, Tina, that I will not share this hotel with you."

"That's your major concern right now? Protecting your assets?" Tina gasped. "Marilyn thought you were only trying to protect her feelings, keep her off the bottle."

"That, too, of course," Lizbeth said.

"And I thought I'd find something better than what I had at home."

"Lizbeth is not like Angela's sisters," Marilyn protested.

"Yes, she is. It's all about *things*. Appearances."

Lizbeth gasped in dismay at the very idea. "You misunderstand."

"Not hardly!"

"Girls, girls," Marilyn crowed. "There are bound to be sticky issues between us, until we get better acquainted. Starting with the fact that I don't wish to be known as *old*. Ever." Her glare had shifted exclusively to Tina, but was softened with a wink. "For now, though, the show must go on. I'm going to have my poncho business featured on TV at any cost. That crew downstairs is on the clock, and I say we put them back to work. Any questions?"

"I have one for Lizbeth," Tina said. "How did Colby react?"

Her expression crumbled. "He hauled me outside and demanded an explanation. Which I gave."

"You dumbbell!" Marilyn howled. "Where is he now?"

Lizbeth bowed her head. "He left with Jerod."

Tina promptly burst into tears. And it was her fretful half sister who rushed to comfort her.

IT WAS THE LONGEST WALK of her life, but Tina landed on Colby's doorstep that evening, wearing his letter jacket. He answered the door himself.

"May I come in?" When he stepped aside she moved into the quiet lamplit room. "Anybody else home?"

"No," he said tightly. "I sent them out for a while."

So he was expecting her. And acting a little too self-righteous in her opinion. Didn't she deserve points for being the one to take the walk in the right direction?

She pulled the jacket tighter, inhaling the comfort of Mennen. "Jerod okay?" she asked softly.

It was just the loaded question to set him off. "I knew this project was trouble!" He pounded the plaster wall. "Every step of the way I had my doubts. Watched my family sink deeper and deeper into it until there was no turning back. I trusted you with my son, Tina."

"He's been safe with me."

"You should have told me what was going on!"

"I tried." She shook her head, looked away. "But I was too unsure. Scared."

"People in love share their secrets. In our case, all you did was pry mine loose!"

"Didn't mean to. But I know that's a hazard of my trade. Look, Cole, I tried to make myself trust you

Sugartown

enough, but I just couldn't take the risk of you pulling the plug on my mission."

"I wouldn't have!"

"You might have. You like to keep your town neat and free of mess."

"Well, it is a miracle that nobody will suffer much from the revelation. The whole town already sees Marilyn as a kook. But if it *had* been one of the trio, their lives might have been greatly damaged."

"The reason I tried to do it secretly, Cole!" She pressed fingers to her temples. "We're just going around in circles here."

"I can't get over your lack of trust."

"Since I discovered my father's adultery, I haven't been able to trust anyone or anything, not even my own judgment. I've been stumbling around without faith or direction. I loved Dad so much, you see. And to find out he lied to me was pretty horrible. I only wanted to try and understand how it all happened."

"I deserved the chance to understand."

"Nobody can tell you anything with the guarantee you'll understand," she said, lashing back.

"Not true. I listen carefully to other opinions."

"And then do what you think is best."

"I'm well liked. Ask anyone."

"You charm your way into getting most things. Then bully for the rest."

"Nobody wants a wimpy police chief. I have to be tough. Because I truly care!"

She was appalled by his naiveté. "I did become lost in your caring for a while. Indulged in the novelty of loving a family man. All I could see was the prize of belonging in your family. I had decided I was willing to please you to the extent of moving here, to juggling my schedule to complement yours, all in order to finally belong someplace! But now I see I would have ended up like the other people you love, nearly smothered by your personality."

On the verge of cracking, his voice grew hoarse. "Congratulations, Tina. You have all the answers now. You can go on home, eat this project and move on."

"Sure, I could do that. But I have too much class to let the town down. This project has always been real. I have plenty of footage to make it work. The show will go on. To three other towns. To a cable program. To a national contest. Without further interference from you."

She tore off the jacket, flung it at him and fled the house.

TINA WAS PACKING HER BAGS later that night when she heard a rap on her door. It was the Bio Mom trio.

"We're sorry!" Violet and Brooke said in unison, bursting inside behind Lizbeth.

Tina smiled faintly. "Thanks for that."

"We wanted to speak to you without Mother," Lizbeth said. "Please don't blame her for anything. We should have handled her fears better than we did. Trying to dump you through Colby when you've been seeing him was especially wrong of us. It's just that we've come to rely on his leadership. Just the same, Colby will get our apology tomorrow."

"As for your snooping into our lives," Violet ventured, "it was rather naughty. But we hope when you left each of us, you generally approved of our motherly qualifications."

"Of course I did," Tina said warmly. "I wouldn't have been the least bit disappointed in any case."

"All things considered," Violet said, "I wish I could call you my own."

"I'd rather not," Brooke admitted. "As you'd be disqualified as a daughter-in-law."

"Guess I'm the luckiest one," Lizbeth said. "I have a new sister."

Violet beamed. "We'd like to talk about Bill sometime. Tell you about the kind man we knew."

Brooke patted her shoulder. "Please don't go on in misery over what he did. No one is perfect. And he was so lonely when he came to us."

Tina nodded. "I will always wish he'd tried to explain himself to me personally. Maybe I could have understood sooner."

"Men aren't the wisest creatures," Violet reminded her. "I, for one, have given up on them completely."

Everyone laughed. And cried. Then Tina snapped her suitcases shut.

"You aren't still leaving!" Lizbeth exclaimed in dismay. "We came to beg you for an extension, to help you make the program better."

"I am thrilled to hear it. Emmy and the crew will be staying on to wrap up any details and will take good care of all of you." Tina tugged her cases off the bed.

"So it is true!" Marilyn barged in, glaring at Tina's suitcase. "You're off."

"I must get back to Angela."

Marilyn took Tina by the shoulders. "I'm proud of the way you're handling her illness. If it helps, I don't believe Angela was a deliberate enemy to either of us. I've seen other fools like her, who never allow themselves any enjoyment. Their losses are the biggest."

"Of course, Marilyn." Tina hugged her. "We're the lucky ones."

"What about Colby?" Lizbeth demanded abruptly.

Tina exhaled. "He was just too angry to reconcile. And I don't have the time or patience to deal with it now."

"You will be back soon, though," Lizbeth asserted.

"Not for a while. I have Angela to consider. Eventually, her estate to settle. And there are three more towns to visit for the project."

Brooke kissed her cheek. "You get over Colby and come back to give Seth a try. He's really a darling."

"He is, Brooke. But the only men I intend to cuddle up with in the near future are Ben and Jerry."

Chapter Seventeen

Two weeks later, into October, Colby arrived home from work to find Jerod and Ronny seated on the sofa in the living room watching television.

He peeled off his jacket, chilled from the cold. "What's for supper? Something hot, I hope."

Ronny raised a hand. "Shh!"

"We're watching the video Tina made," Jerod explained. "It's the end now."

Colby scowled at Seth waving to the camera. "It's the end, all right."

"She sure must be busy," Jerod went on. "Because she never calls us."

Colby grimaced. He still hadn't the heart to tell his son how badly he'd left things with Tina.

Ronny cleared his throat. "Drove Marilyn to AA today. Guess Tina's mom died day before last."

"Oh." Colby felt a lump rise in his throat. "Thought she had more time."

"Those things are always iffy."

Jerod gasped. "Gramps, you didn't tell me her mom died!"

"I was going to. Wanted to enjoy the film first."

Jerod squeezed Ronny's hand. Colby sat down, wanting to squeeze somebody's hand, too.

"I figure I better take a ride to Brooklyn," Colby said finally.

"Marilyn's expecting you by the hotel round eight tomorrow."

Colby gazed at Ronny over Jerod's small head. "Marilyn on a road trip? Still ranting on about Vietnam and the saccharin ban?"

"A just penance for your stubbornness."

Mindful of Jerod, Colby spoke carefully. "I was out of line. But I am ready to go back to the bargaining table to try to fix things."

"Not this trip. Just go, comfort Tina and keep your big mouth shut."

Colby ruffled Jerod's hair. "So, let's see this movie."

"It's not a movie. It's a documentary."

Colby reached for the remote on the coffee table and pressed Rewind. The segment began with Jerod at the hotel, then went through all the stops, with unexpected extras, like a more-vibrant-than-expected Lizbeth in new footage, Violet's beekeeping and a short glimpse of the off-the-record water balloon fight. Jerod fidgeted as the last segment at the school began.

Jerod looked great in his costume, moving through the building, giving a glimpse of a few classrooms. The square dance music preceded the camera inside the gym. Jerod gave the intro, handing off to Ronny, the proud caller, also in costume. The music swelled louder then and the children poured off the bleachers. And to Colby's dismay, Jerod skipped into the line of boys, taking his old place in the dance formation.

The kid danced! After all Colby's trouble to get him another position in the shoot, Jerod went on behind his back, did it his way anyway.

Colby watched the display with apprehension. Jerod and Ronny, in contrast, joyfully clapped along to the beat of the music. Mercifully, Jerod only tripped a little bit. And when he did, others were there to cover for him.

When it was over, Colby let loose. "I can't believe you danced. You weren't supposed to."

"I wanted to dance, Dad," he said simply. "So I did."

"But you were happy being the narrator."

"That was awesome. But I wanted to do both things."

Colby shook his head in disbelief. "You could have fallen."

"I did fall. They fixed the film. It's called editing."

"Why didn't you tell me?"

"It's hard to tell you stuff sometimes." Jerod hung his head. "You get bossy."

This was the living end. His own eight-year-old son, hiding something this big from him. "I always try to do what's best."

Jerod stood and patted his shoulder. "I know, Dad. I'm sorry you get it wrong." He dashed off to the kitchen.

"Am I really that bossy, hard to talk to?" Colby asked Ronny bleakly.

Ronny nodded slowly.

"And wrong?"

"Plenty of times, son."

Suddenly a new reality struck him. "But never as bad as Dizzy, though, right?"

"Just like her."

"No, Dad, no."

"It's partly my fault for making you kids go independent before your time. Kids can be poorly affected by parents, you know. Take a sad girl lied to by her daddy, rejected by her mama. It would take guts to search out her biological mother for a loving relationship, risk another letdown."

"I could have helped her," he grumbled.

"Like the boy said, it's hard to tell you stuff. And in

a way, I think she was trying to protect you by not putting you in the middle of a situation. This way, if something went wrong, nobody could blame you."

"Certain people have been wearing me down with hints these past couple of weeks," Colby admitted. "But I didn't want to believe it. Until now. Until my own sweet little boy…" He stared off numbly to the kitchen.

"We all can be stupid, Cole. But only the real morons continue to deny it indefinitely."

"Sounds like the beginning of a great poem for the Think Tank."

"TEE! YOU'RE NEEDED down here."

Tina moved to the top of the staircase at the house on Hillerman Street to find Emmy standing at the bottom with hands on hips. Both were dressed in shabby clothing like the rest of her current Four Corners crew, who were helping her prep the Mildenderger house for sale. She was going to protest the summons but realized Emmy was sending a strange signal. There seemed no choice but to trot down for a look.

Her heart was like lead to discover her aunts Peggy and Jean had arrived.

"The funeral was only yesterday!" Jean whimpered. "Already you pillage."

"If you'd had the courtesy to speak to me yesterday, I would have told you of my plans to move forward," Tina replied.

Jean gasped in outrage. "Can't wait to profit, can you?"

"Can't wait to pay Mom's bills. Some are overdue, and I've been getting rude phone calls."

Tina noted the generally jaded Michael and Alan looking on now like a couple of traumatized schoolboys. She, too, was upset that anyone should see this thorny display. Especially since her aunts knew deep inside she was a good person, worthy of their affection and respect. Yet they still chose to project their anger over Angela's untimely death and Bill's indiscretion onto the only living target left.

"Well, you know the meaning of rude," Peggy accused, "putting a security system on the house, siccing your lawyer on us."

"I could hardly trust you alone here after the last time, the way you were grabbing for things. And Warren hardly came after you. He told me you ran into him at the nursing home, where he was visiting Angela as both a friend and my representative."

"To discover an outsider like him was privy to our family business," Jean bemoaned. "It was so humiliating. So insensitive of you."

Tina's eyes moistened. "Look, I don't need this flak. I am grieving, too. Angela was my mother and I respect her for all the good things she did, raising me in comfort and security, treating Dad, me—everyone who visited here—with respect. You two are the insensitive ones for never accepting me, never coaxing her to give our relationship a break. She would have been a lot happier if she'd met me halfway."

Peggy and Jean exchanged a brief look, but Tina wasn't surprised when they skimmed right over her observations.

"What about your running off without a single word of warning?" Peggy complained. "That was completely insensitive."

"Just following your orders, Peggy. Last time we spoke here in this house, you ordered me not to call you."

"But you vanished. Where on earth did you go?"

"She came looking for me," a husky female voice inserted.

Tina's eyes grew huge as Marilyn glided inside, wearing an emerald pantsuit, her hair done in a classic chignon. And right behind her stood Colby, wearing casual khakis, a navy-blue shirt and a no-nonsense expression that would scare a hardened criminal half to death. She didn't welcome more witnesses to this sad embarrassment, but it did feel good to see her aunts cringe a little.

"We came as quickly as we could, dear," Marilyn said, grasping Tina's arms, kissing both cheeks.

"It's you!" Jean pointed a shaky finger at Marilyn. "We set a whole box of pictures of *you* on fire!"

Marilyn's hard eyes flashed. "Then introductions are unnecessary. Please know I'd just as soon set your hair on fire this minute."

Tina moved her hands like an umpire calling a runner safe at home. "Enough. Please. Enough."

"Who is he?" Peggy blurted out, shifting her uneasy gaze to Colby.

"I am the man who loves Tina," he stated, now looming over the aunts like a dark thundercloud. "I am the man who intends to take her away from the sorry likes of you."

"You're welcome to her," Jean blustered, jumping back a little.

"As you're welcome to exactly what I've packed for you," Tina said briskly. A nod at Michael and Alan had them springing into the dining room for two fair-size boxes. "This is Winston stuff. Yours free and clear. Just please go on with your lives and let me go on with mine."

Alan and Michael continued out the door with Peggy and Jean quickly trailing after their possessions.

Suddenly the foyer was clear around Tina and Colby. He wasted no time embracing her, burying his face in her hair. "How I've missed you."

"I've missed you, too."

He lifted his head and took her face in his hands. "If only I'd known about the funeral in time."

"I purposely waited to call Marilyn. Figured she would have come for my sake and I didn't have the extra strength to protect her from the Winstons."

"You poor baby." He pressed his lips to hers, lingering for a long sweet kiss. "Marilyn told me so many things on the drive here. I can't believe what you've gone through. But even back at home, I've been paying for my sins. A cherished little boy innocently announced that it is hard to tell me stuff. That I am wrong and bossy. A mediocre poet has informed me that only a moron doesn't know when he's acting stupid."

She smiled. "How are Jerod and Ronny?"

"Enjoying a new mutt bought by a new and improved police chief. Missing you like crazy."

"You haven't even mentioned the square dance. Hope you aren't too mad about Jerod's decision to participate."

"It was his decision," Colby conceded. "The new me is much more flexible in so many ways."

"Have you come to see why I felt so stuck with my secrets?"

"Yes. Your many fans have weighed in on my mishandling of it all."

"I have fans in Sugartown?"

He rolled his eyes. "More than you can imagine. Once word got out about your mother's illness, Deedee swung her vote in favor of replacing the playground equipment, adding a bench dedicated to your family. All the shops have money jars to boost civic funding."

"Why would she do that, Cole?"

"To ensure your return, give me another chance with you. She always did claim to know what's best for me."

"I am overwhelmed."

"Enough to take a chance on me? Give me your trust?"

She rocked on her heels. "Very tempting offer."

"Will it help to hear that I love you more than ever?"

She bobbed her head. "Yeah."

"How about that I don't expect you to make all the compromises. That I am willing to spend some time in your world, maybe grow a goatee?"

She arched a brow. "You'd actually leave Sugartown for an overnight stay?"

"Sure. Sometimes. A little bit. I do have officers with experience, who deserve a chance at more duties."

She gave a soft cry of surprise and touched his forehead. "Hey, who's taken over our chief? Little green men?"

"I've been taken over by a passion for you." He kissed her harder this time, pressing her firmly against him.

She finally wrenched her mouth from his, her blue eyes full of innocent hope. "You really think this can work?"

"Marry me and find out."

Tina's hands were trembling as they lay on Colby's chest. "Hey, crew!" she called out brightly. "I know exactly what your next gig is gonna be after Four Corners!"

Everybody conveniently spilled through doorways.

"Back in Sugartown?" Emmy guessed.

"Yup. Just picture through your viewfinders a bride, a groom, a pastor and a church."

Colby rubbed his hands together with churlish glee. "Don't forget the water balloons."

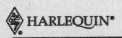

® HARLEQUIN®

American ROMANCE®

The McCabes of Texas are back!

**WATCH FOR SIX NEW BOOKS
BY BESTSELLING AUTHOR**

Cathy Gillen Thacker

The McCabes: Next Generation

Available now:

A TEXAS WEDDING VOW
(#1112) On sale April 2006

SANTA'S TEXAS LULLABY
(#1096) On sale December 2005

THE ULTIMATE TEXAS BACHELOR
(#1080) On sale August 2005

Coming soon:

BLAME IT ON TEXAS
(#1125) On sale August 2006

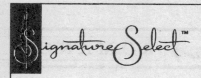

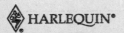

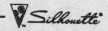
SPECIAL EDITION™

DON'T MISS THE FIRST BOOK IN

PATRICIA McLINN's

EXCITING NEW SERIES

Seasons in a Small Town

WHAT ARE FRIENDS FOR?

April 2006

When tech mogul Zeke Zeekowsky
returned for his hometown's Lilac Festival,
the former outsider expected a hero's
welcome. Instead, his high school fling,
policewoman Darcie Barrett, mistook him
for a wanted man and handcuffed him!
But the software king and the small-town
girl were quick to make up....

SPECIAL EDITION™

PRESENTING A NEW MINISERIES BY

RaeANNE THAYNE:

The Cowboys of Cold Creek

BEGINNING WITH

LIGHT THE STARS
April 2006

Widowed rancher Wade Dalton relied
on his mother's help to raise three small
children—until she eloped with "life coach"
Caroline Montgomery's grifter father! Feeling
guilty, Caroline put her Light the Stars
coaching business on hold to help the angry
cowboy...and soon lit a fire in his heart.

DON'T MISS THESE ADDITIONAL BOOKS IN THE SERIES:
DANCING IN THE MOONLIGHT, May 2006
DALTON'S UNDOING, June 2006

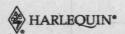
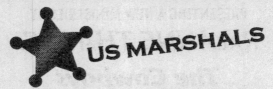